Fire
ON ICE

KIM KANE

ISBN: 979-8-9877235-1-7

For Theresa,
You have saved my sanity more times than I can count. I can never thank
you enough for your encouragement throughout this journey. Your
unwavering support, opinions, and round-the-clock technological
assistance have meant the world to me. I wouldn't be here without you.

CHAPTER 1

I didn't want to be in Miami. It was everything I loathed, hot, sunny, overpriced, and pretentious. My day wasn't off to a great start. The string of mishaps started the night before. It was Halloween, and the first snowstorm of the year struck Syracuse. Where was global warming when I needed it? The early onset of winter weather made it difficult to get an Uber. I faced massive delays by the time I reached the airport. I arrived in Miami shortly after one and discovered my baggage was coming in on the next flight. I felt like something the cat dragged in by the time I reached my hotel three hours later. Usually, I would have arrived in town early and gotten the lay of the land before starting a new position. However, my rapid hire didn't grant me that luxury.

I never expected to get the job as an NHL sportscaster when I applied. As a college football announcer, and a young one to boot, my hockey knowledge was minimal. Fortunately, my boss knew Leora Prescott, the managing director at Southern Sports, and put in a good word for me. The no-holds-barred approach she saw in my broadcasts impressed Leora, who was anxious to fill the unexpected vacancy. I felt like the luckiest woman in the world when she decided to take a leap of faith and offer me the position.. That luck ended my first day on the job.

I woke up early, despite my exhaustion. I was the girl who

preferred a natural look over makeup, and jeans and flats to dresses and heels. Wanting to make a good impression, I settled on a floral print wraparound dress that fell just above the knee. I switched from four to two-inch heels, hoping I wouldn't tower over my co-workers, especially the men. I threw loose curls in my long blond hair, blotted my red lipstick, grabbed my laptop, and headed to the car. I thought I left plenty of time to get to the station and settle in. I was wrong.

Sitting in traffic tops my list of pet peeves, and I encountered more than expected, even for Miami. *Was there a road in this city that wasn't under construction? Don't panic*, I told myself. *You still have plenty of time.* A layer of perspiration coated my skin as the bumper-to-bumper traffic came to a screeching halt. *This isn't good*, I thought, tapping my nails against the steering wheel. I stretched my neck trying to catch a glimpse of what lay ahead. The only thing I could see was the reflection of flashing red lights. I stared at the clock on my dashboard, watching the minutes slip away. Easing my foot off the brake, I edged closer to the car before me as if riding his bumper would speed things along. It took twenty minutes before a lane was cleared. Courtesy went out the window as I zig-zagged in and out of traffic cutting off one car after another. Barring any more unforeseen circumstances, I would still make it on time. That was before I encountered a broken traffic light.

This can't be happening, I thought, banging my hands against the steering wheel. *Move, move!* I yelled at the line of cars in front of me. My heart raced as my anxiety rose. I was three blocks from the office, fighting the urge to abandon my car and sprint to the station when the traffic cop waved me through. *I'll just make it*, I thought, breathing a sigh of relief. I wiped the bead of sweat from my forehead and made a hairpin turn into the parking garage. Oblivious to my surroundings, I carelessly threw open the car door. The sound of a bang and a man's voice snapped me back to reality.

"You hit my car!" the driver blurted out, rushing to inspect the damage.

"I'm so sorry. I wasn't paying attention."

"That's an understatement. You nicked my door," he said, rubbing his hand over the paint. "Shane, buddy, I have to run. Some ditzy woman just dented my car. I'll call you later, my friend. Keep the faith. You'll get through this." The stranger ended the call and released a heavy sigh. "I didn't think this day could get any worse," he said, throwing his hands up in exasperation.

"I'm so, so sorry," I reiterated. It's entirely my fault. I'll be happy to pay for the damage."

"Do you have any idea how much this will cost?" he asked, his voice elevated.

My eyes scanned his car. *Nice job, Layla. Only you would hit a Porsche.* "Listen," I implored, trying not to sound impatient. "I'm late for the first day of a new job. I would be eternally grateful if we could exchange contacts and I'll arrange to pay you after you get an estimate."

"That sounds like a you problem not a me problem," the man replied unsympathetically.

Refusing to be deterred, I took a screenshot of my license. "What's your phone number? I'll text you my information."

"Do you have your insurance card?"

"This is a rental car. I just arrived in Miami last night. My car, with my insurance information, is in transit. I know you have no reason to trust me, but I swear, I won't ghost you. Here, put your details in my phone. Send me the bill, and I promise to reimburse you. If I don't get going, I may lose this job before I start. That wouldn't bode well for you getting paid." I placed the palms of my hands together in the form of a plea.

The stranger looked at me skeptically. I thought he was going to shut me down when he hissed, "Fine. This is the last thing I feel like dealing with right now."

"Thank you so much," I replied, shaking his hand with my clammy one. I grabbed my things and raced into the building. I was about to hit the elevator button when a voice yelled, "Hold it." I didn't have time to wait. The doors were almost closed when an arm pried them open, enabling the owner of the Porsche to step inside. His eyes rolled at the sight of me. The feeling was mutual. We stood side by side in silence that hung heavier than the humid Miami air. I glanced up at the stranger as the elevator ascended at a snail's pace. He was giving me the once-over before his eyes rested on my cleavage. I diverted my attention to my watch. It seemed like an eternity had passed before the elevator finally dinged. It was nine o'clock on the nose.

"Good luck with your job. From what I've seen, you're going to need it," the arrogant stranger said, without a backward glance. I headed in the opposite direction, ducking into the restroom to freshen up. I washed my hands, smoothed my dress, and dabbed the shine off my face before entering the Southern Sports reception area.

"Hi, I'm Layla MacKenzie, and I'm supposed to be at a staff meeting with Leora Prescott. Today is my first day, and I'm not off to a strong start. I would be forever in your debt if you steered me in the right direction and got me one of those," I said, pointing to the cup of coffee on the receptionist's desk.

"Hi, Ms. MacKenzie. We've been expecting you. I'm Ava. Let me be the first to welcome you. You can join the meeting after I give you a temporary ID." My stomach clenched as I realized I would be late for my first staff meeting.

"I'll be right in with your coffee," Ava said, as I followed her to the conference room. I took a deep breath and smiled as I opened the door. Fifteen sets of eyes glanced up as I stepped into the boardroom.

Hi, I'm Layla MacKenzie. I'm so sorry I'm late. I've had some logistical issues this morning, but it won't happen again," I said, sounding self-assured.

"It's good to see you, Layla," replied a familiar voice at the head of the table. It was Leora Prescott, the managing director, who hired me. "Why don't you take a moment to settle, and I'll introduce you?"

I headed to an empty chair toward the end of the conference table. Ava reappeared with my coffee. I would have given her my firstborn; I was so grateful. I nodded at her in appreciation as I set my computer down. That was when my day went from bad to unspeakably worse. I panicked when I realized the man sitting next to me was none other than the one from the elevator. My hand twitched as I opened my laptop, knocking over my coffee cup. I watched the hot liquid run off the table onto the Porsche owner's lap. A groan of pain permeated the air.

"What the hell is wrong with you?" he snapped.

Everyone jumped up, but there wasn't much to be done. I grabbed my cardigan and threw it on the table to sop up the remains of the coffee. Ava returned with paper towels and handed them to the man clutching his groin. He grabbed the roll and quickly exited the room. *Why couldn't the floor open and swallow me up?* My cheeks turned as red as the roses in my dress as every face fixated on mine.

"I'm so sorry!! It was an accident. Do you think he's okay? Should someone go check on him?" I asked in a panic.

"He'll be fine. He's tough. I'm Chase, one of the producers. Believe me when I tell you he's been through worse."

Seeing my embarrassment, Leora intervened. "All right, everybody, let's refocus. Layla, welcome to our weekly staff meeting. You'll concentrate on player statistics, conference standings, game highlights, etcetera. You'll work with Jameson, the media liaison to the Predators. He'll give you a heads-up on who you'll be interviewing between periods and after the game. This is Gabriela. She handles fundraising and community events." I looked at Gabriela, searching for empathy from the other female in the room. The smirk on her face implied, better you than me.

"Darius will be your cameraman," Leora continued, nodding in his direction.

"It's a pleasure to meet you, Layla. I'll happily take you to the broadcast booth and show you the ropes when you're ready."

I was just starting to relax when the conference room door flew open. The man I scalded had changed into running pants and a tight-fitting T-shirt. He glanced at the scene of the crime and noticed Ava had brought me a replacement cup of coffee. The silence was deafening as my victim abruptly situated himself on the far opposite side of the table. I felt myself shrinking beneath the weight of his scrutiny.

He might have caught me staring if I wasn't too ashamed to meet his gaze. In my earlier haste, I failed to notice the man was drop-dead gorgeous. Standing six-foot-two with mile-wide shoulders and a thick neck, he had a beautifully chiseled face with high cheekbones and an angular jaw. Thick black lashes that would be the envy of any woman framed the most piercing, beautiful blue eyes I had ever seen. He possessed a firm mouth, full lips, and a razor fine jaw. His joggers hung low on his hips accentuating a sculpted six-pack. The tight T-shirt modeled his bulging biceps and sculpted torso. Fortunately, Leora's voice interrupted my increasingly inappropriate train of thought.

"Layla, allow me to introduce your co-commentator, Cole Pasternak."

My stomach plummeted as my body broke into a sweat. It was bad enough that I was late for my first day. That, topped by the realization I scalded my partner after damaging his car, was unbearable. I thought I would be sick as my insides cramped. *Take a deep breath, Layla. It was an accident. It could happen to anybody,* I tried to reassure myself.

"I'm so sorry, Cole. Are you okay? Is there anything I can do for you?"

"Haven't you done enough?" he replied in a scathing tone.

My blood ran cold. Cole's reply mimicked steel, hard and unforgiving. "I have a question for you. How did you get this job? What are your qualifications aside from being clumsy and clueless?"

I was speechless. I'd never had anybody speak to me like that. Cole's words felt like a kick in the gut.

"I have media experience," I stuttered. "I was an announcer for Syracuse University's football team." *I hope that didn't come across as pathetic as it sounded.*

"Football, college football, no less. Are football and hockey the same sport?" he growled.

"No, of course not," I said defensively.

"Do you know anything about hockey?" Cole asked in an accusatory tone.

"Cole, calm down. I realize you've had a tough morning, but that's no reason to attack Layla," Leora said, coming to my defense.

"It's okay. He has a right to know," I replied. "Honestly, my hockey background is minimal, but what I lack in knowledge, I make up for in motivation. I am hoping you will help me fill in the gaps."

"I don't recall babysitter or teacher being in my job description," Cole replied through clenched teeth.

"I don't recall personnel director being in your job description either," Leora interjected.

"Lucky for her, I'm not because her CV would land in the trash."

"Cole, why don't you take a break, and I'll meet you in your office after the meeting?" Leora replied.

Hostility pervaded the room as my co-workers shifted their eyes to avoid mine. The extent of Cole's anger astounded me as he balled his hands into fists and stormed out. Here I struggled to earn respect as an attractive blonde my entire life. Yet, the only emotion I evoked within the first ten minutes at my dream job was an overwhelming sense of pity.

"It may be best if we reschedule this meeting for tomorrow. We all seem a bit distracted. Layla, why don't I show you around?" Leora suggested.

When we got to my office, Leora shut the door behind us. I should have kept my mouth shut and played it cool, but I tended to wear my heart on my sleeve. My penchant for people-pleasing trumped my professionalism as I blurted out, "Why does Cole hate me?"

"He doesn't hate you, Layla. Shane McPherson, the man you are replacing, is on medical leave. We just got word that his prognosis isn't good. Shane and Cole are close. His condition came as a surprise to us all, but it's been particularly hard on Cole. I think you're witnessing Cole displacing his anger and frustration onto you. With that said, his behavior today was inexcusable. I plan to speak with him after we finish up here."

"Please don't do that! I'm a big girl. I'm sure we can work it out, especially since I know Cole's anger may be misdirected. Leora, I realize you've taken a great leap of faith bringing me on board. I want you to know that I won't disappoint you."

"I'm sure you won't, Layla. My door is always open if you need anything. I have a very talented staff, and we work as a team. Don't be afraid to ask questions and seek their expertise. Welcome aboard," Leora replied in a reassuring tone.

As Leora left, another face appeared at my door. I hoped it would be Cole, but it was Connor from IT. He helped me get acclimated to the network and set up my accounts. Unlike Cole, he was kind and extremely patient. When we were done, I went to Human Resources to complete the onboarding process. I found Ava waiting for me when I returned to my office.

"I wasn't sure if you brought lunch. Here are some menus from local restaurants if you want me to place an order for you."

"Thanks, Ava. You've been a real lifesaver. I saw a coffee shop up the block. I may take a walk and clear my head."

At the mention of food, I realized I hadn't eaten breakfast. I was hungry, but my stomach was still upset from the morning's events. I decided that before I did anything else, I needed to try to rectify the situation with Cole. His office was three doors down from mine. I knocked on his door and waited for him to acknowledge me. Cole left me in the hallway, refusing to look up from his computer screen.

I took a seat across from him as my insides tightened with trepidation. "Hi, how are you feeling?"

"I was feeling fine until you arrived," he replied contemptuously.

"You can't imagine how sorry I am. I'd like to make it up to you. Can I buy you lunch?"

"I lost my appetite," Cole growled.

"How about a cup of coffee? I was hoping we could get to know each other better."

"Why bother? You won't be here very long."

Cole's comment put me on the defensive, a place I was unaccustomed to being with my colleagues. "Look, I've been upfront about my limited exposure to hockey, but I'm a good commentator. I graduated with honors from the Newhouse School of Communications at Syracuse University. It is one of the best programs in the country."

"I don't care if you were the valedictorian at Harvard. You're not qualified to be an NHL sportscaster. However, I am curious about one thing."

"What's that?" I asked in a hopeful tone.

"Who did you screw to get this job?"

My face flushed as my blood began to boil. This guy had some set of balls. "Apparently, you don't have a high opinion of your boss because she sees something in me worth taking a chance on."

"On the contrary, I have the highest regard for Leora. I'll chalk hiring you up to a momentary lapse of reason on her part. I don't know what makes her think you can hold a candle to your predecessor."

I sighed in frustration. "Okay, I get that you're not happy I'm here, but wouldn't it make sense for us to try to get along? I know I have big shoes to fill, but I'm a quick learner and the hardest worker you'll ever meet. It seems like it would be to your advantage to help me."

Cole shook his head. "The only thing I'm going to help you do is to fail," he replied, with eyes as cold as ice.

I was stunned. I couldn't tell whether I was angry, sad, or both. I never had anyone treat me with such disdain and disrespect. I prided myself on always having great relationships with my coworkers. Refusing to let Cole get the best of me, I chose to take the high road.

"I'm sorry you feel that way. Hopefully, you'll change your mind with time because I have no intention of failing."

"We'll see," he replied curtly, staring back at the monitor.

"Your feelings for me aside, I still feel bad about the coffee incident. Is there anything I can do to make it up to you?"

Cole lifted his eyes off the computer screen to meet mine. "You can catch the next flight back to wherever it is you came from."

I was done dealing with this arrogant asshole. Needing a breath of fresh air, I decided to take a walk and pick up lunch. While I was waiting for my order, I called my best friend.

"Hi, Skylar. Thank God you picked up."

"Layla, I'm surprised to hear from you. How's your first day going?"

"It couldn't be worse. I couldn't make this shit up if I tried." I replied, relaying my series of mishaps. When I told Skylar about spilling coffee on Cole's crotch, she burst out laughing. "Skye, that isn't funny. He could have been seriously hurt."

"I know. You're right, but it sounds like he's okay."

"Aside from Cole's blind hatred for me, he seems fine."

"I'm sure he doesn't hate you, Layla. You're the nicest person I know."

"I'm telling you, Skye, he's pissed I got this job. He doesn't think I'm qualified, and he's right, but he won't even give me a chance. He had the gall to ask me who I slept with to get it."

"That's unbelievable! This guy sounds like a first-class dick. What do you know about him?"

"Not much. I found out the person I'm replacing has cancer. Apparently, he and Cole are tight."

"Are you telling me this guy is your co-announcer, and you didn't Google him?"

"I guess that would have made sense, but you know I prefer to meet someone before making judgments."

"Listen, Layla, don't let this jerk get you down. You earned this opportunity, and you're going to be great. Besides, I've yet to meet anyone you can't win over. Just be yourself. I'm sure Cole will come around."

"Thanks, Skylar! I needed this pep talk. I've got to get back to work before Cole accuses me of being lazy."

"Call me later. I'm going to do some digging. Remember, keep your friends close and your enemies closer."

"Love you, Skye!"

"Right back at you, Layla."

Skylar and I had been friends since freshman year in college. We sat beside each other in my Intro to Mass Media class. We had been inseparable ever since. Skylar graduated with a degree in Journalism. She landed a job at the Post Standard in Syracuse as a local reporter. Her long-term goal was to move to Manhattan and work for Cosmopolitan. Once established, she planned to write non-fiction novels focusing on women's issues. She was more of an activist than I was, but the thing we were most passionate about was our friendship.

Feeling renewed, I finished my lunch and took a studio tour with Darius. I met Wyatt, my production assistant, who was nice enough to get me some old footage from past Predator games. The rest of the afternoon was spent watching videos and taking detailed notes. The day flew by. It was almost eight o'clock when I ordered dinner. I planned to stay at my desk and work until I couldn't keep my eyes open. At eight-thirty, I was shocked to see Cole standing in my doorway.

"Do you normally work this late?" I asked.

"Not usually, but thanks to you, getting laid isn't an option, so I thought I'd catch up on a few things."

"I don't know how many ways I can apologize for that," I replied, in frustration. "I'll cover your medical expenses if you need to see a doctor."

"I guess that means they're paying you big bucks for being unqualified, and here I thought you came cheap."

"You know we are uncharacteristically underpaid starting out in this business. I'm just trying to do the right thing," I replied, trying not to let him bait me.

Cole walked into my office and dropped a bag on my desk. "I ran into your delivery guy on my way out. I think this is your Chinese food. I'm surprised you're still here."

"I was reviewing some old broadcasts. Next, I will dig into the player's profiles. Leora arranged for me to meet the team tomorrow. I thought it would help if I knew something about them."

"You look like hell. I recommend you get some sleep. Trust me, you'll still be clueless in the morning," Cole replied flippantly.

"What makes you so qualified to do this job?" I asked indignantly. "You can't be more than twenty-six or twenty-seven, which is younger than any other NHL sportscaster I've seen."

Cole's face flushed with fury. "For the record, I'm twenty-nine, and experience makes me qualified! Since I was four years old, I've been playing hockey. If you knew anything about the Predators, you would know I'm a former member."

"Well, you couldn't have been very good if they bounced you off the team."

I thought Cole's head was going to explode. "They didn't fire me. I had to abandon my professional career due to an injury. If you followed hockey, you would know that, even if you weren't a Predator fan!"

Sadness seeped into his eyes, causing my anger to dissipate. "I'm sorry. I didn't know. That must have been devastating."

"You have no idea!" he snapped.

"Maybe I do," I replied sympathetically.

"Don't patronize me," Cole snarled.

"Did it ever occur to you that you don't know anything about me either?"

"I know enough. You're the type that things come easily to, whereas I had to work my ass off for everything I have, and it was still taken away."

There was no point in arguing. Anything I said would just infuriate him more. "I have to get back to work. Thanks for bringing me my dinner."

Cole turned and stormed out the door. I pulled up the team roster and started digging for information. I felt exhausted and overwhelmed as my adrenaline high faded. I picked up the phone and called Skylar.

"Hey, Layla, I was just about to call you. I was doing some research on your co-host. Did you know he played for the Predators?"

"I do now. If I had known that ten minutes sooner, I would have saved myself from further humiliation."

"Oh, that doesn't sound good. I gather Cole is still being a prick."

"Yeah, but it isn't entirely his fault. He pissed me off, and I said something stupid. So, what did you find out?"

"Not only did Cole play for the Predators, but he was the runner-up for the Calder Trophy for rookie of the year. He had twenty-six goals, forty-nine points, and one-hundred and fifty-eight shots on goal in fifty-five games."

"That's just great," I sighed. "Not only did I insult him, but I cemented his belief that I'm a complete idiot. Cole said an injury ended his career. Did you find out anything about that?"

"He was in a fight with a player from the Tampa Bay Thunder. I'm sure you know by now that those teams are arch-enemies. Apparently, Cole took a stick to the eye and suffered permanent vision loss."

"That's awful. I never would have suspected that. Cole's eyes are disarmingly beautiful. You know blue eyes are my weakness."

"He has beautiful everything! I was expecting to see a picture of Beelzebub when I Googled him. Cole could always model if broadcasting falls through. I'm glad he's not my partner. I would find it distracting working next to such a hot guy."

"Fortunately, his arrogance and vehement disdain for me kills the attraction."

"Maybe that's better," Skylar laughed. "The last thing you need is an office romance gone bad."

"Is he married?"

"It doesn't appear that way. Cole keeps a relatively low profile on social media, unlike Tristan O'Shaughnessy, who seems to have a parade of women, one more beautiful than the next."

"Who's that?"

"He's the winner of the Caldor Trophy and the guy Cole had the fight with. I'll send you the clip. It was more like a brawl. It was brutal, even by hockey standards. They were both ejected from the game."

"What caused the fight?"

"They didn't say, and believe me, I looked."

"Thanks, Skye. Can I ask you one more favor? If I send you a few players' names, can you find me a quick fact or two for each? I'm meeting the team tomorrow and want to make a good impression. Normally, I'd do it myself, but I'm running short on time. Besides, you're so good when it comes to research."

"Flattery will get you everywhere. Send me the list."

"Thanks again. Did I tell you how much I miss you?"

"I know. I miss you too. Don't let this jerk get to you, Layla. Tomorrow is a new day."

Skylar sent me the link to the fight. Violence usually didn't faze me, but what I watched was disturbing. Cole targeted Tristan. I'd have to watch the game to see what transpired in the first two periods, but this looked personal on both sides. The ice was splattered with blood. Even the referee didn't escape unscathed. Tristan and Cole were taken to the hospital. Both men were fined and benched for several games. The commentators were at a loss as to what started the fight. They admitted both sides had taken cheap shots throughout the game, but nothing that would warrant such a brutal outburst. I shouldn't be surprised. Cole clearly had anger issues. Maybe I was just his latest scapegoat. I vowed to keep digging until I uncovered the cause of the disagreement. I was sure someone on the team must know. For now, it was back to the fact-finding mission on the players. Before getting into bed, I set the alarm on my phone and arranged for a wake-up call. There was no way I would oversleep again!

CHAPTER 2

I woke up exhausted yet strangely invigorated. It was a new day, and I would do what I did best, win people over. The fact that Cole underestimated my abilities was something I would use to my advantage. I got to the office uncharacteristically early. As a night owl, I needed every minute possible to get ready in the morning. Still, today, I wanted to leave myself extra time to review some of my research from last night and be on my "A" game when I met with Leora and Cole.

At nine-thirty, I headed to Leora's office. Before I could knock, I heard Cole's voice emanating from behind the doorway.

"I don't understand why you hired her. I'm sure there were more qualified female candidates if you felt the need to hire a woman," Cole said in an indignant voice.

"Cole, I don't understand your issue with Layla."

"My problem is I'm working with a dumb blonde who clearly admits to being clueless about hockey. Forgive me if I think that should be a prerequisite for a job as an NHL commentator."

"I don't appreciate your stereotypes, Cole," Leora replied with displeasure.

"You can't deny that she arrived late, interrupted our meeting, and dumped coffee on my crotch. Those are the actions of a woman in over her head."

"She had a rough start," Leora replied, with a shrug. Everyone is entitled to a second chance, a concept I think you, of all people, would understand."

"I suppose," Cole replied wistfully.

"Besides, every time you insult Layla, you inadvertently disrespect me since she was my hire."

"I don't mean to do that. You know I think the world of you, Leora, and I'm eternally grateful for all you've done for me. I just can't comprehend what you see in her."

"Layla has skills that can't be taught. Her demeanor puts people at ease which makes for compelling interviews. She thinks fast on her feet and can go off script when necessary. I found her commentary from the football games to be on point and insightful. Most importantly, she has a riveting presence on camera, which translates to ratings. She's bright, and it's not like she doesn't have a sports background. Layla's has a direct, tough, competitive style that works well regardless of what sport she's announcing. I doubt she knew much about football when she started, but she learned quickly. I'm sure we'll see a repeat performance with hockey."

"So, you admit to hiring eye candy," Cole replied in an accusatory tone.

"Cole, you're not listening. I know you're upset about Shane. We all are, but it isn't like you not to give her a chance. Tell me what's going on," Leora implored.

"Shane will get better, and when he does, I want him to have a job to return to. One look at Layla and our predominantly male audience won't care if she speaks in tongues. It's unfair to Shane and sullies the show's reputation."

"Cole, if you were objective, you would see that Layla is good at what she does. Contrary to your opinion, I hired her because she is talented. Her looks are a bonus, especially in the entertainment industry. If Shane gets well, and I wish for that every day, he will always have a job at this network."

"I notice you're not saying what that job will be."

"Let's take it one day at a time. In the meantime, I want you to take Layla under your wing. You're to be her mentor and a source of support. I better not hear any more of these demeaning statements coming from your mouth. Layla would have every right to report you to human resources. If she does, don't expect me to defend you. Do we understand each other, Cole?"

I couldn't hear his response. I'm assumed he nodded in agreement. After all, what choice did he have? I felt better knowing Leora had my back, but I feared her comments would further enrage Cole. My mother always told me that it was hard to pick a fight if your opponent didn't engage, and that was what I planned to do moving forward. Where Cole Pasternak was concerned, I would be the bigger person.

I went to the ladies' room to give Cole and Leora a few minutes to wrap up their conversation. "Good morning," I said in a voice that was so cheerful it even surprised me. "Are you ready to start our meeting, or should I come back?"

"No, we're ready. So, Layla, how was your first day?" Leora inquired.

"It ended much better than it started. The staff is so helpful and welcoming. I was touched by the warm reception," I said, flashing a smile at Cole that would melt ice in the winter. "By the way, you look like hell. I'm hoping you're not still ailing from the incident yesterday."

"I'm fine," Cole growled.

"Are you sure? You look tired. I guess you're not used to working late." So much for the high road. I guess I couldn't get past Cole's dumb blonde comment.

I hated to admit it, but I lied about Cole's appearance. I couldn't take my eyes off him. His tousled hair and five o'clock shadow gave the impression of someone who recently rolled out of bed after a night of great sex, a look I found hot at any time. Cole was wearing a tight polo shirt that was open at the collar, revealing the cleft between his well-defined pectoral muscles. His shirt accentuated his blue bedroom eyes. His hair was still damp, and I watched as he periodically ran his fingers through it to keep the front piece from dangling in his face. It was so unfair. Men look the same or even better than they did the night before. Whereas women woke up looking like a pale, undefined, older version of themselves, leaving men to wonder what happened to the person they took to bed.

Cole looked at me with daggers in his eyes. "My night got better as soon as I left the office. How about you? You look incredibly refreshed for a woman who was supposed to be busy studying. I'm interested to hear what you learned."

"I'm sure Leora has more important things to do than hear my takeaways from old game footage." Cole's face had a smug grin, like a kid who had just tattled on his classmate. "However, I have a list of questions I was hoping you could answer. Maybe you have some time following the meeting?" Cole was ready to blow me off when Leora interrupted.

"We were just discussing how Cole could be of assistance before you came in. He's actually a wonderful mentor."

I nodded in agreement. "I'm sure Cole is a wealth of knowledge, and I'm excited to work with him. Cole, I'll grab my list and head down to your office after the meeting," I said, mustering a smile. I thought he was going to choke. He couldn't resist getting in a parting shot.

"Layla, do us both a favor and leave the coffee behind."

I was curious to see Cole's attitude behind closed doors. I decided to put up with the occasional jab if he willingly let me pick his brain. I downed another cup of coffee, grabbed my notes, and headed to Cole's office. "Is this a good time?" I asked, peering my head through the doorway.

"A good time for what?" he asked, feigning ignorance.

"To go over my questions."

Cole sat up in his chair. "Let me make something perfectly clear," he said, folding his arms over his chest. "I have no intention of answering your questions or contributing to your success in any way. As a matter of fact, if I'm instrumental at all, it will be in accelerating your demise."

My gut wrenched. What happened to Cole's promise to Leora? Was he a liar too? I was searching for an appropriate response when I was saved by a knock on the door.

"Hey, Ash, I wasn't expecting you."

"Sorry to interrupt, Cole, but I'm in a jam and need your help."

I turned to see a stunning woman at the entrance to Cole's office. This must be his girlfriend. She could pass for a model at five-foot-eleven, with long legs that looked amazing in her skinny jeans and strappy sandals. She had dark hair that fell right above her hips. Her eyes were blue/green like the sea. She had high cheekbones and flawless tanned skin.

"Cole, are you going to introduce us?" the woman asked, nodding in my direction.

"Ashley, this is Layla MacKenzie. She's filling in temporarily for Shane."

"Layla, like the song?"

"It was my mother's favorite," I replied.

"Your mother has great taste in music."

"What are you talking about?" asked a clueless Cole.

"My mother named me after the rock classic 'Layla' by Eric Clapton. You must know it."

"I can't say that I do."

I stared at Cole in disbelief. "Everybody knows it. Haven't you heard of Eric Clapton?"

"I know he's a guitar player."

"He isn't just a guitar player. He's a legend!"

Ashley giggled at my response. "I'm afraid Cole's not into music."

"There's not being into music, and then there's living under a rock!" I replied, causing Ashley and me to break into laughter.

Cole was clearly annoyed. "I didn't have time for music. It's not that I don't like it. I was just too busy playing hockey to have time for anything else. Ashley, what brings you here, anyway?"

"I need a favor, Cole. I have a job interview, and my sitter canceled. Can I leave Katelyn with you for a couple of hours? Please!"

"You know I can't say no to you," Cole said, throwing his hands up in resignation. "Where is my favorite niece?"

"Ava took her to get a donut. So, Layla, do you like music?" Ashley inquired.

"I love it!"

"Would you like to grab a drink and see a band with me one night?"

"I don't think that's a good idea, Ash," Cole interjected.

"What's your problem, Cole? My brother doesn't want me to have a social life," Ashley quipped.

"It's not that. I just don't like your choice of company."

Ashley took a long look at me. I could see the wheels turning as she replied, "I think I know why." At that moment, Ava walked in the door with an adorable three-year-old.

"Uncle Cole!" Katelyn screamed as she ran right for him. Cole scooped her up and tossed her in the air.

"Hey, kiddo, I hear we'll be spending the afternoon together."

"Yay," she exclaimed, throwing her arms around his neck. Cole's eyes lit up as he planted kisses on Kate's cheeks. He clearly adored her. I was pleasantly surprised by this side of him. Maybe there was hope for Cole after all.

"I've got to run. Ava, give Layla my number. Layla, don't let my brother fool you. Beneath that gruff exterior lies a big softie. Katelyn, be good for your uncle. I'll see you later."

"Bye, Ashley. It was great meeting you. Good luck with your interview." I turned to Cole, who was fawning over Kate. "I don't want to intrude on your time with your niece. We'll finish this conversation later," I said, turning toward the door.

"I consider this conversation over," Cole replied.

"Your sister looks like you. Too bad you're not more like her," I snarled as I walked out.

I wasn't shocked that Cole wouldn't help me, but I didn't think he would go as far as sabotaging me. Ashley alluded to knowing the reason behind his contempt. I had to find out more. I would arrange to meet with her and pick her brain.

I headed back to my office to get some work done. Fifteen minutes later, Katelyn snuck through the door. She crawled under my desk and put her finger to her lips. "I hide," she said with a voice that melted my heart. Cole appeared shortly afterward. He paused in my doorway, and I pointed beneath my desk.

"Newhouse, have you seen my niece? I seem to have lost her."

"Sorry, I haven't seen her," I replied innocently.

"Where could she be?" Cole asked in an animated voice.

"Katelyn, where are you?" he called, slowly stomping around my office. "She's not behind the couch. She's not behind the TV. Where else could she be?"

Cole got down on his hands and knees and crawled on the floor in my direction. I slid my chair back as he popped his head under my desk. Katelyn let out a shriek of joy as Cole grabbed her. He tickled her all over, causing Kate to squeal with delight.

"C'mon, sweetie, we need to let Newhouse concentrate. She has a lot to learn."

I watched Cole put Katelyn on his shoulders and disappear out the door. Watching him with her gave me renewed hope. Cole had a heart, after all. He even gave me a nickname, "Newhouse," after my college program. That was either a sign he was softening toward me or another way to demean me. I was sure I'd find out which one it was soon enough.

CHAPTER 3

"Are you guys ready to go?" Chase, our producer, asked.

"It's six o'clock already? My day flew by," I replied.

"It always does. Cole, are you ready?" Chase called out.

"Yeah, I'm not sure why I need to go, but I'm coming," Cole replied begrudgingly.

We headed over to Sunrise arena, the home of the Predators. Their practice had ended, and the guys were finishing up in the locker room. Cole strolled into the dressing area, and I made the mistake of following him. He turned to me and snapped. "Where do you think you're going?"

"I thought I was going to meet the team," I replied innocently.

"We're meeting the team in one of the conference rooms," Cole replied, in a raised voice.

"I didn't realize that. I was following your lead."

"Listen, Newhouse, the locker room is no place for a woman."

I sighed in exasperation. "That's right, Cole. We should all be at home, barefoot and pregnant."

"I didn't say that. It's just that hockey players aren't overly refined. I wouldn't want you to see or hear something that offends your delicate sensibilities."

"A bright man would have deduced by now that I'm not easily offended."

"Well then, I don't want to pressure the men to act differently because a woman is in their presence. Chase, take Layla upstairs. I'll round up the guys and see you shortly."

I was excited and nervous at the prospect of meeting the team. I glanced into my purse at my cheat sheet of player information. I hoped seeing them didn't make me forget everything I had memorized over the last twenty-four hours. My heart beat with nervous anticipation as I heard the players coming down the hall like a roll of thunder. Cole was right. The guys were far from dainty. They ushered past me, taking seats. All of the players acknowledged me, whether it was with a head-to-toe inspection, a welcome wave or nod, or prolonged eye contact that made me uneasy.

My knees began to shake. I quickly pulled over a chair, hoping not to appear visibly nervous, as Chase got everyone's attention. I noticed Cole chose to sit with the team.

"Hey guys, thanks for meeting with us. This won't take much of your time. As you know, Shane McPherson is on medical leave. We feel fortunate to have Layla MacKenzie as the new face of our network. She will be working closely with Cole as your new commentator."

"That is until Shane returns," Cole chimed in.

"It goes without saying we are all pulling for Shane's speedy recovery. Layla will be doing most of the player intermission and post-game interviews. I know you guys will make her feel welcome. Let me turn it over to Layla," Chase said, waving his hand in my direction.

"Hi, everybody." I managed to stand and face the twenty-two pairs of eyes staring a hole through me. "It's an honor to meet you. I feel so grateful to be here. I just wish it were under better circumstances. As a young girl, I was a hockey fan, but my broadcasting career centered on football. I'm looking forward to getting back to my hockey roots. I know I have a lot to learn. Still, I plan to get to know you individually, ensuring you get the best possible media exposure. As a first step, I would like you to stand and tell me your name. I've tried to learn something about each of you, and if there is something you would like me to be aware of, please feel free to share it.

"Sebastian Dvorak, I know you are currently our lead goal scorer with nineteen points, twelve goals, and seven assists. Andre Pointe, you were our number-one draft choice this year. You are the youngest member of the team and a star rookie with eight goals and four assists. You'll be a Calder Award contender if your current performance continues. Travis Goodrow, you are our top defenseman and a critical part of our 'kill team,' which has the best record in the league. Alexander Koulak, you are our fastest skater at an incredible thirty miles per hour. You hold our current record for most shots on goal, and you are one point behind Sebastian in the standings. Jordan O'Shea is our beloved team captain. In addition to being an inspiration on the ice, your family foundation does so much for the community. From what I've seen, you do a great job clearing the puck from our end zone. Mathieu Perrault, you have a sixty percent faceoff win percentage, making you fourteenth in the league. You also spend the most time in the penalty box."

The guys chuckled. "I would like to say that your beautiful face will be a welcome change from Cole's ugly mug," Mathieu replied.

"Hey, I resent that remark!" Cole chimed in.

"Pierre Paquet, you recently came to us from the Bombers. What fascinates me about you is that you speak five languages. Brett Gillies, we have something in common. Rottweilers are our spirit animal."

"Like me, they're so misunderstood. I'm really a pussycat underneath my tough exterior," Brett replied, with a smile.

"I don't mean to contradict you, but your cross-checking screams anything but pussycat," I said, laughing. "Brady Caulfield, you were the recipient of the Bill Masterson Award based on your determination, dedication, and how you inspire your teammates through your performance and approach to the game."

I went on until I managed to say something about every team member. Ultimately, I saluted Coach Shanahan for his successful stint in the NHL, which transitioned into an even more remarkable coaching career, with one Stanley Cup to his credit. I breathed a sigh of relief as I wrapped up my presentation. I was stunned when the guys gave me a standing ovation. Out of the corner of my eye, I saw Cole shake his head in what I could only surmise was disapproval.

"Hey, Cole, a few of us are going to grab a bite. Why don't you join us?" Jordan O'Shea asked. "Layla, that goes for you too."

I was surprised by Jordan's invitation. "It's nice of you to include me, but I should get back to work."

"Nonsense, right, Cole?"

"Layla doesn't want to hang out with you thugs," Cole replied, glaring at me.

I decided to go, motivated by the fact that Cole didn't want me there. "I suppose it would be rude not to join you, especially after that warm reception," I replied.

We met up at Fleming's steakhouse. I nearly died when I glanced at the menu. This was way out of my price range. I could tell the Predators were regulars by how the hostess greeted the team. We were escorted into a private room with a long table. Somehow, I got stuck sitting next to Cole. I was glancing at the menu when he whispered, "Nice dog and pony show. The guys were impressed."

"Thank you," I replied, taken aback by what I thought was a compliment.

"Don't thank me. You memorized a few tidbits of information. It takes a lot more than that to dazzle me."

"It may seem like a small gesture, but I find a personal touch goes a long way. By the way, I learned something about you too."

"What's that?" Cole asked, looking bored.

"I learned that your career-ending injury resulted from a brutal fight with Tristan O'Shaughnessy."

"That's far from a newsflash," Cole replied sarcastically.

"What I can't figure out is what started the fight. I understand you guys were in heavy competition for the Calder Trophy."

Anger flashed across Cole's face as he turned to address me.

"Do you think I'm so shallow that I would beat the shit out of a guy over a little competition?"

"I don't know. You tell me. I watched the footage. That fight was personal."

"Not that it's any of your business, but Tristan and I were friends. We played in the same circles. I respected his skills on the ice and was a better player in his presence."

"Then what caused you to knock his teeth out?"

"That's none of your damn business," Cole snapped, turning his back toward me. I decided to let it go but Cole's reaction made me even more determined to uncover the cause of the fight.

The tab for dinner must have been ten grand, and the guys were just getting started. Jordan O'Shea picked up the bill like a drop in the bucket, and we took the party into the bar area. Within minutes, several beautiful women descended upon the guys. I never realized that hockey players had groupies until I watched the women swarm them like bees to honey. Each scantily clad girl was more attractive than the next. I decided to sit at the corner of the bar and observe. I saw Cole talking with his former teammate, Jackson Kane. They were glancing over at me and whispering. I hoped Cole wasn't trash-talking me.

"Cole, are you hitting that?" Jackson asked, nodding in my direction.

"No way, man."

"Would you mind if I give it a go?"

"I don't care if the whole team screws her. Maybe Layla will get a reputation as a slut, and Leora will bounce her for violating her morals clause."

Jackson sat beside me and motioned to the bartender to bring me a drink. "I really don't need another drink. I plan on working when I get home," I said politely. We had a pleasant chat. I thought Jackson was just being friendly until he placed his hand on my thigh and suggested we move the party to his place. I guess I should have seen that coming, but I tended to be naive, especially regarding men.

"Jackson, I would like to get to know you better regarding your strengths on the ice and your contributions to the team. However, I have a policy of keeping my work relationships confined to business. It's nothing personal."

"I understand. I hope I didn't offend you."

"No, not at all. I'm flattered."

"If there is anything I can do to help you, let me know," he said, giving me a wink.

As I watched Jackson walk away, I noticed one of the groupies draped all over Cole. She was hanging off his shoulder and on his every word as she giggled and batted her big blue eyes. She couldn't have been more than eighteen years old. I was perplexed by what he saw in her, or was I? She had shoulder-length blonde hair with pink streaks framing her face. Her breasts were disproportionately large for her tiny waist. The low-cut blouse tied above her belly button revealed toned tan abs. I was convinced she had to lie on the bed to zip her skintight jeans. Although, I was confident that Cole would have no issue getting them off. How remarkably predictable yet disappointing that he would find clueless, compliant women attractive. Why did I care anyway? This reaffirmed my belief that Cole Pasternak was shallow, immature, and chauvinistic. Needing a distraction, I began talking to the bartender. He was a welcome reprieve from the pack of alpha males in the room, who were becoming louder and increasingly intoxicated. Cole called out to me as he ushered his groupie out the door.

"Hey, Layla, shouldn't you be home studying?"

"I'm on my way out. Thanks for calling my attention to the time. Enjoy your evening."

I finished my conversation with the bartender and headed to my hotel. I crawled into bed and watched ESPN for league highlights. Unfortunately, visions of Cole with that bimbo kept invading my thoughts. Why did it bother me? I told myself I didn't care who he dated as long as it wasn't me.

CHAPTER 4

Today, Darius was doing a photo shoot of Cole and me as an introduction for the fans and promotion for tomorrow's broadcast. I stared into my tiny hotel room closet, trying to figure out what to wear. I was told to bring several outfits that would work in different settings. What the hell did that mean? Men were always so vague. They didn't seem to understand that women stressed over these things. I reluctantly took out a floral print dress. Floral patterns are standard in the south, but I hated them. Did I want to look super feminine, or should I wear the royal blue dress and look more powerful? I opted for the blue. I had no issue being in front of the camera when it came to doing a broadcast, but for some reason, photoshoots freaked me out. They felt unnatural and staged. When I was broadcasting a game, my focus was on my audience. Today, the focus would be on me, and I didn't enjoy being the center of attention. I bet my egomaniacal partner loved it.

I had an hour to myself before the photo shoot, so I went back to devouring old footage of pre-and post-game wrap-ups. At ten o'clock, I went to the studio. Cole arrived ten minutes late in a Predator jersey and tight jeans. We were clearly on a different page as to wardrobe choice.

"Nice of you to make it. Did you have to drop your girlfriend off at high school before coming to work?" I asked, my voice dripping with sarcasm.

Cole smiled in amusement. "For the record, she was twenty."

"Was that what it said on her fake ID?"

"Not that it's any of your business, but she's a junior at the University of Miami."

"What is she majoring in? How to snag a hockey player 101?"

"Actually, she just finished taking her LSATs for law school and felt like blowing off some steam."

"Just because she took the test doesn't mean she'll pass."

"True, but that's not really my concern."

"Your concern should be getting arrested for screwing jailbait."

"She's nine years younger than me. There are plenty of guys who date younger women. To my knowledge, that's not a crime."

"She's not even legal drinking age. That is a crime."

"That's not my problem either. I didn't serve her."

"Nine years is a big difference between an adult male and a college student. What could you find to talk about?"

"It wasn't her conversational skills that held my attention."

"What's the matter, Cole? You can't handle a woman your own age?"

"I can handle more than one woman at any age. I'm just saying age isn't a factor for me."

"What is?"

"It depends on what I'm looking for. If I wanted a relationship, my standards would be different, but that's not what I want. Right now, I'm content just having a good time. That's something you should consider, Newhouse. You seem tightly wrapped. I guess your bartender couldn't get you there. I'm not surprised. That happens when you choose a boy to do a man's job."

"Milo is more of a man than all the guys in the bar combined," I replied, defensively.

"That's one person's opinion. From where I stood, he looked one hundred and thirty-five pounds soaking wet. I guess you like to be the dominant one in your relationships."

"Milo was four years old when his family fled Cuba due to the refugee crisis in 1994. His father died on that journey, leaving Milo's twenty-two-year-old mother to raise him and his six-year-old sister."

Cole's demeanor changed as I saw an emotion resembling empathy cross his face. "That must have been hard."

"It was. Milo's mom didn't speak a word of English. There were nights when she would go without eating so her children wouldn't starve. Yet somehow, she managed to survive in a strange place with nothing but the clothes on her back. Luckily, she landed a job as a dishwasher at a local restaurant. She was a hard worker, and the boss eventually promoted her and employed her children. Milo worked his way up from dishwashing to bartending. He dropped out of school to help support his family. He got his GED and enrolled in community college. Milo is about to complete his bachelor's degree in business administration. Then he plans to go on for his MBA."

"Good for him. What happened to the rest of his family?"

"His sister is a paralegal who is working toward a law degree. She plans to specialize in immigration law. Milo's mom formed her own business cleaning office buildings. It's a great story. I'm going to have my friend Skylar reach out to him. She's a journalist back home and loves writing human interest pieces, especially those involving strong females. When I went into broadcast journalism, I wanted to cover this type of narrative, but somehow, I landed in sports."

"I can only guess why," Cole replied, staring at my legs.

"I've had to deal with people like you my entire career."

"I assume you mean bright, captivating, and intrinsically charismatic," he replied with a grin.

"Hardly. I was thinking more along the lines of judgmental and shortsighted. Contrary to your opinion, my appearance hasn't been an asset. People have a hard time taking a pretty face seriously."

"That's bullshit," Cole barked. "Your looks landed you in front of the camera. Hundreds of women would trade places with you in a heartbeat. If you're looking for sympathy, you've come to the wrong place."

"I'm not looking for sympathy. What I want is respect."

"Respect has to be earned."

"That's the first thing you've said that we agree on."

I walked away from Cole, needing to regain my composure. I was relieved when Chase finally arrived. "Hey, guys, sorry I'm late. I've got some ideas I'd like to run by you. I'd like to shoot a few promos here in the studio and then head to the arena for a couple of action scenes. Layla, honey, you look gorgeous. Cole, do you have any dress clothes upstairs? Your jersey will be great for the promos at the arena."

Cole sighed in annoyance. "Yeah, I have a suit in my office. I'll be right back."

"In the meantime, I printed off some talking points for you to look at," Chase said, handing us each a copy.

I was reviewing the suggestions when Cole returned in a tight-fitting charcoal suit with a light gray dress shirt and a blue and gray tie. I felt my jaw drop. "Pull it together, Layla," I told myself. I wasn't a formal gal. Men in business suits weren't my thing. My preferences ran toward faded jeans, boots, and flannel shirts. Items I would never find in this palm-tree-infested haven of humidity. Cole gave me a new perspective as I envisioned grabbing his tie, pulling his body on top of mine, and ripping his clothes off with my teeth.

The scenes in the studio went by without a hitch. Cole should have won an academy award for his performance. You would think he was looking forward to working with me. Then it was on to the arena. Chase arranged for T-Bone, the Predator's mascot, to meet us for a few cameo shots.

"Layla, what size skates do you wear?" Chase asked.

"Size nine. Why?"

"I thought it would be fun to get a couple of shots of you and Cole on the ice. Why don't you go into the Predator store, grab a jersey, and throw on some jeans? I'll scour a pair of skates from the ice girl's locker room.

"Do you even know how to skate, Layla?" Cole asked, in his usual smart-ass demeanor.

"I can hold my own," I replied, in a frigid tone.

I changed and headed toward the rink. We met up with T-Bone and were instructed to get into a group hug. Cole's hand accidentally grasped my arm. His touch was so warm and firm that it sent a slight shiver down my spine.

"Why don't you guys head onto the ice," Chase suggested. "I thought it might be fun to take some action shots. Layla, maybe you could pretend to shoot the puck. I'll go grab some equipment from the locker room."

Cole was rolling his eyes as I stepped on the ice and began to skate around the rink. My muscle memory came flooding back as I started picking up momentum. Cole watched me intently from behind the glass. I decided to teach that arrogant prick a lesson. Picking up speed, I launched into a single-toe loop. I didn't have the height I was used to getting on that jump, but I landed on my feet. Cole's eyes were riveted as I circled the rink again, skating backward before completing another single-toe loop followed by a double-toe loop.

"Darius, are you getting this?" Chase called out.

"There's no way I'd miss it, boss."

I ended my routine by going from an upright, to a camel, to a sitting spin. I heard applause and saw some of the Predators standing in the players' box. I skated over to them for a fist bump before returning to mid-ice, where my eyes found Cole. Now it was his turn to pick his chin off the floor. Cole grabbed the hockey sticks and puck from Chase and handed them to me without saying a word.

"Okay, let's do this. I see the guys are waiting to get practice underway. Cole, Layla, why don't you go to center ice and pretend to face off against each other? Good, now each of you take a few slap shots from the blue line," Chase instructed. Cole sank all three of his shots. I was pleasantly surprised when my last one found its way into the net.

"Why don't you guys stand side by side, crossing your sticks?

That looks great. Now lean back-to-back, holding your sticks up," Chase directed. I felt the warmth from Cole's body emanating onto mine. Even at five-foot-ten inches, I paled in comparison to his massive frame.

"For the finale, I think it would be cool if Cole plays goalie and Layla takes a shot at the net."

"Chase, you're killing me, man," Cole whined as he crouched in the goaltender's box. I skated back and forth a couple of times, trying to plan my approach. As I got closer, I aimed for Cole's left side. Cole kicked out his leg and blocked the puck with his skate. I instinctively skated behind the net, picking up the rebound. I stuffed it in as I rounded the corner to the front of the net. I heard more cheers from the player's box as I skated back for a second fist bump. Cole leaned against the goalpost, shaking his head in disbelief.

"Okay, that's a wrap. Let's clear out so these guys can practice," yelled Chase. We got in the car and headed back to the studio. "Layla, that was quite a show you put on. The fans are going to love it!" Cole groaned in response to Chase's enthusiasm. "Hey, buddy," Chase said to Cole. "You did a great job. Thanks for humoring me. You guys have great chemistry on camera."

"That's three hours of my life I won't get back," Cole muttered. I didn't say a word. I just sat quietly, savoring what I perceived as a victory. I returned to my desk and began reviewing more game footage when I heard a knock at my door.

"Do you mind if I come in?" Cole asked.

"Have a seat."

"Today wasn't just a fluke. When did you learn to skate?"

"I started skating on a small lake near my house when I was five. I loved it, so my mother enrolled me in lessons. It wasn't long before I started working with a trainer, who told me I had the potential to skate competitively."

"Why didn't you?"

"At the end of ninth grade, my father walked out and never returned. I managed to skate for another year until we ran out of money, and my mother needed a second job. My trainer offered to reduce her rates, but it was still cost-prohibitive. Besides, I had no way to get to practice, and I needed to pitch in more at home. So, you weren't the only one forced to give up your dream."

Cole paused. "I see your point, but it's not quite the same."

"You're right. At least you got to realize your fantasy and play for NHL. I'll never know what I could have accomplished. I had to abandon skating for a more practical goal."

"Did your dad ever come back?"

"I haven't seen him since the day he left. My mom tracked him down once. She tried to sue for child support, but apparently, he was working off the books."

"That must have been hard," Cole said, with something that resembled sympathy.

"It was, but we managed. I got a job when I was fifteen. My grandmother helped. My mother didn't make much money, which enabled me to get financial aid for college. My grades also qualified me for scholarships."

"You seem to have landed on your feet."

"So did you," I replied evenly.

"I think it's time for me to be heading out," Cole said, rising from his seat.

"While you're here, would you mind if I ask you a couple of questions?"

"Sorry, there's a bar stool with my name on it waiting for me. You're a resourceful girl. I'm sure you can find the answers."

My victory on the ice was short-lived. I felt like a balloon that had just been stuck with a pin.

"Once a dick, always a dick," I said to Cole. He turned to me and smiled as he walked out the door. I waited until Cole exited the building to call Skylar.

"Hey, Layla, I was just thinking about you. I reached out to Milo's sister, and she agreed to a phone interview."

"That's great, Skye."

"What's going on? You sound upset."

"You watch shows like Criminal Minds and CSI, don't you?"

"I admit they're my guilty pleasure."

"Do they tell you how to kill someone without leaving a trace? Wasn't there a show where a woman put antifreeze in her husband's drink?"

"Yes, and she got caught. What did Cole do now?"

"I was having such a great day, Skye. We did some promotional work for the show at the arena. I saw a modicum of respect in Cole's eyes when he saw me skate. Some of the guys from the Predators cheered for me. My producer was thrilled with the footage. When we returned to the office, I told Cole about my dad leaving and how I had to abandon my dream of becoming a professional skater. I thought we shared something. I sensed a shift in our relationship."

"So, what went wrong?"

"I asked if he would answer a couple of questions, and he totally blew me off. He reverted right back into the smug asshole who makes my blood boil. I went from feeling like I was on cloud nine to being dirt beneath his feet. He'll give me a stroke if I don't kill him."

Skylar laughed. "It's not funny, Skye."

"I know. I'm sorry. Layla, I don't know why you let this guy get under your skin. It sounds like you had a great day. Has it ever dawned on you that maybe he feels threatened?"

"Not on your life. He's not smart enough to feel threatened."

"Now there's my girl. Listen, you need to stop worrying about what Cole thinks. Remember, the one who cares less wins."

"But I do care. It would be easier to kill Cole."

"Then I suggest feeding him to the alligators. They won't leave a trace. Call me when it's done so we can work out an alibi."

Just the thought made me laugh. "Thanks, Skylar. You always know how to cheer me up."

I looked at my list of questions and went in search of answers. Then I made a set of flashcards with hockey terms and definitions. That night I dreamed of slowly lowering Cole into a pit of ravenous crocodiles. I fell asleep with a smile on my face.

CHAPTER 5

Today was my big premiere. I uncharacteristically woke up before the alarm. That only happened when I was nervous about the day's events. Damn Cole, I should be excited, but he had successfully undermined my confidence. Fortunately, the rest of my colleagues were more supportive. Leora was the first in a line of people who popped by to congratulate me on the promos.

"Great job yesterday, Layla. Are you ready for tonight?" Leora asked.

"As ready as I'll ever be."

"You'll do great. I'm glad to see you and Cole are getting along."

"What makes you say that?" I asked, trying to contain the surprise in my voice.

"I can see it from the footage. I knew he'd come around. Well, good luck tonight."

An hour later one person I wasn't expecting, arrived at my door. "What is it, Cole?"

"Shane is here. He's wondering if he could grab a few things he left in the office."

"Of course, I'd love to meet him."

"You must be Layla. May I say you're even prettier in person?"

"Thank you. It's so nice to meet you, Shane. I've watched so many of your broadcasts. I feel like I know you. You have left me huge shoes to fill."

"Shane, buddy, I'm headed back to my office. Let me know how things are going and tell Addison to message me when he wants to catch practice."

"Thanks, Cole, you're the best."

Cole walked over to Shane and gave him a big bear hug. "Things just aren't the same here without you."

Shane stepped into the hall and returned with a box. "I see you still have my pictures up."

"It looks like you have a lovely family," I replied. "I'm assuming these are your kids."

"These are my daughters. Sophie's in her first year of college. Sage is a junior in high school, and Addison is a freshman. Cole has been great with him. Addison's a huge hockey fan. Cole brings him to watch the Predators practice."

"Does Addison play?"

"He plays for his high school team. He's gotten much better since Cole took him under his wing and started coaching him. Cole tries to attend his games when his schedule permits."

"Yeah, that Cole is a real standup guy," I replied, trying to hide my sarcasm. "How are you feeling?"

"Some days are better than others."

"My grandmother had cancer. It's an awful disease, but they've made so much progress. I hope you get well soon. I know everyone here misses you, especially Cole."

"Unfortunately, I don't see myself returning in the foreseeable future. I just applied for disability."

"Hopefully, that's only temporary. I want you to know your job is always waiting for you."

"That's very kind of you, Layla," Shane replied with a doubtful expression.

"I put the rest of your things in the bottom of my file cabinet" I said, reaching into the drawer and loading them into Shane's box. "While you're here, do you mind if I ask you a couple of questions?"

Shane was so forthcoming and helpful, especially in lieu of the fact that I was his replacement. Why couldn't Cole take a page from his book? After Shane left, I decided to see Cole and review the logistics for tonight's broadcast. It was clear he wasn't going to reach out to me. I took a deep breath and walked down to his office.

"Hey, is this a good time to review a couple of things?" I asked.

"Not really."

"I ignored Cole's response and sat down."

"What do you want, Newhouse?" Cole asked in a perturbed tone.

"I just wanted to review some procedures for later." To my surprise, Cole answered all my questions without one snarky remark.

"Cole, I want you to know that I told Shane I would step aside and give him his job back when he's feeling better." I foolishly thought my admission would soothe Cole, but it appeared to have the opposite effect.

"Then you're even dumber than I thought," Cole said disdainfully. He must have seen the shocked expression on my face. "You know how hard it is to get a job in this business. Why would you willingly give up a great gig?" Cole asked suspiciously.

"Because it's the right thing to do. Karma's a bitch. I try to stay on her good side."

"That's easy to say when you know the likelihood of Shane returning is slim to none."

"Why do you say that?"

"Shane told me his cancer has spread to his lung. His treatment doesn't seem to be helping. There is an experimental drug his oncologist would like to try, but the insurance company won't cover it."

"I'm so sorry to hear that. Is there anything I can do to help?"

I thought I saw a tear well up in Cole's eye. "Not unless you have the winning lottery numbers," Cole replied in a choked-up voice.

"He must have money saved."

"He does, but he has three kids with college educations and weddings to pay for, and his wife doesn't work. He doesn't want to wipe out their savings, especially when there is no guarantee he'll get well. I offered to help, but he refused."

It was hard seeing Cole so visibly upset. As someone who deeply valued the friendships in my life, I was touched by his pain. I was toying with giving Cole a hug as he quickly wiped the tear from his eye. My sanity returned when Cole's voice erupted in my face.

"Get out of my office, Newhouse," he snapped. Cole clearly wasn't comfortable showing emotion. At that moment, I felt helpless. I certainly wasn't the one to comfort him, so I left. I tried to return to work, but I couldn't stop thinking about Shane. Then I was struck by inspiration. I walked down the hall and tapped on Leora's door.

"What can I do for you, Layla?"

"Shane just stopped by to pick up some of his things."

"I know; I saw him."

"Did he share his situation with you?"

"He did," Leora replied.

"There must be something we can do for him."

"I'm open to ideas."

"I thought the network could do a fundraiser. We could get the Predators involved. Cole and I would promote it. I could reach out to the team's sponsors and our network advertisers. What do you think?"

"I think it's a very thoughtful idea, Layla, but it's a lot of work. Do you really have time to take that on right now?"

"I could, with the help of my co-workers. I promise to do most of it in my spare time. It wouldn't take away from my work here."

"That kind of networking could benefit your career. Reach out to Gabriela and Jamison and see what they think. Is there anything I can do?"

"Could you see if the station would be willing to offer a discount on our advertising rates?"

"That's going to be a hard sell."

"I know, but maybe a one-time promotion tied into a home game."

"I'll see what I can do."

"Thanks, Leora."

The idea of running a fundraiser excited me. Since losing my grandmother to cancer, I had wanted to do more than make a monetary donation. I'd always been taught that you should answer the door when opportunity knocked. Upon meeting Shane, I knew I couldn't shy away from my chance to make a difference. It wouldn't be easy. I was overwhelmed as it was without adding this to my plate, but event planning was within my control. At the very least, my involvement might prove to Cole that I was not the enemy.

CHAPTER 6

It was almost time for the pre-game show. "Cole, I'm going to head over to the arena early. I'd like to introduce myself to some of the fans."

"This is a hockey game, not a popularity contest Newhouse, but feel free to knock yourself out."

My nerves were under control until I pulled into the stadium. I reminded myself that part of delivering a great sportscast was knowing my audience and being passionate about providing the best possible sportscast. With that in mind, I approached the crowd of people waiting behind the broadcast booth for the pre-game show. I introduced myself and interviewed the fans about their most incredible Predator memories and favorite players. Some fans shared that they were at the game to mark a celebration. I jotted down some notes and vowed to recognize some of these occasions if the opportunity arose. Talking with the fans calmed my nerves until I heard them call Cole's name. I turned and saw him strolling up in a midnight blue suit. He waved to the fans, shooting them a smile that slayed me. Maybe I should be grateful he hated me. I didn't know how long I could look at that grin without having to nibble on his succulent lower lip.

We took our seats in the broadcast booth, and the camera began to roll. "It's a battle for the Metropolitan Division as the rivalry in the Eastern Conference heats up between the Carolina Cobras and the Florida Predators. Hi, I'm Cole Pasternak, and filling in for Shane McPherson is Layla MacKenzie. Thanks for joining us for this much-anticipated rivalry."

I felt a jab as Cole pointed out that I was filling in, especially after the update on Shane's health.

"Layla, what do you expect to see happening tonight?" Cole asked, catching me off guard.

"I think we're in for a great game. The Predators are in second place, and the Cobras are trailing them by three points in the division, so this is a critical win for both sides. From what I've seen, these two teams are evenly matched. The Predators have a better kill record on the power play. Still, the Cobras have a higher winning percentage on the faceoff. Both teams aren't afraid to use their physicality. The Cobras are coming off two tremendous victories on the road, one in overtime at Ottawa and one in Boston. It helps that one of their best defensemen, Jordon Fox, is out on Covid protocol. Blake Lundgren is still out with a lower-body injury. As you know, Brendan Hammond has done an outstanding job in goal with a Goals Against Average of 2.2, so that will be a challenge for our offense. The Predators just finished a brief rest period. They beat the Cobras earlier in the season, and we have the home-ice advantage. Our top offensive line has been red hot with Sebastian Dvorak scoring three goals in the last two games, and Alex Koulak with a goal and two assists in three consecutive games."

Cole responded with a slight nod. I was pleased to see a hint of surprise in his beautiful blue eyes. "I agree. I'm anticipating a great game."

I breathed a sigh of relief. So far, so good. I should have known it was going to go downhill from there. The first period ended in a one-to-one tie.

"Layla, tell me what adjustments you think the Predators need to make for the second period," Cole implored.

"We need to do better scoring off the rush and controlling loose pucks. The players need more traffic in the crease. Our offense is trying to set up the shots, but the Cobras have almost twice as many shots on goal. The Predators have done a great job being tenacious with the forecheck, but they must curb those penalties. They gave the Cobras three power plays to their one. We are fortunate that our Kill Team only let up one goal."

I survived the first period and had a great interview with Andre Pointe, who put the Predators on the scoreboard. Unfortunately, my confidence was shattered when my subsequent downfall struck during the second period. I called icing on the Cobras during a Predator's powerplay. Cole was quick to jump all over me.

"Layla, I guess you missed the unit on 'Icing' in Hockey 101. Otherwise, you would know that a team can't be penalized for icing when short-handed."

I felt my face flush. "Thanks for pointing that out, Cole. I always appreciate your input," I replied, gritting my teeth.

It went from bad to worse when Sebastian scored a goal ten minutes later, making that the third game in a row where he scored. I couldn't contain my excitement as I blurted out, "That is a personal record for Sebastian this season. His tie-breaking goal couldn't have come at a more opportune time. This is the catalyst our offense needed."

"Layla, if you followed the play more closely, you would have noticed that Kriecic hit the puck out of the rink. Sebastian played it on a bounce off the netting. Sebastian knows it. Why do you think he isn't more excited about scoring? He knows the goal won't count."

"I stand corrected," I replied, feeling my throat closing. "At least the Predators will have a power play with a delay of game call."

"Wrong again," Cole chided. "The removal of the goal serves as a penalty. Listen to the ruling by the referee and learn."

I felt like crawling into a hole and dying. Thank goodness the period was about to end. I would have a brief interview with Sebastian, hoping to restore what was left of my composure. As the intermission was winding down, I gave a shout-out to a few fans. I congratulated the Marshalls on celebrating their twenty-fifth wedding anniversary, Dave on his fiftieth birthday, and Sergeant Reyes for her service to the Marine Corps. "I'd also like to congratulate Emily Dickson, who just won a Predators jersey auto-graphed by Sebastian Dvorak. She was the victor in tonight's *In the Know* competition. Emily named all nine planets compared to the Predator's Pierre Paquet, who listed four."

"I hate when they make the guys participate in these ridiculous competitions, especially in the middle of the game," Cole complained. "Besides, Pierre is from Finland."

"What does that have to do with anything? The solar system is the same no matter what part of the world you live in. I think you're just making excuses because Pierre lost to a woman," I retorted, releasing some pent-up hostility.

Now Cole was on the defensive. "I'm not saying that. I know from experience that Pierre has more important things to think about with the Predators being down by a goal going into the third period than having to recollect the names of the planets."

"You're just making excuses because you know women are the smarter sex."

"That's ridiculous," Cole said, shaking his head.

"What did you score on your SATs?" I asked, clearly striking a nerve.

"That's irrelevant! I didn't study for them. Standardized testing was a formality in the recruitment process," Cole countered.

"So, you scored poorly," I said challenging him.

"I would have done better if I cracked a book, but why bother since my score didn't matter?"

"Do you know that women consistently outscore men on IQ tests?"

"That's ludicrous. Women just spend more time studying. It's a proven fact that men have larger brains."

"Yes, but women have thicker cortices, which is the area of the brain linked to intelligence testing. Women's cognitive skills and memories also decline slower than men's. I'll bet I'd beat you if we play *In the Know* at the next game."

"Are you trying to embarrass yourself?" Cole asked.

"I won't! Women also hold up better under pressure because cortisol, the stress hormone, increases more rapidly in men."

"Believe what you like, but we'll see who cracks under pressure in two days. Maybe you should use some of your brainpower to learn more about hockey, even though memorizing all the statistics in the world can't trump experience."

We glared at each other. I would've breathed fire on Cole if I had opened my mouth, incinerating him into ashes. In retrospect, I wasn't sure challenging him was a good idea, but I enjoyed his distaste at being backed into a corner.

The third period was a rough one. The Predators tied up the game with two minutes left, sending the game into overtime.

"What's your prediction here, Layla?"

"This has been a real nailbiter Cole. I think the momentum has shifted in the Predator's favor."

"I agree. I think the combination of being on the road, last night's overtime win, and the level of physicality in this game has caught up to the Cobras. I'm sure they'll lead with their top-scoring line. Still, they've already done longer shifts than usual because of the power play opportunities in the third period. Our defense has done a great job wearing them down. I can tell you; I've been where they are, and it's challenging to skate at your maximum capacity."

"I can only imagine what a struggle that must be," I said empathetically.

"That goes without saying since you never played hockey," Cole replied condescendingly.

The low blow caused my blood to simmer. "That's true, but as you may recall, I was a competitive figure skater. I know the training and strength needed to perform on the ice."

"There's no comparison between the two," Cole said in a dismissive tone.

"You're right. Hockey players are on the ice for forty-five-second shifts. The average figure skating routine is two minutes and forty-five seconds and incorporates acrobatics. Long programs last up to five minutes."

"Hockey players are on the ice for three to four times that long during a game. That's real stamina," Cole retorted.

"Do you know when I was training, I practiced three to four hours a day, which didn't include conditioning and dance lessons?"

"Dance lessons! You can't be serious right now. You're going to compare taking dance lessons to having your body checked continuously into the boards?"

"With a little training, I bet I could hold my own against you on the ice stamina and speed-wise."

"That's ridiculous. My thigh is the size of both your legs, and I'm almost double your weight."

"Do you know a woman's muscles can produce the same force as those of a comparably fit man? The fact that we have a lower muscle mass and still produce similar strength means females are actually as strong or stronger physically."

Cole was clearly annoyed by my unwillingness to back down. "Now I know you're certifiable," he snapped.

"Okay, since you're a little less than twice my size and weight, I bet I can skate half as fast and as long as you."

"You're deluding yourself."

"Do you care to make a wager?"

"Only if you want to be humiliated."

"Good! Then it's a bet."

"The guys are coming back on the ice. Why don't you review the overtime rules for our viewers and give them a break from this nonsense? I know I need one," Cole sniped.

Thankfully, I knew those regulations and recited them without a hitch. Two minutes into overtime, Alex ripped a shot to the top right corner, scoring the winning goal. I couldn't contain myself from cheering out loud. I finished my evening with a post-game interview with the hero of the night.

"Layla, congratulations. That was quite an opening broadcast," Darius said as he turned off the camera.

I wasn't exactly sure what he was implying, so I limited my response. "Yeah, it was an exciting game."

"The station crew usually grabs a drink after the game. I think you should join us and celebrate."

"Would you mind if I take a rain check? It's been an exhausting day."

"No problem. You'll join us next time."

"Thanks for including me, Darius. Enjoy yourself."

The idea of a drink sounded appealing, but I needed to get away from Cole. I knew he wanted me to fail, but I didn't think he would stoop so low as to publicly embarrass me.

I returned to my hotel and raided the mini bar in my hotel room out of frustration. I used a small bottle of vodka to wash down a Milky Way and a bag of peanut M & M's. Cole invaded my being like poison in my blood, depleting my oxygen until I couldn't breathe. I needed to drive him out before him out before he suffocated me. I would purge myself of Cole the only way I knew how, by beating him at his own game.

CHAPTER 7

"Cole, Layla, in my office now," Leora snapped. I was sitting down to eat my granola parfait when I realized I was about to be served a dose of admonishment with a side helping of humiliation for breakfast. I choked down my coffee and headed to Leora's office.

"Hey guys, would any of you like a donut? A lady friend of Cole's just dropped them off," Ava asked.

Cole shook his head. "You know I don't eat that crap, Ava. What did she say?"

"She said thanks for last night and to call her later."

Cole let out an exasperated sigh. "Did she leave me her number?"

"She said you had it."

"Well, she's wrong. I don't even know her name."

"Her name is Zoie. Do you want me to call security if she comes back?"

"No, I'll handle it. Thanks, Ava. Please put these donuts in the staff room."

"Unbelievable," I whispered under my breath but loud enough for him to hear.

Cole was preparing to launch a cutting retort when Leora interrupted. "Would you two like to explain what happened in that broadcast last night? Let's start with you, Cole. Why did you feel the need to publicly humiliate Layla?"

Cole stammered. He was clearly still foggy from partying. "I corrected Layla's mistakes. That's the only way she is going to learn."

"Did you find it prudent to teach Layla a lesson in the middle of a live broadcast?"

"I wasn't thinking about Layla at all. My allegiance is to our listening audience who relies on us for a factual accounting of the game."

"You also have a responsibility to Layla as your co-host. Maybe you and I have different definitions of the term mentor. Mine does not include denigrating another person for making a mistake."

"Layla, has Cole been giving you the information you need?"

My first response was to bury him, but that's what he was expecting. "Cole has answered all the questions I've asked of him," I replied, which wasn't a lie.

Leora didn't need to know that I refrained from asking him anything to spare myself the indignity of being ignored.

"Leora, I apologize for my inaccuracies. I had opening night jitters and made some rookie mistakes. I assure you the next broadcast will be better."

"Layla, may I ask what prompted some of your commentaries? I felt like I was watching a battle of the sexes instead of a hockey game."

"I admit to getting sidetracked. My reaction was a result of Cole putting me on the defensive."

"I want to share some feedback from our viewers," Leora replied as she rustled through some papers on her desk. "Apparently, social media is blowing up with comments about the broadcast. Layla, your interaction with the fans before the game and their inclusion in your commentary is a big hit." Cole groaned. "Furthermore, the fans seem to enjoy your he said/she said banter. Our female audience is impressed by the way Layla advocated for women. They want to know more about your skating career. Both men and women are interested in seeing who will emerge the victor of the next *In the Know* competition."

"I'm not wasting time on that stupid contest," Cole protested.

"That's where you're wrong," Leora replied, vehemently. "Apparently, polls are trending on Instagram and Twitter from both sexes about who will win. That's only the beginning. Our audience already loved the initial promos we released with the two of you on the ice. Now they're demanding to see the skating competition Layla proposed."

"I told you, Leora, this amateur has successfully hurt our credibility in just one show. This is hockey, not Live with Kelly and Ryan!"

"Calm down, Cole," Leora replied. "Initially, that was my reaction, but the audience feels differently."

"You're talking about reality TV fans, not hockey fans."

"May I remind you, Cole, hockey is a form of entertainment, and this network is in the entertainment business. Whether you agree or not, the fans responded to your let's spin it as 'playful banter.' I don't understand it, but the big boss wants to take it further and see where it goes."

"I object," Cole snapped.

"Duly noted but overruled," Leora retorted. "Now, I want the two of you to spend time reviewing old footage together. Cole, you highlight important talking points in the commentary. Layla, overall, I think your insights were on point. You've clearly integrated a lot of valuable information in a short time."

I nodded, not knowing what to say. This wasn't the conversation I expected, and I wasn't sure whether I should be elated or horrified. The meeting ended, and Cole bolted out the door. I could smell his cologne wafting through the air as I walked down the hall. It was a warm, spicy, woodsy blend with musky undertones that infiltrated my senses to arousal. I walked into my office and found him waiting for me.

"Listen, Cole, I know you're not happy, but can I at least eat my breakfast before you give me indigestion?"

"I have one question for you. Why didn't you throw me under the bus with Leora?"

"This isn't elementary school Cole, and I'm not a tattletale. If you choose to be a prick and not help me, I'll deal with it, but I would appreciate it if, in the future, you chose to 'enlighten' me in a more private forum. I made mistakes, but how you handled, it was a poor reflection of your character."

"I'll consider your suggestion if I can offer you one."

"I doubt I could stop you even if I wanted to."

"I'd think better of baiting me publicly or otherwise. Odds are you won't get the outcome you hope for," Cole warned, with an acidic tongue.

I holed up in my office for the rest of the day, watching old footage until I was bleary-eyed. I opted to leave work early and take a nap before my night out with Ashley.

"Hi, Katelyn, guess who's here to babysit?" Cole said, holding his arms out.

"Uncle Cole," Kate replied, throwing her arms around his calves.

"Thanks for doing this for me, Cole. I desperately need to get out of the house."

"Sure thing, Ash. You know I love spending time with my niece."

Can you get the door if the bell rings? My friend should be here shortly. I'm going to finish getting ready."

"Ashley, please try to dress appropriately," Cole implored.

"What are you, my father?" Ashley called out from the bedroom.

"No, I'm your overprotective big brother."

"Don't remind me."

Cole heard a knock on the door. "I'll get it," he said, twisting the knob.

Cole was so annoyed to see me that he left me standing in the doorway. The walls in Ashley's apartment were thin, enabling me to overhear the siblings' exchange.

"Why is she here?" Cole asked, confronting Ashley in her bedroom.

"Because we're going out."

"Didn't I tell you that wasn't a good idea?"

Ashley shrugged. "I disagree. Layla is new in town, and I'm too busy working, going to school, and being a mom to make friends. I like her. I think we'll have fun."

Cole marched back into the living room. I could feel his eyes surveying me, taking in my black leather mini skirt, white off-the-shoulder top, black lace choker, and black heels that tied up my calves.

"I'm not happy about this," Cole said, expressing displeasure.

"There are plenty of things that bother me where you're concerned, but your sister isn't one of them," I retorted.

"I'm ready if you are," Ashley said with a smile.

"For Christ's sake, Ash, could you at least put on a bra?"

"You don't wear a bra with a halter dress, Cole."

"Then change!"

"Cool your jets, big brother."

"You girls are asking for trouble going out looking like that."

"That's ironic coming from a guy who sleeps with a different woman every night," Ashley quipped.

"I don't have a three-year-old at home! Cole countered. "Promise me you'll be careful. Text me to let me know where you are, and call if you need me."

"Will do," Ashley said, rolling her eyes.

We headed out to a local club. Ashley seemed to know all the hot spots. She took my hand, and we waded through a sea of people to the bar.

"Hey, Ash."

"Hi, Kenny."

"Are you having your usual?"

"I am."

"What can I get for your beautiful friend?"

"I'll have a dirty martini. Thanks."

"Are you a regular here?" I asked Ashley.

"I bartend during the day at a place around the corner. There's no shortage of bars or restaurants in Miami, and the employee's paths tend to cross. So tell me, How are you settling in?"

"Fine, I guess. I've been so busy that I haven't had time to think about it. I do miss home and the seasons."

"Yeah, it's pretty much summer three-quarters of the year here. You'll get used to it."

"Where are you from?"

"Buffalo."

"Really, Cole never mentioned that, although he doesn't say much of anything to me unless it's disparaging."

"I'm sorry he's giving you such a hard time. That's not like him."

"Ashley, you implied you knew why Cole was treating me poorly. Is that something you can share?"

Ashley studied my face for a moment. "You bear a strong resemblance to Haley."

"Who's Haley?"

"Haley grew up across the street from us. She and Cole were always together. They started going out when they were fourteen. They dated for years. They were crazy about each other. I thought they would get married."

"What happened?"

"Cole's first love is hockey, which took up most of his time. When he went to college in Minnesota, Haley hooked up with his best friend. Cole was her only boyfriend, and I think she was curious about other men. Unfortunately, Cole found out and blew a gasket. He was heartbroken."

"Cole, the man with the revolving door to his bedroom?"

"His promiscuity is a recent development. He never cheated on Haley, and he had plenty of opportunities. Cole never fully recovered from the breakup. I think he's afraid of getting hurt again, so he keeps people, especially women, at a distance."

"What happened to Haley?"

"She wound up marrying Cole's best friend. Let's say that's one wedding Cole didn't attend. I know Haley regrets what happened, but she knew Cole would never forgive her."

"Do I look that much like her?"

"You both have long blonde hair, big brown eyes, and a perfectly freckled complexion. Your hair is longer with more waves. Haley is shorter with a more athletic build, but you're both natural beauties."

"I have always hated my appearance."

"Why? Women would kill to look like you."

"I feel like I need to work twice as hard to prove I'm not an airhead. People think leggy blondes missed out in the brains department. It's maddening. I always wanted to look like you. I find dark hair with blue eyes to be a captivating combination. You know, Cole accused me of being a dumb blonde. He asked who I screwed to get my job. I'd like to say that's the first time I've heard those types of comments, but it isn't."

"I'm so sorry. I watched the broadcast the other night. I saw Cole make some unnecessary jabs. I hate to say it, but the fact you look like Haley isn't the only strike you have against you. In Cole's eyes, you're replacing Shane."

"That couldn't be further from the truth. What was I supposed to do, Ashley, not take the job?"

"Of course not, but if Cole embraces you, he'll feel like he's betraying his buddy. Cole is fiercely loyal to the people he cares about, and Shane is like a father figure to him."

"Where is Cole's father?"

"Our dad is an alcoholic. He left my mother when Cole was eight. He would have an affair and come back when it ended. He'd stay a few months and then disappear again. Honestly, it was better when he was gone. The only contribution he made to our family was money. Things were rough, but at least Cole could continue playing hockey. My mother went to every one of his games, which is more than I could say for our father. I know Cole wanted things to be different, but my father continually disappointed him. Thank God for our mother. She was an amazing woman."

"Where is she now?"

"She died of cancer the year before Cole was injured. That was another huge blow to him. She was the only person he truly trusted."

"How awful. I was raised by a single mother too, and my father was a deadbeat dad. We have so much in common. I wish Cole would give me a chance. I think we could help each other."

"Give him time, Layla. I can tell you he's the best big brother a girl could have. Even when he was busy playing hockey, Cole was always there for me. When he wasn't around, he had his friends watch over me at school. Cole has been a saving grace with Katelyn. He helps me financially. I don't know what I would do without him."

"Thanks for sharing, Ashley. You gave me some valuable insight."

Ashley and I had a great night. We danced and laughed and met a ton of guys. By the time we got back to Ashley's place, I couldn't see straight. Cole must have heard us coming. He threw open the door to watch us stumble down the hall. He shook his head in disapproval, a look I had become accustomed to seeing.

"Do you know what time it is, Ashley? Why the hell didn't you answer the phone? I was worried."

"The music was blasting, and I didn't hear it," Ashley said, kicking off her shoes.

"How much did you have to drink?"

"Enough," Ashley replied defiantly.

"I think I better get going," I interjected.

"You're not going anywhere in your condition Newhouse. You'll stay here until you sober up."

My head was spinning, and I was nauseous. "Which way is the restroom?"

"It's down the hall on your right," Cole barked.

I raced to the bathroom, collapsed onto the floor, and grasped the sides of the toilet. I knew I would feel better if I got sick, but I didn't want to give in. Too late! As I bent my head over the bowl, I felt a hand gather my hair and gently sweep it away from my face. When I was done vomiting, I heard the bowl flush.

"Are you feeling better?" Cole asked.

I did my best to nod. "I'm so embarrassed. I haven't thrown up since I was a kid."

"It happens to the best of us. Can you stand?"

"I think so."

Cole helped me off the floor and told me to lean over the sink. He soaked a towel in cold water and placed it on my neck, which seemed to help. "Thanks. Could you call an Uber? I should be getting home?"

"You're not going anywhere. I'll help you to the couch. Take my arm," he insisted.

I made my way back to the living room and sat on the couch. Cole fluffed a pillow for my head and eased me onto it. He lifted my legs onto the cushion and removed my shoes. The room was still spinning as he returned with a blanket that he placed over me.

"Here, take these," Cole said, handing me a glass of water and Advil. "Do I need to put a wastebasket next to you, just in case?"

"No, I think I just need to get some sleep. Where's Ashley?"

"She passed out as soon as you got home. Ashley will be fine. She can hold her liquor."

I shut my eyes and prayed for a quick death. How did I do this to myself, especially in front of Cole? I heard some rustling on the floor next to me. I thought I felt a hand brush the side of my cheek. That was the last thing I remembered until I woke up the following morning.

"Oh, look who's rejoined the land of the living."

I sat up to find Katelyn watching TV and Cole making breakfast.

"What time is it?"

"Ten o'clock. I was about to wake Ashley up. Why don't you throw some water on your face and come eat?"

"I don't know if that's such a good idea."

"You need to rehydrate and replace some of the vitamins you

lost. Drink these." Cole placed juice, water, and coffee in front of me, along with two Advil. He followed that up with an omelet, hash browns, and toast.

"You cook?" I asked.

"I can make breakfast. Eat. You need the carbs."

"He's pretty good with the grill, too," Ashley said, wandering in from the bedroom.

"I'm surprised you're still here. Did you sleep on the floor? I asked, noticing the pillow next to the couch."

"I did. Someone had to take care of Kate," Cole replied indignantly.

"I knew you would be a bad influence, Newhouse. I would hate to think what would have happened if I wasn't here."

"It wasn't Layla's fault," Ashley chimed in. "She cut me off at five drinks and two shots. She also stopped me from going home with a hot guy, which I didn't appreciate at the time."

"He was a creep. He had trouble written all over him," I replied.

Cole studied me for a moment. "How much did you drink?"

"I had three drinks and one shot, which is a lot for me."

"I was trying to goad her into drinking more. Layla was the voice of reason between the two of us," Ashley admitted.

"Thanks for making sure Ashley came home. She doesn't have good judgment when it comes to men," Cole said in a conciliatory tone.

"Thanks for helping me last night. It wasn't my finest moment."

Cole gave me an affirmative nod. "I'm going to pick Addison up and take him to the rink. You ladies, have a nice day."

"I don't care what Cole says, last night was fun. We should do it again soon," Ashley suggested.

"We will. I've got to get going. I'm looking at some apartment rentals, and then I want to meet with some local businesses about an upcoming fundraiser. Thanks for last night, Ashley. I hope to use what you shared to improve my relationship with Cole."

"Cole is a great guy. I think you two would be good together if he'd let his guard down."

"I don't foresee that happening, although I did see a different side to him last night. Take care, Ashley. We'll talk soon."

My day off was productive despite my slow start. I found a furnished apartment and convinced some local businesses to participate in the fundraiser. I spent what was left of my evening going for a run, researching our local sponsors, and learning more about hockey. The pieces were falling into place. The only thing I had difficulty reconciling was my feelings for Cole. My attraction to him was manageable as long as he was a complete dick. I wasn't one of those women who would screw a man just because he had a pretty face or a nice body. What haunted me were the glimpses I caught of his humanity. The way he cared for his family and co-workers. How his former teammates still responded to him like he was a brother. The pain of loss Cole covered with false bravado. These attributes did more than stir my body. They warmed my heart and intrigued my mind, a lethal combination. I wanted to dig deeper. I needed to penetrate the walls that protected his shattered heart as long as I could do it without endangering mine.

CHAPTER 8

I stopped by Cole's office when I returned to work the following day. He was leaning against his desk with his legs crossed and his hands in his pockets. His shirt was rolled up at the sleeves and unbuttoned at the neck. He looked tan, relaxed, and sexy as hell. Across from him stood Gabriela in an outfit two sizes too small. If I looked closely, I could spot a line of drool dripping down the side of her face. She was batting her fake eyelashes and laughing over some trite remark when Cole spotted me in the doorway.

"Did you want something Newhouse?" he asked in annoyance.

"I wanted to talk to you, but it can wait," I replied turning to leave.

"No, on second thought stay. Gabriela just finished telling me about her proposal for a fundraiser to honor Shane."

"Oh really," I said, trying to pick my jaw off the floor.

"Isn't that a great idea?"

"Absolutely! I wish I had thought of it," I replied, trying to contain my sarcasm.

"Hey, Gab, why don't you come up with some ways I can help?"

"That would be great, Cole. Let's have lunch tomorrow and brainstorm?"

"That sounds like a plan. It will be my treat."

"Thanks, you're a doll," she said, leaning over and putting her hand on Cole's thigh.

"And you're incredibly thoughtful," he replied.

I had the overwhelming urge to puke. Gabriela turned and gave me a sardonic smile as she sashayed out the door. That conniving bitch! How dare she take credit for my idea. I reminded myself that it was Shane who was important, not who received credit for helping him. If I told Cole the truth, I would look petty, and Gabriela would be pissed off. I needed her help to promote the fundraiser, so I decided to let it slide.

"What did you want to talk about, Newhouse?"

"I wanted to apologize for my behavior the other night and thank you for taking care of me."

"I don't see where I had much choice. If I let you leave in that condition, you would have killed yourself, or worse yet, someone else."

"Regardless of your reasons, I still wanted to thank you."

"Are we done?" Cole asked impatiently.

"Why didn't you tell me you are from Buffalo?"

"What does it matter? I don't live there now."

"I thought finding common ground might improve our working relationship."

"Listen, Newhouse; I'm not your bestie."

"I know that I just thought......"

"At the risk of sounding redundant," Cole said interrupting me. "I don't care what you think."

"You've made that abundantly clear," I said, storming out.

I went back to my office and shut the door. I felt my frustration coming to the surface in the form of tears. Knock it off, I told myself. This man could barely go twenty-four hours without turning back into a first-class jerk. Pull yourself together, Layla. You have a staff meeting in an hour. I took some deep breaths, wiped my eyes, and started to make phone calls to calm down. That lasted until the staff meeting rubbed more salt in the wound. Cole publicly thanked Gabriela for her work on the fundraiser. Gabriela sat across from me, gloating. I don't know why this woman thought I was her competition. I didn't want Cole.

When it was my turn to speak, I shared that I spoke with Pressed On-T-shirts. "I negotiated a good deal. I will work with them to formalize a design once we settle on a date and time for the event. I also recruited several restaurant owners with food trucks who would be willing to attend and donate ten percent of their profits. Leora, did we hear back from management regarding a discounted price for advertisers?"

"The network is willing to give fifteen percent off to new clients and ten percent to repeat clients. It's not great, but it's something."

"I can work with that. The discount, combined with free advertising and a shoutout at one of the games, should be enough incentive."

"I have two times we can use the rink and three players willing to attend the event." Gabriela chimed in.

"I think it would be great if we could get the team to do a half-hour scrimmage for the audience. Afterward, we can use the rink for an ice-skating event for kids. The players who volunteer can autograph tee shirts and pose for photo opportunities along with T-Bone. Wyatt, is that something you could handle while Darius is filming the event?"

"Absolutely, Layla."

"I don't know if I can get the team to commit to a scrimmage. That's a big ask," replied Gabriela.

"Leave that to me; Cole chimed in. Additionally, I'll see if they can donate any old equipment or apparel for an auction."

"That's a great idea, Cole," Gabriela replied in a sickeningly sweet voice.

"Let's finalize a date. This way, Cole and I can start promoting the event on tonight's broadcast."

We settled on a date and time. Gabriela agreed to finalize the details with the facilities management at the arena. I offered to meet with Aaliyah, our graphic designer, to draft promotional materials.

"I'd like to say something before we adjourn," Cole interjected.

"I want to thank everyone for their willingness to help and donate their time. I especially want to thank Gabriela for her thoughtfulness. The fundraiser will mean so much to Shane."

"Meeting adjourned. Great job, everyone," Leora said rising from her chair. "Cole, may I speak to you privately for a moment?" Leora waited until the conference room cleared out before addressing Cole. "Why did you assume Gabriela was spearheading this fundraiser?"

"Gabriela said it was her idea. She approached me this morning and suggested we work on it together."

"That's strange."

"Why?"

"Because it was Layla's idea. She pitched it to me last week after meeting Shane. I told her to enlist Gabriela's assistance, but it was Layla's proposal."

"Layla was in my office while I was talking about the fundraiser with Gabriela. She didn't say a word."

"Maybe she didn't want to embarrass Gabriela, or maybe Layla isn't the type of person who does things for recognition. I just thought you should know."

"Thanks, Leora. I appreciate that."

I didn't see Cole until the pre-game show for our broadcast. Once again, I arrived early to network with the spectators. If possible, my butterflies were worse tonight. I needed to redeem myself for my previous mistakes, but as they say, "you don't know what you don't know." It was the unknown that scared me. Then there was the added pressure of facing off against Cole in the trivia competition. My fears came to light when I mispronounced one of the Toronto Terrapin's names. Cole, of course, couldn't let it go. I tried downplaying my mistake by saying I needed to brush up on my French.

"That wouldn't be much help considering he comes from Russia. Not all hockey players come from Canada, Layla. I thought you would know that is one of the top myths in the NHL."

"The majority of them do," I asserted.

"Less than half," Cole snapped back, "followed by the U.S., Sweden, Russia, and Finland."

"Forty-eight percent may be less than half, but it is still far more than any other country on your list," I argued.

I told myself it wasn't the end of the world that my Russian wasn't exact. I made some excellent observations regarding the Predator's need to get cleaner exits out of the zone and better defense at the blue line. I complimented our skill at reading the opponent and clearing the puck from the defensive zone. That didn't stop Cole from going for my jugular when I suggested the offense take more slap shots instead of spending so much time setting up the puck.

"Slap shots are the easiest type for a goaltender to defend. They may be hard and fast, but he can see them coming."

"He couldn't if there were more traffic in the crease," I maintained.

"If there's a player in the crease, he's better off taking a quick-release wrist shot. It surprises the goaltender, and it's hard for him to defend against."

The final nail in my coffin came when I praised Travis Goodrow's skill at skating backward.

"Travis is a great skater, but the defenseman should always skate forward, not backward, against his opponent," Cole sniped. The sting of his words cut through me like the metal blade of a skate. "Having the defenseman keep pace with the opposition inhibits him from making passes and taking shots. It also cuts off the forward's angle, forcing him to shoot from the outside."

Once again, I stood humiliated. My only shot at redemption was beating Cole at tonight's segment of *In the Know*. I met Abby, the in-arena host, in the sound booth. Cole went to the Predator's locker room, where his performance would be transmitted to the jumbotron.

"Tonight's trivia topic is rock bands," Abby declared. My guardian angel was alive and well after all. Cole knew little to nothing about music. I would crush him. The only thing missing was my ability to see his annoyed expression. I rattled off band after band without a hitch.

"Nice job, Layla, you really know your music. How do you think Cole will do?" Abby asked.

"I think Cole's going down in flames," I replied gleefully. I turned to watch the jumbotron. Cole's expression went from disinterest to distaste when he heard the topic. The butterflies in my stomach went from doing a happy dance to somersaults when Cole failed miserably.

"Layla, I hear this competition resulted from a bet between you and Cole."

"As you know, Abby, women are remarkable people, and I'm tired of seeing their talents underestimated, especially in the workplace. I wanted to prove to Cole and anyone else who doubts that women are the stronger sex emotionally that they're wrong."

"If I recall, you made some claims about women being physically superior to men."

"Studies show that women have a stronger immune system making us more likely to survive tough conditions like famine, extreme climate change, and epidemics."

"I wasn't aware of that," Abby replied.

"We are also better at identifying and controlling our emotions. For example, a woman will experience more pain initially after a breakup. In contrast, men will appear more rational. However, their inability to experience their feelings makes them less likely to heal."

"Interesting," Abby replied, nodding.

"As you know, women have a higher threshold for pain. Imagine one of these big strong alpha males giving birth or getting a bikini wax."

Abby laughed. "I would love to see that. My boyfriend won't let me pluck his eyebrows because he says it hurts too much. Hold on, we have Cole on the line. Hey Cole, it's Abby. That was a tough loss. Layla blew you away. On behalf of our female audience, I want to know if you're ready to concede that women are the emotionally stronger sex."

"Abby, you know I think the world of women, and I don't deny they are strong emotionally. However, you can't make that determination based on this contest. I admit to not knowing much about music. It's simply not a fair assessment."

"Just like I don't have your hockey knowledge no matter how many games I watch because I never played," I retorted.

"Well, folks, it sounds like the battle of the sexes is to be continued. I heard you guys talk about taking this competition to the ice. When is that taking place?" Abby asked.

"We haven't ironed out the details. Cole is a gym rat. He would have to give me a couple weeks to train while he takes some time off."

"Would you be willing to do that, Cole?"

The displeasure on Cole's face was evident. "Sure, Abby. I could give Layla all the time in the world, and it wouldn't make a difference in the outcome."

"I'm sure I speak on behalf of our viewers when I say we look forward to seeing how this feud plays out. Congratulations on tonight's victory, Layla."

"Ladies, I'm getting back to the broadcast, lest we forget that our fans want to hear about hockey."

"Cole is right. Have a great night, Abby."

"You too, Layla."

The game ended in a victory for the Predators, who were now one point out of first place. I started to head for the parking lot when Darius said, "Hey, Layla, you bagged on my last invitation. Tell me you'll join us for a drink tonight."

"That sounds good, Darius. I'd love to."

The production crew, including Darius, his assistant Wyatt, his interns Clayton and Tevon, Morgan, our male in-house host, Chase, and Cole, headed to one of the local bars for a wind-down drink.

"Do you guys do this after every game?"

"More often than not," Darius replied. "Sometimes a couple of the guys from the team join us. It depends if they're catching a flight."

"That would explain the crowd of single ladies," I mused. "Which reminds me. I'm flying out tomorrow afternoon to Philadelphia, and then we're headed to Pittsburgh. I'm glad my shipment of winter clothes arrived in time. Do we have a camera crew that comes with us?"

"Wyatt and Clayton are going. My wife ended my traveling after we had our second baby. It's rough being on the road."

"I'll get back to you on that. My last job didn't involve much travel. I'm looking forward to experiencing some winter weather. It's strange watching hockey in seventy-degree temperatures."

Darius handed me a martini. "I'd like to make a toast to Layla. Welcome to the team. It's been a pleasure working with you thus far. Congratulations on completing your first two broadcasts."

All the guys raised their glasses except Cole, who sipped his whiskey while eyeing a beautiful groupie.

"Thank you, although I'm not sure if congratulations are in order. My performance is still a little raw, to say the least."

"Deficient is more like it," Cole mumbled under his breath.

I brushed my hair back from my face, rubbing my cheek with my middle finger. Cole laughed as he registered my meaning. His attention was quickly diverted as the woman Cole was eying walked toward him and slipped her hand around his waist. Why is he such a superficial, vindictive prick? I decided to focus on getting to know the guys. I was finishing my drink when Cole stopped by on his way to the bar.

"Isn't it past your bedtime Newhouse?"

"I'm getting ready to leave. Should you be ordering another drink?"

"I wasn't the one praying to the porcelain throne the other night."

"Point taken, but that was an anomaly for me. You've already had three drinks to my one."

"Unlike you, I can hold my liquor. However, I'm flattered that you care enough to keep track. Don't you think studying the roster for tomorrow's opponent would be a better use of your time?"

"Perhaps. Judging by tonight's dismal performance, maybe you should start listening to music aside from the eighties rock anthems played at the stadium."

"Why bother, so I could beat you at a stupid contest that means nothing?" he snapped.

"That's the reply of a sore loser."

"When it comes to things that matter, like being able to pronounce the player's names, you don't qualify for the competition."

"At least I admit when I make a mistake, something your overblown ego won't entertain."

"It would if the situation arose, but it hasn't."

"I would continue trading insults with you, but I fear your date is growing restless. Is this one of legal drinking age?"

"She's old enough. Maybe you should consider getting laid. It might help you think more clearly."

That insult was the straw that broke the camel's back. I said good night to the guys and made a hasty exit. I returned to the hotel and packed for my upcoming road trip, fuming as I threw my clothes in the suitcase. Cole was the most irritating, arrogant man I'd ever had the displeasure of meeting. So, why couldn't I stop thinking about him? By now, he was home with his date doing unspeakable things to her body. Was I jealous? I couldn't be. I wouldn't dare sleep with such a conceited jackass. Narcissistic guys like Cole weren't even good in bed. They were focused on their own pleasure. Deep down, I knew that Cole was the exception to that rule. One look at Cole Pasternak, and you could tell the man was built to fuck.

CHAPTER 9

I woke up at the crack of dawn exhausted. I threw on a sweater, jeans, leggings, and boots and caught an Uber to the airport. I grabbed a quick breakfast and made it to the gate just in time to board the chartered plane to Philadelphia. The team had just piled in from the Admiral Lounge. I couldn't believe how animated they were at five-thirty in the morning. Despite my sleep-induced coma, my slitted eyes immediately landed on Cole. He was sipping coffee and talking with Brady and Jordan. His thick mop of hair was still damp from his morning shower. Cole was remarkably alert for a man who couldn't have slept more than four hours. I didn't know how he managed to work, drink, and have sex until the wee hours and still function effectively.

I decided to let the team board, not knowing if there was any type of seating protocol. When I got on the plane, I noticed the front of the aircraft had a few empty rows. If I used my headphones, there was a chance I could get some work done. I was grateful to see Cole sitting with the players instead of being upfront with the station crew. I closed my eyes for a few minutes until I could access my laptop. I was just beginning to relax when I felt something hit me.

"Cole, you startled me. What's this?" I asked, picking up the manual he carelessly tossed on my lap.

"That manual contains the coaches' names on page seven and player rosters. I thought you might find it useful after last night's debacle. Now you can't say I never helped you."

"Thanks, Cole. You're a real standup kind of guy," I said sarcastically.

"So, I've been told," he said smugly, returning to his seat. Upon flipping through the directory, I realized it was a helpful resource. Was this Cole's way of extending an olive branch? I decided not to get my hopes up and take it for what it was worth.

We landed in Philadelphia, and the team jumped on a charter bus to the arena for a quick practice. I longed to take a nap at the hotel but decided my time would be best spent exercising. I threw on workout clothes and headed to the hotel gym. I walked through the door to find Cole lying on a bench lifting free weights. He raised his head in my direction and then continued without a word.

"I guess great minds think alike," I said.

"I don't like distractions while working out, Newhouse."

"I didn't think you viewed me as a distraction."

"Let me phrase this in a way you can comprehend. I'm not up for mindless chatter."

"That makes two of us. I guess your little girlfriend didn't give you enough of a workout last night."

"Let's say I utilized a different muscle that doesn't require additional strength or conditioning."

"You're so damn cocky. I'll have you know that contrary to what men think, women aren't hung up on size. It's more important for us to be romanced and treated with respect."

"I have the utmost respect for women."

I laughed. "How do you rationalize screwing someone without even knowing her name as being respectful?"

"That was an unusual circumstance. I'm sure she told me her name. I just didn't recall it."

"How romantic," I quipped.

"Yeah, she was so offended by my actions that she brought me donuts. You can think what you want, Newhouse, but I don't get any complaints from the females I hook up with. I don't even approach women. They come to me, and when they leave, they leave satisfied."

"Do you ever think these women would like something more substantial than a quick lay?"

"That's not what I'm offering. I take pleasure in worshipping a woman's body. There's nothing quick about it."

"I would feel used if a man just wanted me for a one-night stand."

"That's you. There are plenty of women out there who, like me, are simply looking for a good time. I'm upfront about what I'm looking for and what I'm willing to give. If they're hoping it leads to more, that's on them, not me."

"When was the last time you felt a real emotion?"

"The day I knew my hockey career was over, as is this conversation," he snapped.

"Fine with me!" I put my earphones in and got on the elliptical. Ten minutes later, Cole jumped on the treadmill next to me. He wore a loose, black Predator T-shirt and form-fitting black shorts. His buttocks were tight and firm. A man's ass wasn't my main point of attraction, but the idea of squeezing Cole's round cheeks was appealing.

We exercised side by side for forty-five minutes when I started running out of steam, whereas Cole was picking up speed. His face was dripping with sweat. I watched as he reached down and grasped the bottom of his T-shirt to wipe his face. My eyes were riveted to his torso as one toned ab after the next was revealed as the shirt slid over Cole's slick body. No wonder women couldn't resist him. He was the perfect male specimen. I must have been crazy challenging him to any form of physical competition. His muscles had muscles. It wasn't fair. He looked like an Adonis, whereas I bore a strong resemblance to a drenched rat.

Feeling self-conscious and inadequate, I made a quick exit from the gym. I hopped in a hot shower and lathered my aching muscles. Unfortunately, the warm water did nothing to soothe the throbbing between my legs as I pictured pinning Cole against the shower door. He would slide his soapy hands between my legs, massaging me until the buildup in my pussy was unleashed. I would run my hands down his chest, falling to my knees to take his massive cock in my mouth. He would bury his hands in my hair, clenching it as he came.

Snap out of it, Layla. I turned the water from hot to cold, hoping my mind and body would cool down. I promised myself that whenever my thoughts of Cole turned sexual, I would recant the awful ways he embarrassed me. I hopped out of the shower and got ready for the evening broadcast. I took my laptop and notepad and headed to the hotel bar for a drink and some last-minute studying. Wyatt pulled a chair next to mine. "Have you seen CP?" he asked.

"Are you referring to the chauvinist pig?" I replied.

"Wow, the temperature in this room is frosty."

"I don't know where Cole is, Wyatt. I'm his co-host, not his personal assistant."

"The chauvinist pig is right here," Cole said, sauntering up to the bar with a grin in a tight black turtleneck with a black blazer and gray dress pants. What did I do to deserve being tormented like this? Did I kick someone's dog as a kid? Did I insult someone's grandmother? This ensemble blew his tailored suits away. I loved this look on any man, but Cole wore it better than anyone I'd seen. How could I curb my impure thoughts when he continued to entice me with his every move?

"I'm going to grab a quick Jack Daniels, and then we can head to the arena. Layla, would you like me to quiz you on the Flame's roster?"

"Screw you, Cole."

"Tell me when and where," he replied with a mischievous grin.

"Wyatt, come get me when you're ready to leave. I'm relocating to the lobby."

"Was it something I said?" Cole asked, feigning ignorance.

"I doubt it since I wasn't listening," I replied as I gathered my things and left.

• • •

My broadcast from the Flame's game gave credence to the adage that the third time's a charm. It helped that the Flames were amid a slump, making it easy for the Predators to steamroll over them. Cole couldn't call me out on strategy or ask what adjustments were needed because our guys brought their "A" game. It was the first time I wrapped up the sportscast, not feeling sick to my stomach. We headed back to the hotel on the team charter bus. When we arrived, Cole headed to the bar, and I headed to my room. My head was longing for the pillow, but I decided to do some more preparation for tomorrow's game, as Pittsburgh would be a more formidable opponent.

I was about to fall asleep when I heard laughter coming from the other side of the wall. It would be my luck to have the only loud neighbors in the hotel. Thinking I was tired enough to tune them out, I pulled the blanket up to my ears and proceeded to get comfortable again. A few minutes later, the laughter turned into moans. This was a sound I couldn't ignore. I turned my TV on low to distract me from the banging of the headboard. How rude could people be? Didn't they realize the walls were paper-thin in these hotels?

The clock continued to tick as the moaning raged on. I had had enough. My frustration gave way to aggression as I gave my side of the partition a couple of blows with my fist. I hoped my not-so-subtle hint would lead to a decrease in the noise level. Unfortunately, it did just the opposite. The woman's voice was getting louder and increasingly erratic. She was on the verge of a climax. I just needed to hang in there a little longer. Her jarring screams were enough to wake the dead. I would think the entire floor was up by now. It wasn't that I begrudged the woman for having a great orgasm. I just wanted her to be more considerate of the other patrons. What did I expect? Common courtesy had become anything but common. At least now, things would quiet down, but not before I had to listen to heavy breathing and the woman's critique of her lover's prowess.

I managed to fall asleep, only to be awakened an hour later by the familiar sound of moans and groans. Not again! Usually, I would have been more tolerant, but sleep deprivation had caused my patience to wane. I banged on the wall, only to be ignored. These people were downright inconsiderate. I had a long day ahead of me, and it was after midnight. They had their fun. Now, I needed my sleep. In a fit of anger, I got out of bed and knocked on the door to the adjacent room. I waited thirty seconds before banging again. This time the noise quieted down as I heard some shuffling from inside. The door opened, and there stood Cole, wearing nothing but tight black boxer briefs.

"Newhouse, what a surprise. What can I do for you?"

I tried to formulate my words but was distracted by his naked torso. His massive shoulders and large pectoral muscles made his stomach and six-pack appear even flatter in contrast. After the eyes, a man's chest was my area of weakness. I was thinking how satisfying it would be to run my fingers through his chest hair when Cole's voice caused me to focus.

"I'm a little tied up right now, so I will get back to my guest if you have nothing to say."

"I wouldn't be standing here if you just responded to the banging on the wall," I replied indignantly.

"Sorry, I didn't hear that. I was busy focusing on more important things."

"Listen, Cole, I don't care if you fuck every woman in Philly, but I don't want to hear it."

Now, he was the one staring. In my haste, it dawned on me that I was wearing a short night shirt that was somewhat see-through. Cole's eyes gave me the once-over, settling on my erect nipples.

"I don't blame you," he replied after a brief pause. "You must be feeling left out lying in your room all alone. Why don't you join us?" he asked as his eyes moved to my mouth. "You know what they say, two is better than one, and three is better than two."

"I've always heard that three's a crowd."

"I've always heard that one is the loneliest number," Cole responded. "Don't worry. I'll make sure you're not feeling left out."

"I prefer to be the sole focus of my lover's attention, not a sideshow for your amusement."

Cole laughed. "It's not funny," I snapped. "You might not require sleep to function, but I do. If you're going to continue fucking like rabbits, could you at least keep the noise to a minimum? I know you don't care about my feelings, but you're probably keeping the entire floor up."

"Yet, you're the only one complaining. I'll see what I can do, but if you ever had an orgasm Newhouse, you would know that some things can't be controlled."

"Try! Better yet, try getting some sleep," I replied, turning my back on him.

"My offer stands if you change your mind," Cole called after me.

I returned to my room and punched the pillow. Dealing with Cole was maddening. How could he be so crass, self-absorbed, thoughtless, and rude? At least the noise level subsided. I never screamed like that when I came. What was he doing to her? My body began to stir as I thought of the infinite possibilities taking place next door. I pictured my face buried in Cole's chest as he pushed his rock-hard erection inside me, filling me until I burst. Sexual frustration quickly overcame my exhaustion. It was a good thing I always kept my bullet vibrator with me. It packed a lot of power for a small yet highly effective toy. I placed the vibrator against my clitoris, rubbing it up and down, in and around. I imagined Cole stroking my hair, sucking my breasts, and kissing my neck as I dug my nails into his ample buttocks. It didn't take long for my body to succumb. My release enabled me to sleep. However, it was nowhere near the level of pleasure that Cole seemed to elicit from one woman after the next.

CHAPTER 10

I was sitting at the front of the plane, preparing for takeoff, when Cole sat beside me. "If it isn't the man who thinks the entire world revolves around him. To what do I owe the displeasure?"

"I brought a peace offering," Cole said, handing me a large latte.

"What's this?" I asked in a bewildered tone.

"I notice you bring Starbucks with you to the office. I called Ava, and she told me what you order."

"Thanks, I think."

"I figured it was the least I could do after keeping you up half the night. You might want to cover those bags under your eyes before going on camera."

"What a thoughtful suggestion," I said with a sneer.

"Seriously, Newhouse," Cole replied, placing his hand on my arm. "My behavior last night was inconsiderate and inappropriate. I shouldn't have asked you to join us. That was the liquor talking."

"I can't decide if you're an alcoholic or a sexaholic."

Cole looked pensive, as he rolled his fingers over his chin. "I'm probably a bit of both."

"Don't you see a problem with that response?" I huffed.

"Not really. I function just fine. Why do you want to save me, Newhouse?'

"If I did, would that be so wrong?" I asked, my voice laced with genuine concern.

"I don't want to be saved. Even if I did, that would be yet another job too big for you to fill."

"What if I saw something in you worth saving?"

"I'd say you need glasses. Enjoy the flight, Newhouse."

This man drove me mad. Just when I was convinced he was downright despicable, he planted the tiniest seed of doubt. However, Cole was right about one thing; it wasn't my job to save him, especially when I was the one treading water.

Pittsburgh was going to be a hard team to beat. They were one spot behind us in the standings, making tonight's competition a big win for either team. I had reviewed footage from Pittsburgh's past games and was familiar with their top line's strengths. As luck would have it, the player I was most familiar with was out on COVID protocol. I was unaware the Pittsburgh coach brought a replacement left wing up from the minors. Of course, Cole got the memo and appeared to know about this guy. He utilized his commentary to expose that I was in the dark. If there was any doubt, I erased it when I pronounced Puljujarvi wrong. Who has four vowels in their name? It was maddening, especially when this guy scored a goal and an assist. By the first intermission, the Predators were down by two goals.

"Layla, tell me what you think we need to do to get back into this game?"

"Well, Cole, I'm sorry to say the Predators have made some soft plays that gave up offensive opportunities. I think we need to play better in the neutral zone. I'd like the defense to make better dumps deep in the 'D' zone. There were periods when our offense chased the puck instead of controlling it. We need more control in the offensive zone to get our forecheck to work, creating scoring chances."

"I agree that our guys need to win more loose puck battles. We also need to make more challenges on the short side."

I had no idea what Cole was talking about, so I buttoned my lip until it was time to interview Jordan O'Shea, the team captain. I asked Jordan to share a moment in his career he would go back and relive. If only I had known that I was the one who would want to relive that moment. It was the end of the second period, and we were going into intermission with a score of three nothing.

"Layla, I'll ask you again, what do you think the Predators need to do in the face of this growing deficit?"

"As you know, Cole, the Predators have been in this position before and were able to make a comeback. They finally started playing more aggressively in the last five minutes of the period. The score would have been three to two if the Pittsburgh goalie hadn't made some key stops. We need to see the Predators score within the first five minutes of the third period to change the momentum." As I prepared to interview Travis Goodrow, Cole ambushed me.

"Layla, maybe you can ask Travis something about this game. I think our audience wants to know what he will do in the final period to regain the lead. Why waste time having him recount a memory from his past that is irrelevant to the present?" I felt my face blush with embarrassment. In this case, the best defense was a quick exit, but Cole wouldn't grant me that either.

"Despite making some great defensive plays, our captain hasn't scored in the last six weeks. I think Jordan might have appreciated the opportunity to address his current slump, which has been a topic of discussion amongst Predator fans and the media, not relive the past," Cole harped.

"Like me, maybe Jordan wanted to focus on something more positive, Cole. If he felt the need to address the slump, he would have. Now, if you'll excuse me, I don't want to waste more of Travis Goodrow's time listening to what you want to hear from the players."

I stormed down to the area outside the guest locker room, trying to burn off some aggression along the way. Player interviews were my area of skill. As a fan myself, I appreciated hearing something personal about the athlete I emulated. Leora and Chase were pleased with my interviewing style. Maybe that was why Cole chose to demean that part of the broadcast. Whatever the reason, I was done with that smug bastard. I decided I wouldn't spend more time with him than necessary.

The game ended with the Predators losing by one goal. I stayed out of Cole's way while we wrapped up and headed to the airport to fly home. It was a tough loss, and the mood was somber, much like mine. I was too angry to sleep, so I spent the return flight working on the fundraiser. I was relieved that I didn't have to be at the office until early tomorrow afternoon for a staff meeting. When the plane landed, I waved a quick goodbye to Wyatt and Clayton and dashed to the parking lot before the team made it off the plane. I headed to my apartment, unpacked, and crawled into bed. Without Cole and his flavor of the month next door, I could finally get a much-needed night's sleep.

The next day, I arrived early for our staff meeting to ensure I wasn't stuck sitting next to Cole. I was still miffed by last night's verbal flogging. The way Cole carried on; you would think he was the Wayne Gretsky of broadcasting. I was relieved when Wyatt grabbed the seat next to mine. "Hey Wyatt, is there any way you could get me footage of the Predator's games back from when Cole was on the team?"

"Absolutely, Layla, just give me a few hours."

"Thanks, and if you don't mind, let's keep my request between us."

Ava came in at the end of the meeting with a birthday cake for Cole. He gave her a smile that would stop traffic before blowing out the candles.

"Hey guys, I'm going out with my former teammates after work. I would love it if you joined us. The drinks are on me."

I was the only one who seemed less than enthused by Cole's invitation. It figures he was a Scorpio. I never put much stock in horoscopes, but Cole's sign fits his personality to a tee. On the plus side, he was hardworking, ambitious, intelligent, confident, or should I say over-confident, and loved to have a good time. On the con side, he was cunning, manipulative, brutally honest, and ruled by passion, aggression, and animal instinct. Cole thought he was smarter than everyone else and had difficulty letting go of the past, which would explain his breakup with Haley and whatever was behind the fight with Tristan.

Scorpio men were supposed to be jealous and possessive. I hadn't seen any evidence of that where Cole was concerned. They are highly sexual once in a relationship. I laughed out loud at that thought. I didn't think the term relationship existed in Cole's vocabulary. The only sex he seemed to like was casual. Scorpio men were known to hold grudges. Ending up on their bad side was a dangerous place to be. I knew that from first-hand experience. Even the stars deemed that I would remain Cole's enemy.

Leora asked Cole and me to stay after the meeting, leaving me no way to avoid him.

"I have some news I want to share with you. I would start this meeting by scolding Cole again for his on-air swipes at Layla's commentary. However, your public miffs seem to engage the audience, especially women. The demand to see this male versus female skating competition is growing exponentially, so set it up."

"Leora, this is ridiculous. You can't tell me that you support this nonsense," Cole griped.

"I support whatever gives this station higher ratings."

Cole shook his head in disapproval. "Fine, you chastise me for correcting Layla publicly, but then you want me to participate in a contest where I'll wipe the floor with her. Forgive me for being confused."

"I may not win, but there is no way I'll be your mop!" I protested. "I'll make arrangements, and we'll start promoting the competition at tomorrow night's game."

"Good, now what about these other comments trending on social media about women having a higher threshold for pain than men?" inquired Leora.

"It's a well-known fact. That's why we give birth instead of men. Abby and I were joking around. We said men couldn't handle what women go through daily, and we used waxing as an example."

"I bet you're right about that. I made my husband get his back done before going on a cruise. He complained for two days afterward and refused to return," Leora replied, laughing.

"I'm telling you now, nobody is ripping hair off my body," Cole snapped. "If you want ratings, I'll give you a show on the ice, but there is no way I'm giving in to this lunacy."

"I think you protest too much. Are you afraid you couldn't handle it?" I asked with a huge grin.

"Of course not. It's the principle."

"I bet both sexes would eat that up, Cole. The women would love to see a man go through the torture we endure, and the men would tune in out of curiosity and solidarity."

"I don't care, Leora. I'm not doing it," Cole replied vehemently.

"I can't believe I'm saying this, but I agree with Cole. As much as I would love to see it, I think that's violating his privacy."

Cole looked at me in astonishment. "Thanks, Newhouse."

"Let's see how the skating competition goes, and we can revisit this later. In the meantime, Layla, feel free to defend yourself on camera. Cole, I know you'll understand what I mean when I say don't cross any lines. Do we understand each other?" Leora asked with a raised eyebrow. Cole and I nodded in agreement as Ava walked into the conference room carrying a manilla envelope.

"Cole, your stalker, left this birthday present for you at the front desk." Cole rolled his eyes and opened the envelope. He reached in and pulled out a lacey black thong the size of dental floss.

"This woman refuses to take the hint."

"Maybe that's because you're leading her on," I replied.

"I assure you I'm not. I was trying not to hurt her feelings. I guess I need to be less sensitive."

"Is that world's smallest violin I'm hearing?" I replied in a mocking tone.

"Think what you want, but I'm not enjoying this."

"You can't deny it's good for your ego."

"My ego doesn't need stroking."

"Wow! That's the second thing we agreed on today. Leora, you're my witness."

Cole shoved the thong back in the envelope and tossed it on my lap. "Here, maybe this will help you get laid."

"Enough, you two," Leora interrupted. "You're worse than kids. Layla, I want to add that I'm pleased with the development of your play-by-play analysis. Now you just need to pay more attention to your enunciation of the players' names."

"I'm developing a system to address that."

"Good. Cole, you seem to be pulling back on your narration. That needs to stop until Layla is more experienced."

"I thought the best way for her to learn was to throw her in the deep end and make her sink or swim."

"It's more like drop me in the shark tank and watch me get eaten alive," I griped.

"I think you're judging me unfairly," Cole replied with a smirk. "You must admit, your last few broadcasts, name debacles aside, were an improvement."

"Gee, thanks for the high praise. I assume you're taking credit for that?"

"No, but I did force you to step up and fill a void."

"Did it dawn on you that I could fill in the gaps because I've devoted countless hours to living and breathing hockey? I've gleaned what I know from reviewing old footage, learning statistics, and watching current games on other broadcasts."

"That's what I'd expect you to do when you have a huge learning curve."

"Well, I'm so glad I'm meeting your expectations, your highness," I scoffed.

"I do hope you take a break and help me celebrate tonight, Newhouse. I noticed you didn't have any cake. That's bad luck."

"I'm watching my girlish figure. Besides, if we are going to have this man versus woman competition, I need to be training, not drinking."

"Layla, you should at least make an appearance. You need to spend time with your co-workers outside of the office."

"Fine, I'll do it for you, Leora. I'll see you both later."

I decided to take the old game footage Wyatt dropped off back to my apartment. After reviewing it, I went for a run and took my time cleaning up to ensure a late arrival at the bar. The less time I spent celebrating the birth of that douchebag, the better. The party was underway when I arrived. Cole eyed me the minute I walked in.

"Hey, Newhouse, I see you chose to arrive fashionably late."

I gave him half a wave and headed to the opposite side of the room. The bar was crowded with lots of faces I didn't recognize. I ordered a martini and talked with Jamison about coverage for the fundraiser. Our conversation was interrupted by Gabriela. Her shirt was so low that her cleavage mimicked a bike rack. To me, she reeked of desperation, but in truth, I was jealous of her more than ample breasts. Jamison's eyes were glued to her chest as Gabriela slipped her hand around his waist and led him away from me. I began to scan the room for someone else to talk to when an attractive man approached me. Several minutes into the conversation, I realized he wasn't from the office. He insisted on buying me a drink when Cole walked over. He came up behind me and whispered in my ear.

"I see that thong is your lucky charm," he murmured.

"That got tossed in the trash."

Cole patted my ass. "I don't see any lines, and those jeans don't leave much to the imagination."

"I decided to go au naturel in your honor," I quipped.

"Be still my heart," Cole said, placing his hand on his chest. My birthday wish came true," he whispered blowing his warm breath into my ear.

A shiver ran down my spine as Cole apologized to the man standing across from me for the intrusion. I was feeling the effect of my second drink rather quickly. It was probably a combination of my run and not eating. My new male acquaintance convinced me to have dinner with him. We adjourned to the dining room, where I had a clear view of Cole conversing with a pair of twins.

Our eyes met several times as he seemed equally interested in the interaction at my table.

It was approaching nine o'clock, and the bar began to clear out. I heard Cole thank everyone for coming to celebrate with him. I looked up to see him leaving with one twin on each arm. Cole's actions were so foreign to me. I couldn't fathom the appeal of screwing a countless array of strangers. I looked across the table at my dinner companion. He asked for my number, and I gave it to him because it was the path of least resistance. I knew I wouldn't see him again. The last thing I had time for was a relationship. I headed back to my apartment and attempted to review some stats on tomorrow night's opponent. The martinis and the vision of those two pubescent blondes, devouring Cole like munchies when you're stoned, distracted me. I decided to get into bed and watch some footage from his old games.

Cole was even more mesmerizing to watch on the ice. He skated down the rink like a motor kicking into high gear. His slap shot was like a laser. The release on his wrist shot had such speed that it was almost impossible to defend against. However, what impressed me the most was his passing ability. Cole's precision when passing the puck was a thing of beauty. I was surprised to see him set up his teammates when he had the opportunity to make a play on his own. The man I knew would want all the glory for himself. The Cole I was watching was very much a team player. He never hesitated to come to a teammate's defense when he was on the receiving end of a cheap shot. Cole was brutal to a fault, getting more than his fair share of penalties. On the flip side, he also managed to draw them, giving his team power-play opportunities. The commentators kept referencing Cole's superior Hockey IQ, especially for such a young player. This wasn't the first time I had come across this term. I stopped watching the film and began reading up on the concept.

Players with a superior Hockey IQ had a keen understanding of the game, combined with ice awareness, pattern recognition, and problem-solving skills. They could predict where plays would happen, enabling them to react faster and use the clock more efficiently. Although it was described as an intangible skill, a player could improve his hockey sense by reviewing old films, practicing mindfulness, blocking out mental distractions, and experience. It was hard to imagine how good Cole would have been if his career hadn't been cut short. That explained why I often saw him making defensive plays despite being an offensive right-wing. He could foresee the opposition's movement and react before they made a play.

I glanced at the clock. It was closing in on midnight, and I needed to go to bed, but I felt compelled to watch more footage. Cole's aggression on the ice was an issue early in his career. I watched in awe at the force he used to drive his opponent into the boards. Cole used his powerful body as a weapon. The commentators reported that Cole was the hardest-working player on the team, according to the Predator's trainer. He surpassed the physical benchmarks the trainers would give him, spending extra time training in the gym, on the ice, and during the off-season. With maturity and coaching, Cole learned to temper his aggression and use his immense physicality to benefit the team.

My mind drifted back to the vision of Cole standing half-naked in the doorway of his hotel room. Despite his career change, he was still in impeccable shape. I imagined what it would be like to lie beneath that herculean body. How safe I would feel enveloped in those big arms. All the evidence supported my belief that making love to Cole would be mind-blowing. I knew it would be far better than any sex I ever experienced. The few former lovers I had, ranged from inept to adequate. They never made me scream with abandon like the woman in Cole's hotel room. However, at least my ex-boyfriends knew my name and took me on dates. I had to remind myself that Cole used women. I knew he rationalized his actions by saying getting great sex was enough for them, but that wouldn't satisfy me, or would it? My body was on a different page from my mind where Cole Pasternak was concerned. This was one problem that wouldn't be reconciled since we couldn't stand each other. Sex was one exchange that Cole and I would never share.

CHAPTER 11

"Predator fans tune in to Southern Sports and watch Cole Pasternak face off against Layla MacKenzie in the battle of the sexes. This is Abby Lang, and I'll be speaking with Layla later in the broadcast for the latest updates on this must-see event."

The Predators were home facing the Montreal Mountaineers. The first period ended with the Predators leading the Mountaineers by two goals.

"I have to say, Cole, that was one exciting first period. I never cease to be amazed by Sebastian Devorak's Hockey IQ. He appeared to be two plays ahead of the defenseman. He could have made that middle-lane drive instead of passing to Alex. But by faking the shot, he knew the Mountaineer's goalie would go down to block the shot he anticipated, allowing Alex to elevate the puck over Brock Mathison's stick."

"I agree; Sebastian has one of the highest Hockey IQs in the league. His ability to read the puck contributes to his explosive breakaway success and setting up Alexander Koulak for the goal."

"I thought there would be a feeling-out process since these teams haven't competed against each other in almost two years, but the Predators were aggressive from the opening faceoff. It's great to watch them playing such tight defense, winning the puck battles against the wall, and blocking coverage in the lane," I countered.

I interviewed Alex regarding his goal and Sebastian's brilliant offensive play between periods. After the way Cole chastised me over my last interview, I decided to avoid questions that didn't pertain to tonight's game. Then I stopped for a brief chat with Abby about my upcoming competition with Cole.

"Hey Layla, I hear the competition is on."

"Yes, Abby, in two and a half weeks. I didn't want to do it after the holidays because I'm officially watching what I eat."

"Two and half weeks isn't a lot of time."

"Tell me about it! I wish I had given myself a longer training period."

"What are you doing to prepare?"

"I'm running five miles a day, working out, and getting to the rink before work to practice my skating. Sleep is a thing of the past."

"I don't envy you. It looks like Cole is in exemplary shape. Does that make you nervous?"

"Cole would be a formidable opponent regardless of when the competition is held. He has agreed to suspend exercising as a way of leveling the playing field."

"So, what will the competition entail?"

"We will each be given two minutes to skate around the rink. Our speed will be clocked. Since Cole is almost twice my weight, I'm expected to score approximately half of what he achieves to win. Thus, proving that although women have less muscle mass, they don't have less strength. I understand you are going to narrate the competition."

"I'm looking forward to it. I wish you all the best on behalf of all the women out there. Now back to the second period."

The Predators won the game four goals to two. I met up with Cole to do the post-game show following my interview with Ryan McEwin, who scored the game-winning goal. Ryan was relatively new to the team and a rising star. I asked him what value he brought to the organization, how he served the community off the ice, and what his most significant challenge was playing in the NHL. I was happy that Cole didn't contradict my line of questioning.

"Cole, I've noticed many of our guys aren't comfortable in front of the camera. Do you think it would help if I hosted a workshop offering skills and suggestions to help them present better when addressing the media?"

"I think that's a ridiculous idea, Newhouse. These guys are hockey players, not actors. If they don't project well, it's because they don't want to do these interviews. It takes away valuable coaching time between periods. By the end of the game, they want to get the hell out of here. They talk to the media, even the fans, to a certain extent because it's part of their contractual agreement, not because they want to. Hockey players want to do one thing, play hockey."

"I understand. I thought it might be helpful since public speaking isn't a natural skill, especially for Coach Shanahan. After four years in his position, I thought he would be more engaging. He looks like he would prefer having a root canal than being on camera."

"Coach Shanahan is a former hockey player, not an actor," Cole replied condescendingly. "He'd rather spend time providing his team with a winning strategy and bringing home a second Stanley Cup, not answering inane questions posed by the media."

"I'm aware of Coach Shanahan's background, but his role has changed. Regardless of what you think, these guys are stars in this community, and they have an obligation to the public. Using the media to ingratiate themselves with the fans will translate into money through ratings, accessory sales, and endorsements," I retorted indignantly.

"You can pitch it if you want to, Newhouse, but I'm telling you it's another bad idea. Why don't you go home and get some rest? I'll blame sleep deprivation for your ludicrous thinking."

Cole was turning to leave when I heard Abby call out his name. "Hey, Cole, what are your feelings on the upcoming competition with Layla?"

"I won't dignify that question with a comment. To our viewing audience, thanks for tuning in for tonight's broadcast. On behalf of Layla MacKenzie, Abby Lang, and Morgan Philips, we look forward to seeing you on the road when the Predators take on the Las Vegas Knights."

I didn't see Cole until the following day, which was still too soon for me after the way he insulted me at the game. I was standing at the front desk talking with Ava when Ashley walked in.

"Hey Ash, it's great to see you. What are you doing here?" I asked.

"Hi, Layla, I'm taking Cole to lunch for his birthday. I was trying to fit it in before he hit the road."

"Speaking of that. Ava, could you make sure my hotel room isn't adjacent to Cole's? Maybe you could put him closer to the team or, better yet, on another floor."

"What did he do now?" Ashley asked, with a sigh.

"Let's say I haven't found Cole to be a discreet or quiet neighbor. Now that he's upped his game to twins, I'll never get any sleep." Cole came down the hall as I was finishing my sentence.

"Twins?" Ashley said, looking at Cole with disapproving eyes.

"You know what they say, 'double the pleasure, double the fun,'" Cole replied with a self-satisfied grin.

"Cole, now that you've turned thirty, you need to raise the age of your conquests," I quipped.

Cole shrugged his shoulders. "According to whom? All the women I see are adults in the eyes of the law."

"Might I recommend women in their mid-twenties as opposed to those old enough to merely vote or drink?"

"You could if I were seeking advice on my love life, which I'm not, especially from a woman who has the sex life of a nun."

"Layla, you should know that I lived with Cole when I first moved to Miami. He was a dating Nazi. Nobody met his approval. I finally had to move out to have a social life," Ashley interjected.

"It's not my fault that nobody is good enough for my baby sister," Cole said, hugging Ashley.

"I see Cole is a fan of the double standard," I replied.

"I see things more clearly than my sister and you do, Newhouse. For example, that guy you had dinner with the other night is a pussy. I hope you're not planning to see him again."

"Cole, you're not my big brother, so I'll see who I want. In the future, please refrain from using a female body part in a derogatory or demeaning manner."

"I don't get your attraction to these wimpy pretty boys."

"I thought you would be happy I'm going on a date. Aren't you the one always telling me I need to get laid?"

"Yeah, but with a guy who can get the job done. You're surrounded by 'real men' who are ready and able to do the honors."

"Like I told Jackson, I don't mix business with pleasure, but thank you for your unsolicited and unwanted feedback on my love life."

"Are you too at it again? Leora asked as she stepped out of her office. Cole, Layla, I'm glad I ran into you. I watched the post-game show last night. In the future, when Abby asks you about the upcoming competition or anything else for that matter, I don't want to hear 'no comment.' Are we clear?" Leora chided.

"Yes, Leora," Cole said, reluctantly.

"Good! Enjoy your road trip and try to behave."

"Layla, why don't you join us? We're just grabbing a burger down the street. I want to hear about the new man in your life." Cole looked irritated by Ashley's invitation.

"No, thanks, Ashley, I have too much to do. Please ensure Cole gets a double helping of fries with a side of arsenic."

"That still won't tip the scales in your favor, Newhouse."

"Why can't you guys play nice?" Ashley groaned. "Layla, what are you doing for the holidays?"

"I wanted to go home, but as you know, we don't have much time off, so I'm flying my mother down instead."

"Then it's settled. You will come to Cole's for Christmas dinner."

"That's very thoughtful, Ashley, but I wouldn't intrude on your family celebration."

"Don't be silly. It's only me, Cole, and Katelyn."

"I don't think Cole would appreciate that."

"Cole is fine with it. Aren't you, big brother?"

"Do I have a choice?" Cole grumbled.

"No, as a matter of fact, you don't. It's a date. Have a good trip, Layla. We'll talk soon."

The team arrived in Vegas close to 11:00 p.m. I felt so overwhelmed between the fundraiser, my competition with Cole, and trying to do my job, that I headed straight for my room. Some of the guys decided to hit the casinos. I had never been to Vegas. I didn't see the appeal since I wasn't a gambler, but I would've liked to take in a show or walk the strip. I guess that would have to wait until next year. I opted for sleep over play. The following morning was spent doing squats, sit-ups, and leg lifts in my room. My breakfasts now consisted of whole-grain cereal or oatmeal and half a grapefruit. I went to the pool and did some laps while the team attended practice. I didn't see Cole until just before our pre-game show.

"Hey, Newhouse, did you get an opportunity to explore Sin City?"

"No, I had too much to do. I would ask you the same thing out of courtesy, but I already know the answer."

"It was a good night. I won five grand on the blackjack table and scored a very talented showgirl."

"Lucky you. Why only one showgirl? I thought you might go for the entire chorus line."

"Even I don't have that type of stamina. However, my showgirl did have a friend who needed some afternoon delight."

"For your information, if you had enough willpower to abstain from ejaculating for one week, your sperm count would improve, and you'd have a better orgasm."

"No need to fear, Newhouse. My sperm is packed with punch, just like my orgasms. Besides, you are the one responsible for my sexual marathon."

"You're unbelievable! How does your inability to keep it in your pants become my fault?" I asked in an incredulous tone.

"Since you banned me from working out, I have to find another way to get my exercise. Until I get back to the gym, I consider sex the best form of physical exertion."

"Try the pool. It works for me," I snapped.

"My poor Newhouse. Just remember who created this nightmare."

It was a challenging game for the Predators. I wasn't sure if Cole was the only guy who went out the night before, but the team lacked juice. Our defense was exhausted. They needed the help of the forewords to get to the finish line. In the end, they beat themselves. Las Vegas had twice as many shots on goal. They chipped away at us shift after shift.

"That's a rookie mistake if I ever saw one. Do you know what I'm referring to, Layla?" Cole asked, baiting me. He knew I had no idea what he was talking about and faking it would only make it worse. I braced myself as I glanced at Cole's face. His countenance mimicked that of a predator about to devour its prey. His eyes sparkled with anticipation at my ignorance as he prepared to pounce.

"No, Cole, I don't know what you're referring to."

"Andre Perrault just played the puck off a high stick. The Kings would have gotten a penalty if he hadn't touched it."

"How would you expect me to know when Andre didn't?" I replied, regretting those words the moment they left my mouth.

"It's inexcusable that neither of you knows that!"

I left myself open for that degradation. Cole set me up, and I fell for it hook, line and sinker. It was bad enough that he humiliated me, but now I was embarrassing myself.

The Predators didn't have time to mourn the five-to-two loss. The team headed straight to the airport to catch a flight to Chicago. We didn't arrive until 3:00 a.m. due to weather delays. We were all exhausted and deflated when we reached the hotel. I went to bed immediately, and much to my surprise, so did Cole.

The Chicago Bombers gave the Predators more competition

than we bargained for, considering their place in the standings. Fortunately, Bryce Andersen, the Predator goalie, kept our guys in the game.

"Cole, I think Bryce has a superhero cape under that uniform with the saves he's making."

"What are you watching, Layla, a Marvel movie? That last save is known as an old-school poke check. Many goalies don't use it, but as you can see, it's very effective."

"That doesn't mean his last couple of stops weren't superhuman."

"I would expect nothing less of Bryce. He is one of the preeminent goalies in the league and the best trade the Predators made."

"I agree. Bryce has a Goals Against Average of 1.65, tying him for sixth place with Eric Sorkin."

"Your statistical knowledge dumbfounds me," Cole said mockingly.

"Let's leave it at dumb," I snarked.

We cut to a commercial break before Cole could lash out with a snappy retort. I walked away to avoid strangling him. In the end, the Predators won, but it was a hard-fought battle. We headed to the airport after the game. Although I was sad to leave the cool climate, I was glad when we touched down in Miami. I had too much to do and not nearly enough time to get it done.

CHAPTER 12

I dragged myself to the rink, despite my exhaustion. Then I headed to the office and stayed behind closed doors, doing my best to avoid Cole. It was the last home game before our competition. I was sitting at my desk when the door opened.

"Haven't you heard of knocking?" I snapped at Cole.

"I was just checking to see if you're alive?"

"Why do you miss me?"

"Yeah, like gonorrhea. I thought you might be avoiding me."

"Don't flatter yourself. I'm just busy."

"What is it you're doing?" Cole asked, walking over to my desk.

I tried to push the index cards beneath my keyboard, but it was too late. Cole picked one up and examined it. I had made a card for each player on the Falcon's roster. I listed the spelling of the player's name, his jersey number, any noteworthy statistic, and most importantly, a translation of how the name should be pronounced.

Cole looked at the cards and then back at me. I was bracing for some form of insult when he surprised me. "I wondered why your enunciation has improved so dramatically," Cole said with approval. "Can you explain this one?" Cole held up Nick Neiterriter's card. Nick was a member of the Predators, and his jersey number was twenty-one. Under Nick's name was the phrase, "I need a drink."

"I confuse some of the guy's jersey numbers on the team. I have a condition called dyscalculia. It means I transpose numbers."

"You mean like dyslexia, except with numbers instead of words."

"Yes, so to help me remember the correct number, I use mnemonics."

"What are they?" Cole asked with genuine interest.

"That is when you associate something you are trying to recall with something familiar, making it easier to remember. For instance, Nick is number twenty-one. Twenty-one is the legal drinking age. Writing the phrase, 'I need a drink' under Nick's name helps me remember his jersey number and that his name is pronounced need instead of neat, as it would appear. You probably think it's silly, but it works for me."

"I'm glad," Cole replied, with a nod of approval.

"Are you, really? The fact that I've overcome this obstacle gives you one less thing to criticize."

"I'm not worried. The list may be shorter, but it's still extensive. I'll see you at the pre-game show, Newhouse," Cole replied, sauntering out of my office.

Tonight's broadcast would be our last opportunity to promote our on-ice competition. I had to admit I was getting nervous about the upcoming event. Abby and Morgan stopped by the booth for a brief interview.

"Layla, it's the eve of the big competition. Do you have predictions about the victor?" Abby asked.

"I can't say for sure. I've worked hard to get in the best possible shape, but I didn't leave enough time to train adequately."

"See, she's already making excuses for why she's going to lose," Cole interjected."

"I'm not making excuses. I'm just stating the facts."

"Cole, who do you think will win?"

"As you know, Abby, there has never been a doubt in my mind that I'll be the victor."

"You sound pretty confident."

"I'm not confident, I'm convinced. There's no way Layla can keep up with me."

"Have you honored the rules of the agreement and not worked out for the last few weeks?"

"I have. There's clearly no need for me to cheat."

"Do you believe him, Layla?"

"I do. If you look at Cole's waistline, you see he's put on a few pounds."

"As you can see, Abby, Layla is so dehydrated that she's hallucinating," Cole replied, motioning to his torso.

"Are you guys aware of how this competition is blowing up social media? People are going as far as to bet on the outcome."

"I've been too busy to follow social media," I replied.

"What are the odds?" asked Cole.

"Right now, they're five to two in your favor," Morgan replied.

"That's because we have a smart viewing audience," Cole replied, with a smug grin.

"Well, my money's on you, Cole. I remember how you destroyed your opponents on the ice. No offense, Layla."

"None was taken, Morgan. Although I can't project the winner, I can guarantee an interesting race."

"Good luck to both of you, and now back to the third period."

I woke up the next day with a pit in my stomach. Me and my big mouth. I should have known Cole wouldn't back down. His superiority complex wouldn't let him. Now was facing off against him in a competition I was destined to lose. Worse yet, it would be publicly televised on the local segment of the evening news. I could handle being defeated if I put up a good fight, but the thought of letting down the female fans rooting for me was hard to swallow. There was nothing I could do at this point. Next time, maybe I'd think before opening my mouth and choking on my foot. Now, all I could do was stay positive, envision my victory, and hope my body followed suit. I ate some toast, hydrated, did some stretches, and grabbed my figure skating costume. I hadn't put one of these on since I was a teenager. Thank God for Amazon because I had no time to shop. I decided if I was going to lose, I might as well look good doing it.

I was relieved when I arrived and found an empty arena. I headed to the locker room to get changed. The Predators were nice enough to give us time on the ice prior to practice. I was debating whether to do a trial skate or conserve my energy when I heard familiar voices. Apparently, Abby and Morgan were outside the locker room talking to Cole. There went my opportunity to hit the ice. I decided to take my time applying my make-up and fixing my hair. The less time I saw Cole, the better. Ten minutes later, Abby came into the locker room, looking for me.

"Hey, Layla. Wow, you look fantastic! How are you feeling?"

"Between you and me, Abby, I'm a nervous wreck."

"I'm sure you'll do great."

"I wish I had your confidence."

"I was hoping to get a couple of comments on camera before we start."

"Sure, whatever you need."

"Thanks. I'll see you outside."

I took a few deep breaths, did a couple of last-minute stretches, and emerged from the locker room. Cole and Morgan were chatting. Cole looked relaxed and well-rested in his old hockey uniform. It figured the one night I needed him to drink like a fish and screw a harem of women, he probably sat on the couch and turned in early.

"Here she comes. I thought you weren't going to show Newhouse," said Cole in an irritatingly cheery voice.

"Newhouse? Why are you calling her Newhouse?" Morgan asked.

"That's the program where Layla boasts of getting her degree. She claims to have graduated on the Dean's List."

"Are you saying you don't believe her?"

"No, I trust she was in the top echelon for broadcasting. It is her hockey IQ that requires a remedial class."

"I thought that's something you can't learn," replied Morgan.

"You're right about that, so I don't know why she bothers trying. I guess our Newhouse is a lover of lost causes."

"Which is why I continue to have faith in Cole's ability to not be a total ass," I chimed in with a smile.

"I see there continues to be a lot of, shall I say, tension between you two. Cole, how do you think that will play out on the ice?" Abby asked with a raised eyebrow.

"First off, Abby, I have no hostility toward my co-worker." I felt my eyes rolling in their sockets. Who did Cole think he was kidding? "If I feel anything for her at all, it's pity. I don't know how often she can fall short of her goals without annihilating her self-esteem."

"I take it from that comment that you're still confident about winning today's competition," replied Abby.

"There's not a doubt in my mind." It could have been that I was feeling particularly insecure, but Cole's reply was delivered with an extra dose of cockiness.

"Layla, what are your thoughts?"

"Well, Abby, it would be foolish for me to be as confident as Cole. After all, he was a professional athlete, and we know the type of stamina that required. I will say that to have speed on the ice, you need a strong relationship between your glutes and your hamstrings, which I have. I'm also very disciplined and don't party like Cole, so I expect a close race."

"Layla, I know you were training to be a professional figure skater at one point. There are people out there who don't consider that a real sport. They don't realize how physically demanding it is or the athleticism it requires. I'd like to take a moment to review a few facts for the audience on the demands of a hockey player versus a figure skater. I know both sports require agility and endurance. The difference is figure skaters skate the entire time they are on the ice, with a routine lasting up to five minutes. Whereas the shift of a hockey player lasts forty-five seconds to one minute. With breaks, hockey players are on the ice for approximately twenty minutes in an hour game. Skaters need agility to perform spins, jumps, and other gravity-defying gymnastics. Hockey players must be agile to maneuver the puck and avoid being checked by opponents. Figure skaters must be able to skate upwards of seventeen miles per hour to launch into their moves. The average hockey player skates between ten to twenty miles per hour. Hockey players have bulkier frames. They need to balance weight and strength to move quickly while still being able to endure physical attacks. It would be a disadvantage for skaters to have that type of bulk. Despite their slimmer frames, skaters also possess incredible strength. I read that figure skaters absorb seven to eight times their body weight on one leg when coming out of a quadruple turn."

"Thanks for clarifying those differences, Abby. People equate hockey players with strength and athleticism. Whereas they view figure skating as an artistic medium. Skaters make their routines look so seamless that spectators fail to realize the endurance and flexibility required to perform them."

"I want to talk about today's competition, so our audience understands the playing field. As our viewers may or may not know, hockey skates are lighter than figure skates. They are also built to turn, stop, and accelerate more quickly. We had Cole put on his old gear to even the playing field, which weighs anywhere from twenty to twenty-five pounds. Each skater will be given two minutes to skate around the rink. Their speed will be clocked at each rotation's end and at the finish. We will take the average speed over the number of rotations, and the skater with the most laps at the fastest speed wins. Since Cole outweighs Layla by approximately one hundred pounds, Layla needs to complete just over half the rotations Cole does with a speed that exceeds his record. I don't know if you guys are paying attention to social media, but the most recent chatter predicts Cole to win with five to three odds. If you look at the jumbotron, I pulled some clips off Instagram and Twitter for you guys to see."

Cole and I glanced at the big screen overhead to see fans holding up signs urging us on. My fans were mainly female, with a few males thrown in. Cole had his collection of groupies, along with the male majority.

"I understand we are about ready to get underway. We'll flip a coin to see who goes first. Cole, do you prefer heads or tails?" Abby asked.

"Ladies first," Cole piped up in a sickeningly sweet tone.

"Layla, heads or tails?"

"I choose heads."

Abby tossed the coin and placed it on top of her hand. "It's heads. Layla, would you like to go first or last?"

"I'll let Cole go first."

"Okay, let's head to the ice. My co-host Morgan Philips will keep time while Tevon Chatfield counts the laps. Darius, are you ready to film?"

"We're all set."

I looked up to see the Predators gathering behind the glass. The sight of them made my stomach plummet. Beads of nervous perspiration formed on my forehead as Cole made one loop on the ice before getting into position. Morgan counted down from three, and Cole was off with a burst of speed. I heard the blades of his skates cutting through the ice, enabling him to establish a fast pace. It had been three and a half years since Cole played for the Predators, but you wouldn't know it by the speed and precision he circled the rink. The first minute had passed, and Cole managed to do five laps. The average hockey player could only do four. I knew he was faster than most of his teammates when he played, but I never imagined he could set this pace. I heard the Predators banging on the glass and yelling at Cole as he passed.

"Cole, get the lead out."

"Cole, I can skate faster backward."

And my favorite, "Cole, you skate slower than Brady's dead grandmother."

I realized the guys were trying to egg him on, but I was expecting cheers instead of taunts. Cole was closing in on the end of the two-minute mark. I was so captivated watching his performance that I lost track of the number of times he circled the rink. I couldn't be sure, but Cole's speed appeared to slow down from the first half of the race. I hoped the decrease was significant enough to give me a fighting chance.

"There are ten seconds left," I heard Morgan call out from center ice. I watched Cole dig deep for one final dash, crashing into the boards as Morgan called time.

"Not bad for an old, out-of-shape guy," Jordan yelled from the sideline. I watched Cole wave his middle finger at Jordan as he stopped to catch his breath.

Abby approached Cole with the microphone. "That was an incredible display, Cole. How are you feeling?"

"Wiped out," Cole replied, panting.

"I know when you skated for the Predators several years back, you exceeded the average player's speed by five miles per hour. Do you have any idea how fast you were going today?"

"I don't. I counted nine laps in two minutes, but my speed dropped after lap five."

"That's a remarkable feat considering the average player in the NHL would complete eight laps in that amount of time."

"As I told you, Abby, I stay in shape."

"Nobody's going to dispute that claim after what we saw today. I see Layla is taking the ice. She needs to get around the rink four and a half times to have a shot at winning, and that isn't taking speed into account. Layla is getting into position."

"Are you about ready, Layla?" Morgan asked.

"I'm as ready as I'll ever be."

I heard Cole call out, "Break a leg, Layla." Could he genuinely wish me good luck, or was that his way of getting rid of me? Either way, I found his comment disconcerting.

I heard Morgan start the countdown. I leaned forward for a more aerodynamic stance. As I homed in on the ice before me, my butterflies were replaced with laser focus. I put one hand behind my back like the speed skaters in the Olympics. I pushed off my back leg and catapulted my body around the ice at break-neck speed. My body kicked into overdrive as adrenaline flooded my veins. My fight or flight mode was all fight as I heard the Predators cheering my name when I soared past the bench. I vaguely heard Morgan call out, "One minute down, one to go." I was a woman with tunnel vision. My sole focus was to make it around the rink as fast as possible and beat the man who continued to undermine, underestimate, and embarrass me. Expanding my fan base and putting a feather in the feminist cap would be a bonus, but beating the chauvinist pig was my driving force.

"Ten seconds left," Morgan announced.

"Bring it home, Layla, you got this!" screamed a voice from the Predator bench. I lost count of how many laps I had done. My primary purpose was pushing my body to cut through the ice. My legs burned as I summoned every remaining ounce of strength.

"Time!"

My body was still in overdrive as I circled to a stop. I felt like I was standing on wet noodles as my legs went limp. My mind was still on an endorphin high when Cole skated up behind me and scooped me off the ice. He hoisted me over his head and proceeded to skate around the rink.

"Cole, put me down! Are you crazy! I'm going to fall. Put me down now," I shrieked. The players went nuts on the sidelines, screaming and clapping. I felt like I was dangling in midair, making a gawky spectacle for the world to see. "Put me down, you bastard."

Cole laughed beneath me as he lowered me to his chest, only to shock me again by tossing me into the air. I screamed, convinced I would hit the ice, but he caught me and set me down in front of him. I stared at his mischievous grin, not knowing whether I wanted to slap or kiss him. Neither came to pass as Abby approached us on the ice.

"That was some show! Layla, are you okay? You look flushed."

"I'll be fine now that I have my feet under me. Cole took me by surprise."

"Cole took us all by surprise. How do you think the race went, Layla?"

"It went better than I expected. I was pleased with the consistency of my form. I don't know how fast I was going. Still, my speed exceeded my expectations, especially by the end when I was running on fumes."

"I think Morgan has tabulated the results. Are you guys ready to find out who won the battle of the sexes?"

"I think I just proved who won," quipped Cole.

"Morgan, do we have a winner?"

"We do, Abby, but I have to say it couldn't get much closer. Cole completed nine laps at an average speed of twenty-two miles per hour. He started off close to twenty-five but lost momentum after the first minute. Whereas Layla's speed was consistent at twelve miles per hour."

"That would give us a tie."

"I agree, Abby, except Layla skated an extra half a lap. Cole had a total of nine laps. Layla needed four- and three-quarter laps to tie. She completed five and a half laps, which, combined with her speed, gives her the win."

"So, if this were a horse race, she would have won by a nose," Abby replied, laughing. "On behalf of all the women watching, let me be the first to congratulate you on a job well done, Layla," Abby said, giving me a hug.

I didn't know who had a more shocked expression on their face, me, or Cole. "Layla, what do you want to say to your fans?"

"I just want to thank all the people who believed in me. This was a hard-fought race. Cole is a great competitor. Watching him out there on the ice, I doubted my ability to beat him. It shows women that we are stronger than we think, and there's nothing we can't accomplish with the right amount of training and belief in our abilities."

"Cole, you clearly looked surprised when Morgan declared Layla, the winner. I guess this is what you would call an upset. Tell us what's going on in your head."

"Well, Abby, I accept that Layla won, but I don't think we were on a level playing field. My speed was fast, even for an NHL player. Still, carrying twenty-five pounds of equipment a minute to seventy-five seconds longer than the average shift on the ice eroded my speed. Considering these factors, Layla needed to beat me by a wider margin."

"That sounds like the argument of a sore loser if you ask me," I interjected. "Cole is six foot-two and weighs two hundred and five pounds. With the additional weight of the equipment, he's up to two hundred and thirty pounds. I'm five foot-ten and one hundred and thirty-five pounds. My math isn't great, but that is a little more than half his weight, making the benchmark seem fair. Cole also forgets that females exhibit more fatigue resistance. Even though women have twelve to fourteen percent less muscle mass than men, they have more muscle mass in their lower bodies. Whereas men have more muscular upper bodies. The muscle groups required for optimum performance in this competition come from lower body strength. As you saw by the way Cole vaulted me into the air, he has an exceedingly strong upper body. There is no way I could have performed a similar feat. Frankly, I would've thought it was a stretch for Cole after the way he exerted himself."

"That sounds like a good rationalization to me, Newhouse. You can't convince me that it requires more athleticism to be a figure skater than it does a hockey player," Cole snarled.

"I'm not saying that. I'm saying the skill sets are different. If you recall, the purpose of this contest was to prove that muscle mass isn't equivalent to muscle strength and that women's lower bodies are stronger than those of comparable males. I think I made that point."

"I haven't played professional hockey in close to four years. Yet, my speed and endurance are still in the superior range."

"I haven't skated in twice that amount of time. Nobody is saying that you're not in impeccable shape, Cole. I'm saying that your excuses don't hold water, and the playing field isn't as uneven as you claim."

"Well, fans, it looks like the battle of the sexes lives on. Thanks for tuning in and be sure to catch more of Cole and Layla as the Predators host the Tornadoes tomorrow night. On behalf of Morgan Philips, Cole Pasternak, and Layla MacKenzie, this is Abby Lang wishing you all a great night. We're out. Great job, guys. I'm returning to the studio to prepare this footage for the local news. We're also going to rerun the race portion tomorrow night at the pre-game show, " Abby replied.

The Predators stepped onto the ice to begin practice. Many of the guys came over to give me congratulatory hugs and high-fives.

"Here come my so-called friends. I think traitors are more like it," Cole said to his former teammates.

"We can't help it, Cole. The team loves Layla, and she's easier on the eyes than your ugly mug," said Bryce.

"Yeah, I get it," replied Cole with half a smile.

"Cole, you were terrific, but on behalf of all the women out there, I must give kudos to Layla."

"You too, Abby? After all I've done for you?"

"Sorry, Cole, you're the greatest, but we females have to stick together."

"I'm going to hit the showers and grab some lunch before heading back to the office. Do you care to join me, Morgan?"

"Sounds great, Cole."

"Newhouse, regardless of whether I think you won or lost, what you did on the ice was impressive."

"Now I can die in peace knowing I managed to earn the almighty Cole Pasternak's stamp of approval. I'm assuming that backhanded compliment is the closest I will get to a concession."

"That's an astute assumption. It's no wonder you graduated with honors. See you later, ladies."

When Cole and Morgan disappeared from sight, I turned to Abby. "Do you mind if I ask you something?"

"Sure, what's that, Layla?"

"Cole implied he's done a lot for you. Was he just throwing that out there to make you feel guilty?"

"No. A bunch of us went out after a game one night. One of the guys in the bar started giving me a hard time. Cole immediately interjected and shut him down. That wasn't the first time I'd seen him do something like that. We were at an end-of-season party where Cole saw some jerk harassing one of the waitresses. Cole threatened the guy. He made him apologize before Cole escorted him out of the bar. Cole's always there when I need a question answered. He's taught me so much. I know your interaction with him seems strained, but that's unusual. From what I've seen, Cole's a great guy."

"That's what I hear. I'm glad you have a better relationship with him."

"I guess it helps that Cole doesn't see me as competition."

"I'm not his opponent!" I replied in exasperation.

"That may be true, but I didn't just beat him on the ice."

"Point taken. Thanks for moderating today, Abby. I'll see you at the game tomorrow night."

Needing to share my good news, I called Skylar on my way home. "Hey, Skye."

"I was hoping you'd call. Who emerged victorious in the battle of the sexes?"

"Much to my amazement, me, by a hair."

"Congratulations!!! One more step for womankind."

"I think you're being overdramatic but thank you."

"Why don't you sound happy? I thought you'd be over the moon at beating that pompous jerk."

"Part of me still doesn't believe I won. You should have seen him, Skye. Cole had such command of the ice. You would think he still plays professional hockey. His stats were better than the average player's. When the competition was over, Cole picked me up over his head and skated around the rink, tossing me in the air for a finale. I can't imagine where he found the strength. His arms are like tree trunks."

"I can't wait to see it. You still didn't tell me why you aren't more elated."

"Cole's reaction put a damper on my spirits."

"What did he say?"

"He said the race wasn't fair."

"Of course he did! You know that's bullshit, don't you? Layla, he was just trying to save face. You can't take him seriously. You need to stop giving this man such control over your life."

"If I could only get my insane attraction to him under control.

When he set me down and looked into my eyes after tossing me in the air, I had an overwhelming urge to kiss him. Maybe it was the adrenaline pumping but being in his arms caused an electric surge throughout my body."

"I think you should screw him and get it out of your system."

"Even if he were on board with the idea, which he's not, I think that would only make things worse. I'll send you the footage from the race once I get a copy. I've got to get back to the office."

"I can't wait to see it. Layla, remember, you worked hard for this. Don't let Cole continually diminish your accomplishments."

"Yeah. Thanks, Skye. I wish I had a snapshot of this face when Morgan said I won. That made every ounce of sweat worth it. At least it's over, and I can breathe a sigh of relief."

"If you feel this bad as the winner, imagine how he would have destroyed you if you lost?"

"You have no idea how much I miss you, Skye."

"I miss you too. Keep your chin up and your tongue sharp. We'll talk soon."

That night, I watched the competition recording again and again before falling asleep. My performance was impressive, but Cole's had me spellbound. I didn't see him again until the following day when Leora called us into her office.

"Have a seat, guys. I just wanted to tell you that we aired the competition on last night's

Highlights in Sports, in addition to the local news. That footage is pure gold. You two really put on a show. Cole, that was a nice touch throwing Layla in the air like that, even if she didn't think so. It played well on camera. Layla, congratulations! I didn't realize you were so athletic. Your list of talents continues to grow." Cole choked. "I can't wait to see the ratings for tonight's game. I want you two to think of other ways to engage each other on air." Cole shook his head in disapproval.

"Do you have a problem with that, Cole?" Leora asked with a glare that dared him to defy her.

"Not at all, Leora," replied Cole with an inescapable hint of sarcasm.

"If we're wrapped up, I'm heading back to my office to do more research on tonight's opponent. Cole, I'll see you at the pre-game show."

"I'll wait with bated breath, Newhouse," he replied, rolling his eyes.

Apparently, some fans saw the competition footage on the news because they were clapping for me as I approached the stadium.

The outcries of support included: "Great job, Layla. You're awesome, Layla. You rock. You showed him, Layla. On behalf of the women out there, great job."

It was the first time I savored my victory. "Thanks, you guys are the best! I did it for you." Cole walked up in the middle of the love-fest. He had a look that was a combination of annoyance and disgust on his face.

"Get your head out of the clouds, Newhouse. This is a big game."

"I'm well aware of that, Cole."

It was the battle of the best two teams in the Eastern and Western Conferences. "Hey Cole," said one of the announcers for the Tornados. I watched as Sienna Matthews gave Cole a warm embrace. I could tell from their body language that this wasn't a platonic relationship. "This should be a great match-up," said Sienna.

"I know. The team's skillsets are evenly matched," Cole replied.

"I'll catch up with you after the game."

"Sounds good, Sienna. I'm looking forward to it," Cole replied, with a wink.

I decided not to say anything. It was none of my business. I shouldn't be surprised that Cole's magnetism crossed state lines.

The first period ended in a zero-zero tie. Cole was unusually civil during our first intermission report. He agreed with my assessment that the Predators had too many turnovers at the blue line. The Tornado's offense was jamming the puck down their throats. The period ended with no score because of superior goal-tending on both sides. The second period was a different story.

After a reckless penalty by Matt Perault, the Tornados scored on a powerplay. Fortunately, the Predators tied the game two minutes later.

"That was a great use of the back of the net by Andre," I announced.

"If you didn't have such limited knowledge of the game, you would know when a player scoops the puck onto the blade of his stick and flicks it into the corner of the net, it's called a lacrosse move. Don't feel bad about your ignorance. I'm happy to enlighten you. As I said a few moments ago, our forwards need to lift the puck if they want to get it past Max Keumper."

My face burned red with rage as I gave Cole an arsenic smile. "Thank you for educating me, Cole. I hope our guys try to be less fancy moving forward. I think it's backfiring on them. They need to settle in and get back to playing their game."

"Their game isn't cutting it against a team of this caliber. It's common sense that you switch it up if something isn't working."

"Personally speaking, I think Coach Shanahan should split up Sebastian Dvorak and Alex Koulak and move Alex to the second line with Andre Pointe."

"That's a ridiculous idea. Why would Coach Shanahan split his top line?"

"Because he has his top two scorers on his first line. Alex is the best passer on the team and can feed Andre. He would also be coupled with Matt Perrault, who wins most of his faceoffs."

"Have you ever coached a sport, Layla?"

"No, and I'm not saying that Coach Shanahan isn't terrific at his job. I'm just giving my opinion. If I'm not mistaken, everyone is entitled to their opinion."

"I guess you're right, even if your opinion is wrong. Are you confident enough in your opinion to make a bet?"

"What kind of bet?" I asked apprehensively.

"Starting tonight, I think we should predict the outcome of each game, along with the breakout player to watch," Cole suggested, knowing I couldn't back down from a public challenge. I didn't have Cole's insight or perspective on other teams. Still, I was familiar enough with the Predators to voice an intelligent opinion. If I chose not to accept his offer, it would look like I lacked knowledge, which was the image Cole was trying to project.

"I'm shocked you're suggesting this, considering you lost both of our previous bets," I replied, sounding more confident than I felt.

"You've been lucky so far. When it comes to knowledge about the game, you're sure to lose. Do I hear you backing down?" Cole asked in a self-assured tone.

"You know better."

"Then tell me your prediction for the end of the game."

"I predict the Predators will win two to one, and Sebastian will make the difference."

"Although I agree with your score differential, I foresee the Tornados coming out on top. I think their captain Keegan Brossard will be the one to seal the deal."

"How much are we betting?"

"I'm not talking money. I think we should bet something far more interesting."

"Such as?" I asked with a hint of trepidation.

"What do you want?"

"I would need a few minutes to think about it. I'll get back to you by the end of the period."

"I think you're trying to bide your time because you're afraid of losing. However, I don't want it to be said that I'm not a gentleman, so I'll allow it."

"How magnanimous of you," I replied sardonically. "Are you telling me you already know what you want?"

"As a matter of fact, I do, but I'm not divulging that information until you're ready with a response."

The fact that Cole knew what he wanted worried me. I'm afraid he thought of yet another way to mortify me, and this bet was just an elaborate ruse to set me up. Call it coincidence or an alignment of the stars, but it was as if Coach Shanahan heard my thoughts regarding the player shift. Midway through the period, he moved Alex to the second line. Alex fed a beautiful pass to Andre, who scored a goal within five minutes. Unfortunately, Mathieu Perrault drew a cross-checking penalty a few minutes later. Keegan Brossard capitalized on the opportunity, ending the period in a tie.

"This is Layla MacKenzie, along with my co-host, the sore loser."

"I wouldn't be so quick to throw labels around," Cole shot back with daggers in his eyes.

"I'm referring to our ice competition from yesterday. However, now that you mentioned it, I recall being on point when I suggested the line change that scored the only goal for the Predators. If I remember correctly, you called my strategy ridiculous. I'm glad Coach Shanahan possesses more vision."

"Don't get ahead of yourself, Layla. As I said earlier, the Predators needed to deviate from their usual game. I wouldn't be surprised if the switch was temporary. Let's see if your intuition is right regarding the game's outcome. Have you decided what you want if you win, or are you trying to stall since Brossard scored for the Tornados?"

"If I win, I want you to clean my apartment."

Cole's expression was a combination of shock and horror. "You want me to clean your apartment? Why would I do that? I don't even clean my own place."

"Then you better start practicing. Like you, I'm busy and don't enjoy cleaning, so yes, that's what I want if I win."

"Do I have to wear an apron?" he asked facetiously.

"I don't own one, but it would be worth it for the entertainment value alone to purchase one. Dare I ask what you want if you win?"

"I want a massage."

"You mean a gift certificate for a massage."

"No, I mean you as my personal masseuse."

"I don't think that's in my wheelhouse."

"Cleaning isn't in mine. Are you welching on our bet?"

"No, of course not."

"Then it's settled."

I couldn't believe Cole asked for a massage. It was enough that

I had to look at his beautifully chiseled face and perfectly sculpted body. Touching him would stretch my willpower to the limit. I'd just pray the Predators won.

The third period seemed to go on forever. We were down to the last minute of play when one of the Tornado players pivoted around Jordan Gillies and put the puck over Bryce Andersen's shoulder. I felt that familiar sensation of my stomach relocating to my feet. I glanced over at Cole, who looked disappointed that the Predators had lost. He peered over at me, and his eyes lit up as he remembered there was a silver lining to the defeat.

"Well, Layla, that was a tough loss for you and the Predators."

"Don't gloat, Cole. I'm going to do my post-game player interview."

"I'll check my schedule and tell you when I'm free for my massage."

"Take your time. I know there's an opening on the twelfth of never."

Cole cracked a victorious smile. As I was leaving, I saw him holding the car door open for Sienna as she stepped into his Porsche. I knew there was something between them. When I got back to my apartment, I Googled her. She had an impressive resume, but it was her recent marriage announcement that caught my attention. I thought the bar couldn't get any lower regarding my respect for Cole, but I was wrong. Did this man have any boundaries? The idea of rubbing my hands over his adulterous muscles made my skin crawl. I guess I should thank Sienna for that. The thought of Cole sleeping with a married woman had me so riled up that I had to pour myself a double vodka to get some sleep.

I was still annoyed when I woke up the following day. Was Cole devoid of a moral conscience? Was it not enough that he had a sea of single women swooning at his feet? I was planning to confront him when I got to the office, but Cole wasn't in. He was probably still in bed with Sienna. Fortunately, Leora appeared at my door and distracted me from that vision.

"Good morning, Layla. I just wanted to tell you that your skating competition with Cole has gone viral."

"I guess that's good."

"It's better than I imagined. Our audience for last night's game reached an all-time high. I'm attributing it to an increase in female viewership."

"It could also be because of the rivalry between the Eastern and Western Conferences," I replied.

"That could have had something to do with it, but it wasn't enough to explain the drastic spike in ratings. Cole, good timing. I was just telling Layla about the surge in ratings for last night's game. I love the idea that you two are betting on the games. That's a great way to keep the audience engaged."

"Did you like how Cole called me out for not knowing what the 'lacrosse move' stood for in hockey?" I asked Leora.

"I can appreciate Cole's actions upset you, but it is those kinds of comments causing women to rally around you."

"Are you condoning his behavior?"

"I'm not, but you seem to be able to handle yourself. If I recall, you called Cole a sore loser. Besides, it would be good for you to develop a thicker skin, especially as a woman in this industry." I wanted to lunge across the room and wipe the smirk off Cole's face.

By the way, Leora, is there any corporate clause I would be violating by giving Cole a massage?"

"Only if he reports you for sexual harassment."

"That's too bad."

"I'll let you two work that out. Apparently, women loved the idea of having Cole clean your apartment."

Cole rolled his eyes. "There are many better ways to utilize my skills."

"You underestimate the appeal of a clean home for the average working woman," I said.

"Apparently."

"I'm going to let you guys get back to work. I just wanted to share the good news."

112

"Thanks, Leora," I replied. "Cole, could I speak with you for a moment?"

"What's up, Newhouse? I know we're flying out later today, but I thought you could give me my massage when we get back from the road."

"Tell me, Cole, are you planning to hook up with any more married women while we're away?"

"What are you talking about?" he asked, sounding clueless.

"Are you going to deny sleeping with Sienna last night?"

Cole stepped inside my office and shut the door. "Not that I owe you an explanation, but I didn't realize Sienna got married. She didn't tell me until after we had sex."

"I guess you missed the wedding announcement and the ring on her finger."

"There is no reason for me to see her wedding announcement, and she wasn't wearing an engagement ring. She had on a band, but that could've been a favored piece of jewelry or something with sentimental value. I would've thought it was her responsibility to tell me she was married."

"Would that have changed what happened?"

"Absolutely! I met Sienna a couple of years back at one of the games. We hit it off, and I spent the night. We had a break before the next game, so I decided to hang out in Colorado for another day to take her skiing. On the occasions that our paths crossed, we would hook up. It was a mutually agreeable arrangement. Besides, I'm not the one who cheated. If you remember, my girlfriend cheated on me. I would never put another man through that."

I saw pain flash through Cole's eyes. He was telling me the truth. "I'm glad to hear that, Cole. Maybe there's hope for you yet."

"I think you owe me an apology."

"I think that's pushing the envelope. You can't blame me for coming to that conclusion judging by your pattern with women."

"I bet you wouldn't judge Sienna so harshly."

"That's where you're wrong. Unlike you, I don't have a double standard."

"I'll see you at the airport, Newhouse. I'm done being berated."

I was relieved to hear that Cole disapproved of sleeping with married women. It shouldn't matter, but the part of me that saw signs of a decent human being didn't want to think I was completely off base in my judgment.

As I boarded the plane later that day, I grabbed a seat next to Ryan McEwin.

"Layla, to what do I owe the pleasure?"

"Hi, Ryan. I'm not sure if you know, but Cole and I are making on-air predictions about the games, and we are picking a 'breakout' player. Anyway, I need your help."

"How so?"

"I'm picking you as my player to watch tonight. I know your performance level hasn't been up to par, and part of that is because you're recovering from Covid. I've been watching you, and I see your frustration. You've had a couple of close calls at the net and some great pass plays. I think tonight will be the night it all comes together for you."

"Thanks for the vote of confidence, Layla. It has been frustrating. I haven't had the stamina I normally do, but I've been training extra hard, and I'm starting to feel like myself again."

"I see it."

"I'm amazed you noticed."

"I have, and I believe in you. Please do whatever you can to execute those plays and get that puck in the net. I can't lose to Cole again."

"Speak of the devil," said Ryan as Cole came down the aisle.

"Are you lost, Layla?" Cole asked, clearly annoyed to find me sitting with the players.

"Don't worry, I'm moving."

"Don't let him chase you off. Why don't you sit with the team? I swear we don't bite."

"Yeah, Layla, come sit with us," Jackson Kane called out.

"Layla's fine sitting up front," Cole interjected.

"Thanks, guys. I'm better off sitting alone if I hope to get some work done. Have a good flight and a great game." As I took my seat, I overheard Brett Gillies telling Cole that he should be nicer to me.

"You can't be serious. Aside from Layla's appearance, what do you like about that woman?" Cole asked, rolling his eyes.

"Do you know when it's our birthday or if one of us is out injured, Layla sends us an e-card?"

"Really?" replied a wide-eyed Cole. "Don't tell me you fall for that crap."

"It's very thoughtful. Layla even stops by to watch us practice."

"I wasn't aware of that, but it doesn't make up for the fact that she knows jack shit about hockey."

"She's learning a lot, and she asks us great questions. Layla works really hard, which is something we all relate to."

"During one of our interviews, I mentioned my son's birthday," Jordan O'Shea interrupted. "Do you know she left a stuffed dinosaur at the arena for him?"

"Are you guys forgetting about Shane? Do you want Layla to push him out of a job?"

"Of course not, but the fact is that Shane can't work. Layla is doing a great job, and yes, it doesn't hurt that she is way better to look at. All we're saying is you should give her a chance."

"Do you all feel like this?"

I turned to see a group of Predator players nodding in agreement.

"Unbelievable! You guys are all a bunch of suckers. Don't be taken in by her. Beneath that sweet exterior lies a shark."

"I disagree," Brady retorted. "Think about all the work she's doing for Shane's fundraiser. Look, Cole, we're not saying you need to be her best friend, just give her a chance."

"I'll think about it," Cole muttered.

My soul was flying as high as the plane. Cole glanced at me as he took his seat. The way his jaw was clenched told me that he knew I overheard that entire conversation, not that the guys were trying to hide it. A warm feeling, the kind you get when you look at a puppy, spread over me at Cole's displeasure.

My feet still hadn't touched the ground when the team arrived at Madison Garden, where the Predators would face the Raptors. I recalled watching the Raptors as a kid. They were a physical team with a great goalie, but they stood three spots below us in the standings.

"Layla, I'm anxious to hear your prediction," Cole said at the beginning of the post-game show.

"Well, Cole, despite the differences in their record, I think the Predators will have a tough time coming off the speed and physicality of last night's game against the Tornados."

"The Predators took a hard loss last night. They're not going to let that happen again," countered Cole.

"I have a theory that top teams tend to play down when facing an easier opponent, while the teams lower in the standings play up. It can catch the stronger team off-guard."

"It happens, but it's not going to happen tonight. I predict the Predators will win three to one," Cole retorted confidently.

"Don't get me wrong, I have faith in our guys. I just don't think it's going to be an easy win. I predict a Predator victory with a score of four to three."

"Who is your player to watch?"

"I'm going with Ryan McEwin. He's had a bit of a rough patch since he's come off Covid protocol, but I think the pieces will come together tonight."

"I assume you know he's a defenseman, don't you? I'm not trying to help you out here, but you'd be better off betting on one of our forwards."

"I'm aware of his position, and I assume you know that our defensemen have scored twenty-two goals thus far this season."

"It's true. The Predators have one of the highest-scoring defenses in the NHL," Cole shot back with a pissed-off look. "I'm going to go with Andre Perrault for my pick. Am I still cleaning your apartment if you win?"

"You are. What do you want? A second massage is not an option."

"You must be psychic," Cole laughed "I'll settle for you washing my car in a white T-shirt."

"How dare you tell me what to wear. This isn't going to be a wet T-shirt contest."

"Not a contest, but I foresee a wet T-shirt."

"You're unbelievable! Your initials really do stand for chauvinist pig."

"Do we have a bet?"

"We do, but I'm going on record that I find your terms offensive."

"Duly noted," Cole replied with a cocky grin.

The Predators won four to three in overtime. It was the battle I expected. Ryan had a great night, scoring one goal and one assist. Travis Goodrow scored another goal, continuing his streak. Andre Perrault had one assist, making me the winner.

"Cole, I just want to point out that two of tonight's four goals were scored by defensemen."

"I'm aware of that, Layla. Our offense was tired coming off last night's game. Our high scorers were out of gas, forcing the defense to step up. At least they held on and came away with the victory."

The camera clicked off, and we prepared to head back to the hotel. "You let me know when you can clean my apartment," I said, gloating.

"First things first. We're flying home on Saturday. I'll expect my massage late Sunday morning, so I can relax before the game that night."

"Make sure you find your way back from your flavor of the night's bed. I have work to do for the fundraiser, and I'm not going to sit around waiting for you."

"Don't worry about me. I'll be ready. I have massage oil, so just bring your hands."

"The guys are getting on the shuttle back to the hotel. Are you coming?"

"No, I'm meeting up with a friend."

"I should have known. Do you have a woman in every city?"

"I didn't say it is a woman."

"Well, is it?"

"It is," Cole replied sheepishly. "She happens to be a friend from Buffalo who moved to Manhattan for work. Our relationship is platonic."

"I didn't think you knew such a thing existed."

"Contrary to your opinion, I don't sleep with every woman I know."

"I'm guessing you're not attracted to her. Am I right?"

Cole hesitated. "You're right."

"I'm also betting that she's attracted to you."

"You'd have to ask her. I'll see you tomorrow, Newhouse," Cole replied, rushing off. My assumptions clearly made him uncomfortable.

"Try to have fun," I called after him. "I know it must be a strain for you to converse without the prospect of sex." I went back to the hotel and called Skylar.

"Hi Layla, I'm sorry I couldn't catch a flight to the city. I would have loved to meet the infamous Cole in person."

"That's okay. I know you're busy."

"How are you doing? I see you won tonight's bet and got in some nice jabs at your nemesis."

"Yeah, it was a good night. The guys invited me to sit with them on the plane. They told Cole he should treat me better."

"That's huge, so what's the problem?"

"I'm giving Cole a massage Sunday morning. The thought of touching him is vile in some ways and exciting in others. I'm afraid my hormones will trump the part of me that despises him for being an atrocious human being. Do you have any words of wisdom?"

"That's a tough one. I'm objective, and I can tell you I'd sleep with Cole if he hit on me. Remember, he's your archenemy. He has done nothing but undermine you from the day you arrived. Jot down a list of things he's said to upset you. Recite them for the next day and a half. If you feel yourself getting excited, picture something that turns you off."

"Hmmm, I could visualize baseball players spitting and rubbing their crotches."

Skye burst out laughing. "That works for me. I've got to get some sleep. Let me know how it goes."

"Thanks, Skye. You should have gone into counseling."

CHAPTER 13

It was Sunday morning at ten o'clock. I got a text from Cole telling me I could head to his place at any time with his address. I had never been to his home before. I was greeted by the doorman, who called Cole to announce my arrival. "Just take the elevator straight to the top," the doorman said. I should have known Cole would have the penthouse. I stepped out of the elevator, where Cole was leaning against the foyer entrance. His arms were folded on his chest. He was wearing low-rise ripped jeans that hung perfectly off his hips. His torso was bare, as were his feet. My eyes drank him in. My God, he was a gorgeous creature. I scaled down his delineated build from his broad shoulders to his firm pecs, flat stomach, and trim waist. He had a trail of hair that led beneath his belly button down to his groin.

"You can't take your eyes off me, can you, Newhouse?" Cole said with a hint of amusement in his voice.

"If you didn't want me to look, you should be wearing a shirt," I said, lifting my eyes.

"Were you planning to massage me through my clothing?"

"That would be preferable."

Cole laughed. "Most women enjoy touching my body."

"I'm not most women.," I replied indignantly.

"We'll see," he retorted with a wink.

Cole motioned me to step inside. I walked into a beautiful space with high ceilings and an entire wall of windows flaunting a spectacular view of the city. The living room had a large sectional with two oversized reclining chairs facing the sofa. One wall was lined with white bookshelves. Between the bookshelves was a big screen TV mounted over a gas fireplace. The color scheme was gray, blue, and white. It was masculine but not dark or over-powering.

"Why don't you give me a tour?" I asked, trying to postpone the inevitable.

The tour included a guest bedroom decorated in a beach motif. Next was the man cave, complete with an even bigger large screen TV, surround sound, wet bar, and a treadmill. The walls were covered in awards and pictures of Cole from his time with the Predators. The kitchen had white cabinets, stainless appliances, a large island, and gray quartz countertops. It flowed into the dining area, which contained a gray-washed wooden table and twelve chairs. Next came the main bedroom, which had a king-size bed with a massive frame. I envisioned countless women tied to the bedpost begging for mercy. The thought caused my temperature to rise. The master bath was marble with an enormous shower. Adjacent to the bathroom was a huge walk-in closet. I stepped and the smell of his cologne struck me. I wondered if his skin tasted as good as he smelled.

"You have way more clothes than I do. They're even organized by color. Do you support the theory that clothes make the man?"

"I have an image to present, and the color coding makes it easy to find things. Frankly, I couldn't care less about clothes. I collect watches, as you can see," Cole said, waving his hand over a series of accessory cases sitting on a built-in dresser."

"It's an impressive collection. I have a total of two, one silver and the other gold. I do admit to having a fondness for clocks. The penthouse is very tastefully done. Did you use a decorator?"

"No, I did it myself with a little help from Ashley."

"You did a nice job."

"Thank you. I'll get a couple of towels and some massage oil.

Would you like something to drink? You should hydrate. You'll be working up a sweat."

"No, thanks, I just finished breakfast."

"I've been up since seven. I already worked out for two hours. I was going to shower, but that seemed silly. I hope I don't stink."

"I'll let you know if you do." Cole came out of the bathroom and tossed me a towel and a bottle of massage oil. I watched as he started unbuttoning his jeans.

"Stop right there." He looked surprised.

"This is strictly an upper body massage."

"You're only doing half the job."

"Be grateful I agreed to this at all."

"If you change your mind, let me know," he said, sprawling out on the bed. "Be sure to rub the massage oil between your hands to warm it up first."

"I see you've done this before."

"I go for regular massages, which is something you should consider. Maybe it would help you unwind."

I stood by the side of the bed, rolled the oil around my hands, and started rubbing his massive shoulders.

"Newhouse, I barely feel you touching me. I know you can do better than that."

"I don't have a lot of upper body strength," I replied, grasping at straws.

"You're strong enough. From our race around the ice, I know you have enough power in your lower body to draw from. It would help if you were in a better position. You need to straddle my butt."

That was the last thing I needed to do, but I never would have made a dent in his shoulders from where I was standing. I got on the bed and sat on top of his rounded buttocks. I started with the part of his neck that wasn't covered by his dark, thick, wavy hair. Now that I was on top of him, I smelled his musky scent. I was hoping it would turn me off, but it did quite the opposite. My hands moved from his neck out to his shoulders.

"Press harder," Cole instructed.

"I don't want to hurt you," I replied, hoping my excuse sounded plausible.

"I'm used to deep massages. Believe me, you won't hurt me." I leaned over, digging into his shoulders with all my strength. I felt his muscles rippling beneath my hands.

"Much better." Cole sighed. I took my palm and rubbed it up and down his back between his lats. I rose to my knees, which were situated along his hips. I rubbed his back in long, flowing motions before going from side to side. I didn't know what possessed me, but I braced my hands against his shoulders and used my knee to rub his back in circular motions.

"Now that's what I'm talking about," Cole groaned. I shifted my body onto his upper back and placed his arms over his head. I languished them with long deep strokes, massaging his palms with my thumbs when I got to his hands. Cole turned his head sideways to look at me. I stared back at him and felt my insides getting wet. I tried picturing spitting, crotch-grabbing baseball players, but they were no match for his temptation eyes. I switched to his other side, hoping to avoid his gaze. His eyes followed my hands as I tugged on his fingers. I imagined his large, graceful hands cupping my breasts. I pictured what it would feel like to slide my body up and down against his moist skin, which wasn't half as slick as my insides. I needed to rein my thoughts in before I did something I would regret. If I made a pass at Cole, I would be forever at his mercy. To regain control, I tried counting sheep. What a stupid idea! That did even less to distract me. I hate dirt, so I conjured images of hoarders' homes stockpiled with junk. Nothing was working, so I decided to use the sides of my hands to plant karate chops up and down his back. At least it expelled some pent-up frustration while getting me away from his eyes.

"Newhouse, could you rub my lower back right above my buttocks? I think I strained it lifting earlier."

"You're pushing your luck, Cole. I'll do that, and then I'm done."

He was right. I was working up a sweat. I straddled his buttocks and dug into his lower back, first with my thumbs and then with my palms. I didn't realize that my pussy was rocking against the top of his ass cheeks until I felt the tension cresting in my clitoris. I couldn't believe I was on the verge of having an orgasm. Why did I let myself rub against him like that? Why didn't I wear jeans instead of these thin cotton yoga pants? I glanced down at Cole's back and realized he was breathing heavily. Apparently, I wasn't the only one getting aroused.

"I need to stop now," I said, sliding off his back.

"If you're looking to regain control, I have handcuffs in the top drawer of my nightstand," Cole uttered.

Shit, Cole knew I was getting aroused. I needed to do something to regain my composure while interrupting his train of thought. Much to our surprise, I opened the drawer and removed the handcuffs. Cole rolled onto his side, watching my every move. I let the handcuffs dangle before me, sliding one onto my wrist.

"Who would these be for, you or me?" I asked.

Cole's eyes were gleaming. "It doesn't matter. Either way is fun."

"They're too big for me."

"They're adjustable," Cole responded evenly.

I slid the handcuff off my wrist and reached back into the drawer. I removed what looked like a leather riding crop.

"That's a flogger," Cole replied in a sultry voice.

I struck my leg with the flogger. "Interesting," I said as I placed it on the mattress. I returned to the nightstand pulling out a blindfold with one hand and a gag with the other. I examined them before tossing them aside. I would never voluntarily take away my ability to see or scream with a man I didn't trust. The last article I withdrew was a whip with a small black handle and multiple leather strands.

"That's called a cat of nine tails," Cole said, breaking the silence. I picked up the whip and lashed the pillow, causing Cole to jump. "I see you're a fan."

"Curious is more like it," I replied as I struck the pillow again.

"I can tell by the maniacal shimmer in your eye that you're

turned on. I'd be happy to show you how to strike someone without leaving marks."

"You're the last person I would experiment with."

"Why is that?"

"For starters, I don't trust you."

"I promise that I adhere to the cautionary colors."

"What does that mean?"

"If you were excited by what I was doing or wanted more, you would say green. You would say yellow if you wanted me to ease up or use caution. Obviously, red means you've reached your limit. I assure you this is one area where I strictly adhere to boundaries."

"Even if that were true, I still wouldn't engage with you."

"Fair enough, but judging by your reaction, I think it's something you should consider exploring."

Unfortunately, playing with Cole's tools of torture didn't give my aching pussy the respite I was seeking.

"I need to go," I mumbled. "I have a lot to do today, and I'm already behind schedule."

I clumsily bolted out the front door, relieved that Cole didn't follow me. I think he was equally out of sorts from our exchange. I was so rattled when I left Cole's penthouse that I found the nearest bar and had a drink. Alcohol was easily found in Miami, even on an early Sunday afternoon. My mind flashed back to the image of Cole's half-naked body as I sipped my martini. I couldn't deny the effect this man had on me. He assaulted my senses, from preoccupying my mind to making my body ache with need. I wished I knew how to purge myself of him. My desires made me feel weak and out of control, which was unacceptable given the man's character. I kept my distance when I saw Cole later that night at that game.

"Hey, Newhouse, it dawned on me that I never thanked you for my massage. You left so quickly; I was worried."

"Save it for someone who believes you," I sniped.

"I'm being serious. I figured this was the first time you touched a real man. I didn't want your body to go into shock or, worse yet, heart failure."

"I was more concerned about getting things done for the fundraiser. Touching you was an unnecessary waste of my time. I wanted to get away from you as fast as possible and move on to things that matter."

"If you say so. Unlike you, I'm not afraid to admit I enjoyed our time together."

"That makes one of us," I quipped.

"I can't wait to hear your prediction for tonight's game, Newhouse."

"I'm warning you, Cole, you better not ask for anything involving the implements in your nightstand."

"Don't worry, you're safe." Cole laughed. "I couldn't get away with referencing that on camera."

I was grateful as the pre-game show began, ending our personal commentary. The night was off to a rough start for the Predators who were down three of their players. One's wife had a baby, and the other two had injuries. The team brought William Blaschuk up from the minors. From what I understood, he scored sixty goals last season. Fortunately, we were playing Dallas, who wasn't high in the standings.

"Layla, are the last-minute changes to the roster impacting your prediction for tonight's game?"

"I don't think so, Cole. I'm confident everyone will step up, and the Predators will come out on top two to one. I'm picking our captain as the player to watch. This is the type of scenario where he'll lead by example."

"I don't doubt that. I'm going with the Predators as well. I'm expecting Sebastian Dvorak to have a good night. Our 'perfection line' has been underperforming the last couple of days, and they're frustrated. Tonight is the night they're going to make things happen. I also have eyes on Will Blaschuk, who the Predators pulled up from the minors."

Sebastian scored a goal by the end of the second period, and Will had a goal and an assist. The Predators were leading three to one. "I'll tell you, Cole, Will has been tremendous thus far. He's fired up the line, and he's all over the ice. He's fast as lightning and has a wicked wrist shot. I don't understand why he isn't a fixture on the Predator bench." That was when Cole unleashed unholy hell on me.

"Of course you don't! That goes without saying. If you knew anything about player development, you would know it is an ongoing process. Even the top draft picks need to spend time in the minors developing penalty-killing and face-off skills. New players have so much to learn, ranging from good dietary habits to establishing mental toughness. Even when players are brought up from the minors, they need to sit on the bench and learn by observing the pros. It takes lots of patience but helps young guys avoid career-ending injuries. It also prevents them from being placed on the fourth line, where they won't necessarily get the playing time they deserve. It's not about getting there quickly, Layla. It's about establishing the good habits and consistency that will increase the longevity of a player's career."

"Please correct me if I'm mistaken but didn't you play for the Predators right after being drafted?"

I could see the contempt in Cole's eyes as he responded. "Yes, I was one of the exceptions. However, I think the coaching staff learned from my experience. I spent a lot of time in the penalty box my first two years because I didn't have patience or discipline when using my physicality on the ice. I was fortunate the Predators always had a great penalty kill. Still, I admit to putting special teams in a tough spot when many of those penalties could have been avoided."

"Knowing your vast ego, I'm surprised to hear you say that. Can you admit it would've made you crazy sitting on the sidelines?"

"Yeah, it would have, but I was young and impulsive, and all I wanted to do was play. Now that I'm more mature—"

"That's a matter of opinion," I said, interrupting him.

Cole ignored my comment. "Unlike you, I understand the reasoning behind the new player protocol. Hopefully, I've enlightened you enough for you to avoid making more erroneous statements in the future."

"I still stand behind my opinion. Maybe you've been watching a different game, Cole. The one I'm witnessing has benefitted from William Blaschuk being on the ice."

"If that's the case, you've misconstrued the information I gave you. If you want to continue spouting baseless statements, so be it. I am only trying to prevent you from looking clueless."

I bit the inside of my mouth to avoid going back at Cole and prolonging this torturous exchange. I turned to review the highlights from the period as I counted the minutes until the game reconvened. The Predators won five to two, and Sebastian scored a goal and two assists.

"Good thing I didn't take my car in to be washed," Cole said, grinning over his victory. "Should I expect you tomorrow?"

"I'm not washing a thing until you leave me with a sparkling clean apartment," I retorted.

"You heard it, Predator fans, that was one disgruntled Layla MacKenzie paying the price for underestimating the Predators. Thanks for tuning in. From all of us at Southern Sports, have a great night."

"If I were a man, you'd be a pain in my balls," I snarled.

"Good thing the cameras are off, Newhouse. That comment might be taken as discriminatory."

"Report me! I'm going home. I'll expect you at my place by ten a.m. Come ready to work and bring me a latte from Starbucks!"

"My, someone's grumpy. Now, who's the sore loser?" Cole asked, with a victorious grin.

"I'm just sick of your condescending attitude. I may have to deal with it on camera, but I'm off the clock. Have a miserable evening." The last sound I heard was Cole chuckling as I stormed out.

CHAPTER 14

I woke up the next day feeling conflicted. On the one hand, the thought of seeing Cole was enough to make my stomach turn. However, knowing he would be miserable cleaning my apartment gave me a warm fuzzy feeling. I decided the idea of tormenting Cole brought me a sense of joy that surpassed my misery. I was busy lining up the cleaning supplies when the doorbell rang.

"You're late," I snapped.

"I see you're still in a foul mood. Maybe this will help," Cole said, handing me a latte.

"Should I assume from your bicentennial eyes that you had a late night?"

"What's that supposed to mean?"

"That means your eyes are red, white, and blue, dumbass."

"It must be allergies."

"Have you developed an allergy to Jack Daniels and loose women?"

"No, only cleaning products."

"Nice try." I turned away from Cole in a huff beckoning him with my finger. "Now, if you're done making excuses, follow me. You can start by stripping my bed and washing the sheets."

Cole begrudgingly followed me over to the bed. He lifted the top sheet to his nose and inhaled.

"These sheets don't smell like they've seen a lot of action. I don't think they need to be cleaned."

"I don't recall asking your opinion. Grab the sheets and follow me." I opened the sliding barn doors revealing my washer and dryer.

"Which one's the washer?" Cole asked, as his eyes darted back and forth between the machines..

"If you're feigning stupidity, hoping I'll let you off the hook, you're mistaken."

Cole threw up his hands in a shrug. "My cleaning woman does my laundry, and I have a delivery service for my dry cleaning."

"My God, you're spoiled."

"I prefer to call it fortunate," he replied in a matter-of-fact tone.

"Do I need to give you lessons, or do you think you can figure out how to use the washer?"

"I used to do my laundry in college. I think I can manage."

"One day, you're going to make someone a useless husband," I lamented, as I smacked him in the stomach with the detergent.

"That would depend on what my wife finds important. I reassure you it will be something more spellbinding than laundry."

"When you're done here, meet me in the kitchen."

"Yes, ma'am," Cole replied, giving me a mocking salute.

I watched from the corner of my eye as Cole started the washing machine. He was clearly busting my chops as usual.

"Are you ready for your next task?"

"I can hardly wait."

"Here is a feather duster. Be sure to clean the blinds," I instructed waving it in his face. "Use this bleach when cleaning the tub. You might want to wear gloves to avoid burning your skin."

"I assume you have a pair."

"Here," I tossed him a pair of vinyl stretch gloves.

"I can't even get my thumb in these," Cole whined as he ripped off the glove. "You have munchkin hands."

"My hands are proportionate for my body."

"Your mouth is certainly big."

"So is my brain. Are you done stalling?"

"Go on," Cole replied, tossing his hands up in resignation.

"Use this on the sink and countertops," I said, pointing to the bottle of Scrubbing Bubbles. "I assume you know how to vacuum. Be sure to go under the couch. This is the floor steamer. All you need to do is plug it in and twist this dial. It gets boiling hot, so watch that you don't burn your feet."

"It's nice you're concerned about my welfare."

"The only thing I'm concerned about is getting sued if you hurt yourself."

Cole smiled in amusement.

"Do you have any questions?"

"It's not rocket science, Newhouse," Cole replied, half asleep.

"You would say anything to shut me up."

"Is it working?" he asked with a glimmer of hope.

"I'm going to sit on the balcony and have my latte in peace." As I turned to walk out, Cole removed his shirt and jeans.

"What are you doing?" I snapped.

"I don't want to risk getting bleach on my clothes."

"I don't want to see you naked."

"I'm not naked. I'm wearing boxer briefs and socks."

"Here, put this on," I said, shoving an apron in his hands.

"You can't be serious."

"Have you ever known me not to mean what I say? Now put it on and call me if there are any issues."

"Don't you want to watch and ensure I'm doing the right job?"

"I'll inspect your work when you're done. The less I see of you, the better."

"I'm surprised the control freak in you finds that acceptable."

"My desire not to be in your presence takes precedence over my OCD," I called out as I walked away.

Cole went to work in the bathroom while I sat on my balcony with my laptop and latte. The agitation in my stomach was just starting to settle when he reappeared.

"That bleach stinks."

"Did you turn on the exhaust fan?"

"I turned it on now. I didn't expect the fumes to make me dizzy. No wonder why you can't think straight."

"I assure you, I see things quite clearly. Why don't you grab a quick drink from the fridge before dusting?"

"Wow, you're quite the taskmaster. Even employees get a break," Cole whined.

"You've barely worked a half hour."

"I'm not used to manual labor. It's exhausting."

"So are you," I said, shoving a bottle of water in his hand. Cole took a swig of water and started work on the living room. "Make sure to move my knick-knacks. Don't be lazy and dust around them."

"I thought you weren't watching me."

"Unfortunately, you need constant supervision." I glanced at Cole periodically and was surprised to see him doing a good job. "Don't forget my windows."

"I don't do windows," Cole protested.

"Don't even try it!"

"All right." He conceded . "I'm only giving in because you have a small apartment. "Judging by the size of this place, I'm guessing your salary must be commensurate with your hockey knowledge," Cole replied condescendingly.

"Maybe I prefer cozy to big and ostentatious. Besides, you know how high the rents are in Miami. Here, use this shammy cloth on the windows. It cuts down on the streaking, and don't forget to dust the fan blades."

I should have left well enough alone. Cole had to stretch to reach the tops of the windows, revealing more of his body from beneath the apron. I had the overwhelming urge to run my nails down his sides to see if he was ticklish. I knew touching him wouldn't have a happy ending, so I improvised. I picked up the feather duster, along with my phone. I snuck behind him and brushed the feather duster against his bare skin, causing Cole to yelp.

"Holy shit, you scared me," he exclaimed.

I flitted the feather duster beneath the apron against his bare navel. Cole jumped back as I videotaped our exchange.

"You are ticklish, aren't you?"

"No, you just surprised me," he replied coyly.

"You're lying. Untie the apron."

"No!"

"I guess I'll see for myself." Cole stepped back from me as I walked toward him. With lightning reflexes, he apprehended the feather duster.

"Stay back," he warned, waving the feather duster in my face.

"I wish you could see how ridiculous you look right now," I taunted him.

"Give me that phone," Cole snapped.

"Come and get it," I replied, provoking him. Cole took two steps toward me, backing me into the couch. I fell onto the cushions, and he pounced on me. I shoved the phone between the seams.

"That's not fair," Cole protested.

"Neither is this," I said, reaching to tickle his torso.

"Stop!" Cole gasped.

"Here, I didn't think you had a sensitive bone in your body. Imagine my surprise," I said with a smirk. I traced the outline of his chest to his waist with my nails. Cole grabbed my hands, pinning them over my head. His breath felt ragged and warm on my face. His eyes were wild as his face hovered over mine.

"Two can play at this game," he whispered, grazing my navel with his free hand.

I was ridiculously ticklish, as Cole was about to discover. Why didn't I think about that before giving in to my urges? I had to get away from him before he realized the extent of my vulnerability. Of course, he uncovered my most sensitive spot in seconds. There was no place for me to escape Cole's touch. He was straddled over my waist, and I was no match for his girth.

"You better stop now if you know what's good for you," I said, sounding tougher than I felt.

"Is that so? It's funny how your tune changes when the shoe is on the other foot."

"Cole, I'm serious," I pleaded to no avail.

Knowing he found my Achilles heel, Cole stroked my navel, causing me to writhe uncontrollably beneath him. My body was out of control as my knee lunged forward, making direct contact with Cole's groin. He released my hands instantly, grabbing his crotch as he doubled over. I felt like I should do something to help but was at a loss as to what. At the very least, I owed him an apology.

"I'm so sorry, Cole! I didn't mean to do that. I lost control."

"Are you trying to make sure I never reproduce?" Cole said, gasping for breath.

"I warned you!"

"I didn't think you would rupture my ball sack," he replied in a scathing tone.

"I'm really, really sorry. Contrary to your opinion, I didn't mean to hurt you."

"At least it isn't as bad as scalding me with hot coffee."

"Is there anything I can do for you?"

"Yeah, stay the hell away from my private parts," he snapped. "Needless to say, I'm done cleaning for the day."

"I understand," I replied with an affirmative nod.

Cole slowly straightened up, rising from the couch.

"Would you like a glass of water?"

"A stiff shot would be more like it," he replied, wincing.

"I'm sorry. I don't have any alcohol in the house."

"I strongly suggest getting some, especially if you plan to kick all your guests in the nuts."

"I will. I promise." Realizing my comment could be misconstrued I added, "I'm talking about getting alcohol, not assaulting my guests."

"I would hope so! I will expect you at my place tomorrow to wash and wax my car."

"I thought I was just washing the car."

"That was before you wounded me."

Now wasn't the time to argue with him. "Fine, I'll see you tomorrow. Cole, once again, I really do apologize," I said contritely.

"Payback's a bitch, Newhouse," Cole replied as he hobbled out the door.

That night, I met Ashley for drinks. I shared the photo of Cole in an apron, along with the unfortunate 'ball breaking' incident. Enough time had elapsed for me to find the story amusing.

"We may be laughing now, but I assure you my brother will show you no mercy tomorrow," Ashley predicted. "He may have been protective of me with other kids, but we did our fair share of roughhousing growing up. He didn't go easy on me because I was a girl."

"I'm fully expecting it. Frankly, I'd rather Cole torture me while I'm washing his car than make a fool of me on camera."

"Don't be surprised if he does both."

"Unfortunately, nothing surprises me when it comes to Cole's deviant behavior. Ashley, I'm sorry I have to cut our evening short. I still have research to do for tomorrow's game. The more I prepare, the less opportunity I give your brother to embarrass me."

"Thanks for coming out, Layla. I'm going to talk to the guy at the bar who's been staring at us since we sat down." I followed the direction of Ashley's eyes until I encountered the dark stare of a sexy Latino.

"Have fun and be safe. I'll talk to you soon."

I woke up the following day and put on the cut-off denim shorts and white T-shirt Cole requested. It peeved me that he had the nerve to dictate my outfit, but it wasn't worth the fight. I pulled into the guest parking at Cole's building and walked over to the doorman.

"Hi, Ms. MacKenzie. Mr. Pasternak is waiting for you around the back of the building." I walked through the parking garage to find Cole filling a bucket with soap and water.

"Newhouse, as you can see, I've been anticipating your arrival. Here's your sponge, tire wash, towels, and hose."

"How are you feeling today, Cole?"

"Never better. Everything was in working order by the time I went out last night. I'm sure you've heard the adage, 'it's hard to keep a good man down.'"

"That may prove true if, in fact, you were a good man."

"Do you think it's a good idea for you to be trading insults with me in your position?"

"Probably not," I said reticently. "Give me the hose. Let's get this over with."

Cole's Porsche had beautiful lines. It reminded me of its owner, sleek and fast. I could see where the car would be a chic magnet, not that he needed one. Cole leaned against the parking lot wall ogling my every move.

"I think you missed a spot along the bottom," he said, pointing his finger toward the back tire.

"It looks clean to me."

"It's clean if you're Stevie Wonder. Rewash it," he barked in an authoritarian tone.

As I bent over to clean the 'so-called' dirty area, I felt my shorts ride up my buttocks and the shirt slide up my back. "Are you enjoying the show?" I asked, turning to face him.

"I'll admit the view isn't bad," he replied, beaming. That's when I realized he was recording me with his phone.

"You can't be serious," I whined, pointing to the phone.

"I'm just leveling the playing field from yesterday."

"Turn it off, now!" I demanded.

"I would get to work on those tires if you want to be on time for the game tonight," he replied, dismissing me.

"Your tires are sparkling. Toss me the towel. I'm going to dry the car off."

"Not so fast. I still see some soap. Hand me the hose." I foolishly placed the hose in Cole's outstretched hand, only to have him spray me from head to toe.

"That's not fair!" I shrieked. "I worked so hard to stay dry."

"You were starting to sweat. I thought you needed to cool off," Cole replied, amused by my distress.

In truth, the cold water felt refreshing. Apparently, my body agreed because I looked down and saw my nipples standing at attention. To make matters worse, Cole could see through my wet T-shirt. I grabbed a towel and wiped the water from my eyes while Cole resumed videoing me in all my glory.

"Cole, erase that. It leaves nothing to the imagination!" I pleaded.

"I know. That's the look I was going for." I stormed over to him, trying to pry the phone from his hand. Unfortunately, my reflexes weren't nearly as fast as his. "I would keep my distance unless you want to be tickled again," Cole threatened.

"Should I remind you how that ended?" I quipped.

"There's no way you're getting your hands on my phone," he replied, staring at my breasts.

"Cole, you can't post those pictures. They're borderline pornographic."

"That depends on what you're going to do with the video from yesterday."

"That's different. The fans will get a huge kick from seeing you in an apron. It's funny."

"I'm not amused. I'm sure spectators will be equally, if not more, captivated by your tan glistening legs and silver dollar-sized nipples."

"Stop staring at my breasts!" I shrieked. "If you don't erase those pictures now, I'm leaving."

"Go right ahead. I'll have you wax my car after you lose tonight's bet."

"I'm serious, Cole."

"Don't have a hissy fit. I'll hold onto the pictures for leverage, but they'll be for my eyes only."

"I don't find that comforting."

"If you don't find my terms acceptable, I could always pass my phone around the Predator locker room."

"You wouldn't dare!"

"It's you who always says I'm not a good man. Do you want to test that theory?"

"You're enough to drive any woman mad!"

"If you mean mad with desire, I agree."

He was on my last nerve. "I'm going home. Let me borrow a dry shirt."

"Do I hear a pretty please?" Cole asked, toying with me.

"No, but I'll refrain from kicking you in the balls."

"Now, who wouldn't dare?"

"Do you want to test that theory?" I shot back with a venomous stare. Cole popped his trunk and tossed me a shirt from his gym bag. "Smart man," I replied.

The thought of Cole possessing those pictures haunted me. The idea of them going viral had me so distraught that I nearly had two accidents driving home. I raced into my apartment, changed clothes, dried my hair, applied my make-up, and called Ashley.

"You'll never guess what your brother did now."

"You can't say I didn't warn you," Ashley replied resolutely. I explained what happened and asked her to talk to Cole about deleting the photos.

"I'll do my best, Layla, but my brother has his own mind."

"At least he'll hear you out, whereas my pleas fall on deaf ears."

"I'll let you know if I have any luck, but I'm not optimistic."

"Thanks, Ashley. I'm sorry to put you in the middle. I didn't know where else to turn. I can't let those images go public."

I stopped by the office to pick up some paperwork for the prospective sponsors I was on my way to visit before tonight's game. My back was to the doorway when I heard a low whistle.

"Cole, you scared me. I wasn't expecting to run into you."

"I left something in my office for Shane's son. I'm on my way to see one of his games."

"It's nice that you do that."

"Why are you here, Newhouse? It looks like you're going on a hot date."

"I'm trying to seal the deal on a couple more sponsors for the fundraiser. They've been dodging me. I hope meeting them in person will yield more positive results."

"You mean you hope that making an appearance in a come fuck me dress will prove more effective."

I sighed. "I admit to using my appearance as a form of persuasion in this case, but only for a good cause."

Cole shrugged. "You're not getting an argument from me. I didn't think an outfit could top the Daisy Duke shorts you were wearing earlier, but this is a close second. I know I'd buy what you're selling."

"Thank you, I think."

Cole's eyes scanned me from head to toe. "You're welcome."

"I hope you know this isn't something I would do if it weren't to help Shane."

"You don't have to defend yourself to me, Newhouse. Women use their looks as a bargaining chip all the time."

"That's not true, especially in my case."

"How can you say that when you just admitted otherwise?" I went to defend myself, but Cole raised his hand to silence me. "Contrary to your opinion, I wish you luck. Although, I doubt you'll need it with those legs."

I let out a sigh of exasperation. Why did Cole see me in this dress? It gave credence to his argument that I was hired for my looks, not my ability. My guilt was somewhat assuaged when all three potential clients signed on the dotted line. I rushed home, changed into something less revealing, and headed to the stadium.

"Hey, Newhouse, how did your meetings go?"

"They went well. Everyone signed."

"Of course they did. Sex sells. I'm assuming your prospects were male."

"They were," I said sheepishly.

"I thought as much," he replied with an all-knowing smile.

"I wouldn't be so proud of that. It proves that men think with their little heads."

"I never said they didn't."

"By the way, here's your shirt," I said, tossing it in his face.

"I got a call from my sister," Cole said, folding his shirt. "You must be desperate to get those pictures back."

I was about to plead my case again when Darius appeared to

begin the broadcast. Part of me was relieved by the interruption as we launched into the pre-game show.

"Layla, tonight the Predators face the Volcanos, who, as you may or may not know, are on a four-game winning streak. Do you think tonight's going to make number five?" Cole asked.

"No, I don't, Cole. I think the Predators will stop them in their tracks, but I'm projecting a close game. My prediction is the Predators will win three to two."

"I'm betting the Predators will beat the Volcanos two goals to one."

"If I win, I want access to your phone," I snapped.

"Why don't you trust me to delete the pictures?" Cole replied. His voice was dripping with sarcasm.

"Obviously not."

"I think we need to fill the viewing audience in on the terms of our bet. As you guys may recall, I owed Layla a clean apartment. She thought it would be amusing to take a video of me wielding a feather duster while dressed in little more than an apron. I returned the favor by filming her as she washed my car. If Layla is right about tonight's prediction, I agree to erase my footage. Subsequently, she agrees to do the same if I win."

The game was too close for comfort, but fortunately, I emerged the victor.

"Hey, Darius, can I get a closeup on my phone?" Cole asked.

"What are you doing, Cole?" I asked, my heart racing.

"I thought it was only fair to show the fans."

"Cole, please," I pleaded as desperation seeped into my voice. He looked at me with an evil gleam before turning to the camera.

"This is my car after Layla washed it. Doesn't she do nice work?" Cole asked, addressing the viewing audience. I let out an audible sigh of relief as Cole glanced over at me and chuckled. "I can see my reflection in this shine," he continued. "Thanks for a job well done, Layla."

"I loathe you. You know that, don't you?" I said to Cole when the show wrapped up. He smiled and blew me a kiss. "Key in your passcode and give me your phone," I demanded. I scrolled through the pictures and deleted everything pertaining to the car wash.

"What am I going to jerk off to now?" Cole asked, licking his lips.

"I would watch my tongue unless you want the world to see you posing as my maid."

"I was only kidding, Newhouse. Messing with you is one of my greatest pleasures."

"May I suggest you find a different hobby? Goodnight Darius. Screw off, Cole." I breathed a little easier that night when I got into bed. Now, if only I could rip the image of a nearly naked Cole from inside my eyelids, I could enjoy a good night's sleep.

CHAPTER 15

"I can't believe it's Christmas Eve," I said to my mother as I picked her up from the airport. "These past two months have flown by."

"Layla, honey, you look exhausted."

"I'm fine, Mom. I'm just so thrilled to see you. I miss you so much. I wish I could have come home for the holidays. It's weird looking at palm trees and people wearing shorts in December. I can't begin to tell you how much I miss being back east, especially at this time of year. I long to feel the crisp air, see the beauty of snowflakes clinging to the trees, and be surrounded by holiday decorations. Their idea of Christmas spirit down here is having a boat parade."

"There are worse places to be than Miami, Layla. It gets harder to handle the cold and snow as you grow older."

"It isn't just that. People seem so fake here. The only people I truly like are Cole's sister, originally from Buffalo, and my boss, from Chicago. I guess I'm just homesick. I'm sure nobody back east is talking to me. I haven't sent one Christmas card or made so much as a phone call."

"So I've heard."

"I'm sorry. Please let everybody know they're in my thoughts.

I'm just so busy. Hopefully, things will ease up after I get this first year under my belt."

"I watch every one of your broadcasts, and I think you're terrific."

"That's spoken like a true mom. A more accurate assessment would be that I'm passable and getting better every day."

"That's all that matters."

"Tell me, did you get everything I asked for?" my mother asked.

"I had it all delivered today. You have every ingredient you need to make lasagna tomorrow. I can't guarantee the kitchen utensils, though. I have the bare basics."

"Don't worry, I know how to improvise. I'm looking forward to meeting the infamous Cole. How bad could he be if he invited us for dinner?"

"He didn't. Ashley did."

"Yet he is hosting, so obviously, he is okay with her decision."

"Cole may be a pushover where his sister and niece are concerned, but he is a backbreaker when it comes to me."

"Well, if it's as bad as you say, I'll just have to set him straight."

"You will do no such thing! You raised me to be a strong, independent woman who can stand up to men like Cole. Now it's up to me to fight my own battles."

"You're right, honey. I'll mind my own business." I walked over to my mother and buried her in a bear hug.

"I can't tell you how good it is to have you here, Mom."

"I'm always there for you, Layla. You are the light of my life," my mother replied, stroking my hair.

We awoke the following day and had breakfast. Mom and I exchanged presents, and she cooked while I caught up on work. At four o'clock, we headed over to Cole's place.

"Welcome, ladies; Mr. Pasternak is expecting you. I believe you know where the penthouse is, Ms. MacKenzie."

"My goodness, Layla, I think they're underpaying you at the station."

"Mom, remember Cole was a professional hockey player before he went into broadcasting."

"How much do hockey players make?"

"More than sportscasters."

Ashley greeted us as we stepped into the penthouse foyer.

"Merry Christmas, please come in. I've been excited to meet you," Ashley said. "Cole, come help me take their things."

Cole was on the floor, playing a game with Katelyn. He wore gray lounge pants that hung low on his waist and a red cotton shirt that hugged his magnificently cut torso. I was convinced this man would look good in a potato sack. It wasn't fair!

"Cole, this is my mother, Theresa."

"Mother Theresa, did you get your sainthood for putting up with Layla?"

"Cole!" Ashley snapped.

"It is the other way around, Cole. Layla is the angel," my mother replied calmly.

"The jury is still out on that one. Sorry, I'm being rude, Theresa. Let me take that from you," Cole said, bringing the lasagna into the kitchen. "You didn't have to cook."

"I wanted to and I never arrive at someone's house empty-handed. Besides, Layla didn't have time to cook. She was busy working, even on Christmas!"

"Why don't you make yourself comfortable, and I'll get you a drink."

"Newhouse, can I take that bag from you?"

"Yes, these are some gifts. This is for Ashley," I said, handing her a small box. "The toy is for Kate, and this is for you." I handed Cole a bottle of Jack Daniel's. He seemed surprised. "I wasn't aware we were exchanging gifts."

"I know what you can give me," I replied.

Cole looked at me suspiciously. "What's that?"

"In the spirit of the holiday, I want us to declare a truce."

"That's a great idea, Layla," Ashley replied.

Cole cocked his head and gave me a cautious glance. "I guess I could behave for the day, but don't get used to it."

144

"I wouldn't dare."

"What would you like to drink, Theresa? I made some mulled wine if you care to try that."

"That sounds wonderful, Cole."

"Newhouse, can I get you a glass, or would you like your usual dirty martini?"

"I'll try the wine as well," I said, surprised that he knew what I drank. "It smells great in here."

"It's the spices in the wine," Cole replied.

"Your tree is beautiful," I said, envious of the twelve-foot Christmas tree trimmed with white lights and blue and silver ornaments to match Cole's apartment. "Did you decorate yourself? "I asked, admiring the fresh pine rope adorning the columns that delineated the dining area from the living room.

"No, I hired someone. I don't have the time or the patience. Why don't you ladies take a seat?" Cole said, pulling out two chairs. "I almost forgot, I picked these up for you." Cole handed my mother a beautiful bouquet of red and white flowers.

"How incredibly thoughtful. You didn't have to do that."

"I wanted to. May I say that I see where Layla gets her looks from?"

"Layla looks like her father."

"I disagree. I see a strong resemblance."

"I think Layla looks like Isabel May," Ashley interjected.

"Looking at you too, I would say your parents are models. Cole, you are even more handsome in person."

"Mom, please, his ego doesn't need more stroking."

Ashley set some appetizers on the dining room table as we took our seats. I was about to bite into the baked brie when I caught Mother staring at Cole.

"Cole, you have beautiful eyes, doesn't he, Layla?"

"Yes, Mom," I replied reluctantly.

"He's exactly your type, Layla."

I nearly choked on my wine. "Is that so?" asked Cole with a raised eyebrow.

"If my type is egomaniacal, you would be correct."

Cole laughed. "So much for our truce." He clearly enjoyed watching me squirm.

"I think you're being harsh."

"I know him better than you do, mom."

"I know him better than anyone," Ashley chimed in. "I can tell you that Cole would give his life for someone he loves. He's loyal, generous, helpful, and honest to a fault."

"The truth, Theresa lies somewhere between the two perspectives," Cole replied.

"I side with Ashley. I have a good sense when it comes to people. I don't understand the issue between you and my daughter, but I can tell you're a good man."

"I think you give me too much credit, but thank you."

"Tell me, Cole, how do you afford this gorgeous penthouse on your salary?"

"Speaking of brutally honest," I said, hiding my head in my hands.

"My stint with the Predators paid for this place, my car, and Ashley's condo."

"How much money can a grown man make playing with sticks?"

"Mom, if you keep this up, I will drop you off at the airport now," I warned, kicking her beneath the table.

"Hush, Layla. I'm curious. You don't mind, do you, Cole?"

"No, it's fine. I made five hundred and seventy-five thousand dollars the year I was signed. After that, I negotiated an eight-million-dollar contract for six years, plus performance bonuses."

"How old were you when you started playing for them?"

"I was drafted when I was nineteen."

"Were you in college?"

"I had just finished my first year at Minnesota State. It was the top hockey program in the country."

"So, you never graduated." My mother's observation made Cole squirm in his chair. I had never seen him embarrassed until now.

"No, I didn't, which is something I regret. Things are different now. A lot of the American draft picks can finish school. I think it's better. Look what happened to me. My career was cut short. I am fortunate that I was able to transition into sportscasting."

"Layla was always a great student."

Great, now my mother is giving Cole more reasons to hate me.

"So I've been told," he replied.

"I couldn't have afforded to send Layla to school if it weren't for her scholarships."

I could see Cole growing increasingly uncomfortable. Strangely enough, I had the urge to protect him. "Mom, please drop this!"

"How old were you when you left the NHL, Cole?" Theresa continued.

"I was twenty-six."

"And how old are you now?"

"Mom, start packing," I warned.

"I just turned thirty."

"Do you have a girlfriend?"

"He has many, Mom. Now knock it off."

"I'm not ready to settle down. If you'll excuse me, I'm going to check on the roast." Cole rose from the table and escaped to the kitchen.

"What's with the interrogation?" I asked, glaring at my mother.

"He said he didn't mind," my mother replied innocently.

"He was being polite!"

"If he wasn't comfortable answering your mother's questions, he would have declined," Ashley interjected. "I agree with you, Mrs. Mackenzie. Cole should have a girlfriend. I've been encouraging him and Layla to date, but I've been overruled."

"Speaking of dates, how was your date with the—"

"Don't say it!" I interrupted.

"With the dick-boy?" Cole called out from the kitchen. At least he was using male body parts for his disparaging name-calling.

"He wasn't my type," I said, trying to sound nonchalant. I watched Cole break into a self-righteous smile as he began carving the roast.

"I hate to say I told you so, but we both know I did. Theresa, I fear your daughter has bad taste in men."

"I'm afraid she gets that from me."

"Just like Ashley got it from our mother," Cole replied.

"I'm going to help Cole in the kitchen," Ashley said, rising from the table.

"Can I do anything?" I offered.

"No, we've got it all under control. Why don't you help yourself to a refill on the wine?" I went in search of the wine but was distracted by a roast beef that was picture-perfect, as were the roasted Brussels sprouts, sauteed mushrooms, and glazed carrots.

"Ashley, I didn't know you could cook."

"I can only take credit for the salad and the appetizer. Cole did the rest."

"He cooks! My God, Layla, he really is a great catch. I don't think your father knew how to turn on the stove."

I let out an exasperated sigh. "Cole, would you mind if I heated the lasagna for a few minutes?" I asked.

"No problem. I'll be happy to pop it in the oven. Is there anything else I can do for you?"

"You can wipe that grin off your face."

"What grin?" Cole asked, feigning ignorance. "By the way, did I tell you how much I liked your mother, Newhouse?"

"There's no need. You love anyone who flatters you." I helped Ashley set the table while Cole finished making the gravy.

"This is delicious, Cole. The roast is impeccable, as are the vegetables."

"Thank you, Theresa."

"When did you learn to cook?"

"I wouldn't say I learned. I started following recipes, and I began improvising as I grew more comfortable. May I say your lasagna is wonderful as well? I'm afraid I'm out of my league regarding Italian food."

"Did you watch your mother cook when you were growing up, Cole?" my mother asked.

"I wasn't around much. I was always playing hockey."

148

"I'm afraid Layla learned to cook out of necessity because I was busy working. I was an administrative assistant by day and a real estate agent on nights and weekends. After Layla's father walked out, it was all I could do to make ends meet. Fortunately, Layla was independent and very helpful. I guess you know she had to give up skating because of me. That's something I'll always regret."

"It's okay, Mom. It wasn't meant to be."

"Cole, did your parents go to your games?"

"The one game my father managed to attend ended in a fight with my coach. He didn't come to another game again until I turned pro. By then, I wanted nothing to do with him. My mom was at all my games except when she watched Ashley play volleyball."

"So, Ashley, you're an athlete too?"

"I was an athlete. I got a partial scholarship to play in college."

"What did you major in?"

"I have a degree in accounting, but I hate it. I worked briefly after graduating from college, but then I got pregnant. I have a bartending job now, and I enjoy that much more. I make good money, which allows me to return to school part-time. I'm studying to be a nutritionist, although I don't know if I'll ever finish my degree."

"Why don't you take some classes part-time, Cole?" I asked, interrupting my mother's line of questioning. "It sounds like you regret not finishing college."

"I would feel silly going back to school now."

"Why? Studies show that adult students outperform their younger counterparts because they are more motivated and focused."

"I wouldn't feel comfortable taking classes with twenty-year-old kids."

"If you go to an all-girls school, you should feel right at home," I quipped.

"Theresa, did you know your daughter missed her calling? She should have been a comedian."

"I thought Layla was going to be a performer. She was great at ballet, and she sang like a songbird. As a child, Layla used to act out skits with her friends. I thought for sure she would major in performing arts in college. She had the talent for it."

"Really? Maybe she could sing the national anthems at one of the games," Cole replied, avoiding my eyes.

"Don't you dare suggest it!" I snapped.

Cole laughed. "I didn't realize you had so many talents, Newhouse. Wouldn't it have made sense to go into a field where you could use them?"

"I consider broadcasting a form of acting."

"That's right, you pretend to know about hockey."

"Kids, remember your truce," Ashley interrupted.

"Why didn't you go into acting?" Cole inquired.

"My mother is blowing my talent way out of proportion. When I was a kid, I performed in some school plays. As an only child, I was lonely before discovering skating, so I created my own reality. Enough about me. Katelyn, what do you want to be when you grow up?"

"I want to be like Uncle Cole," she murmured.

"I will get her involved in the local girls' hockey league when she's old enough," Cole replied, beaming.

"I'll kill you. Let Kate play volleyball like me," Ashley interjected.

"We'll let her choose when it's time. Tell me, Theresa, what else was Layla passionate about as a kid?" Cole asked.

"Layla is an animal lover. She was always feeding strays and trying to find them homes. After giving up skating, Layla became a dog walker. She expanded into a pet-sitting business and made decent money for her age. I would come home to find five or six animals in the house."

"Cole also has a soft spot for animals," Ashley chimed in. "I remember him climbing a tree to rescue our neighbor's cat. Our dog was a stray that Cole found on the side of the road."

"You don't strike me as an animal lover," I said to Cole.

"That's because you think I have a black heart. I love animals.

Unfortunately, I'm never home enough to have one. I'm going to get Katelyn a dog when she gets older. Would you like that, Kate?"

Katelyn nodded in excitement.

"Don't you dare show up with a dog without talking to me. This is what Cole does. He plays the hero, and I'm the one who gets stuck taking care of it," Ashley snapped. "When you settle down, you can get a dog."

"You mean when hell freezes over," I replied.

"Speaking of relationships, if you haven't been busy dating this guy, why haven't I seen more of you? We need to plan another girls' night."

"I know. I'm sorry, Ashley. I've been so swamped working on the upcoming fundraiser for Shane."

"How is that going?"

"Really well. I have six food trucks committed. The T-shirts are done, and I signed four new clients for advertising space. I spoke to Pearl Paint, the art supply house, and I'm getting several huge rolls of white paper, markers, and crayons for the kids to make a mural for the team. Cole, I thought you could run a hockey skills clinic for the kids, following the players' scrimmage."

"I would love to do that. Can I ask Shane's son Addison to help? I know it would make him feel good doing something for his dad."

"I think that's a great idea. We could split the rink in half and run clinics for two different age groups. I've arranged for the delivery and donation of a bouncy house. I'm not in charge of marketing, but Gabriela and Jameson have done a great job promoting the event. Aaliyah and I finalized the ticket design and signage we will need for the various events. The tickets go on sale in two days. I just received a list of items the team is donating for auction. Morgan agreed to handle that portion for me since he knows what the equipment is worth.

"Now, I must focus on prizes for the raffle. I have three sets of tickets for upcoming Predators games to auction off. The arena box office is donating two sets of tickets to the Harlem Globe Trotters and another two for Disney on Ice. Next week, I have appointments with several of our sponsors, including R & W Brewing, Josh Cellars, and Pimlico Vodka. I want to see if they'll rent a couple of concession stands so the parents can drink. The more they drink, the more they'll spend. I hope to get some gift baskets or a case of liquor to raffle off. Next week, I have several meetings with more corporate partners to discuss renting booths for advertising and additional donations.

"You're unbelievable, Layla. Don't you think she's amazing, Cole?" Ashley asked.

Cole stared at me with a bewildered look on his face. "How did you find time to do all of this?"

"I took sleep off my to-do list. I work through every lunch break and on my days off. Don't get me wrong, I've had a lot of help."

"There goes my daughter being modest. She was always a great organizer."

"It's just a lot of multitasking. Fortunately, our community is full of loyal hockey fans, so the businesses have been receptive to my pitch."

"I can't believe you've done all this for Shane."

"I told you I would help him if I could. As usual, you have underestimated me."

"I've learned my lesson. Seriously, I'm blown away by all your hard work, Newhouse. Thank you."

"I didn't do it for you. I'm doing it for Shane, even if it means losing my job. It will be worth it if he gets better."

Cole got up, poured himself a whiskey, and headed into the living room with Katelyn. The women chatted amongst themselves for a while before doing the dishes. I looked over to see Cole pouring yet another drink. He sat on the couch and stared into the fireplace. A solemn look crossed his face. I took a seat beside him. "Are you okay?" I asked.

"I'm fine."

"No, you're not."

"What makes you say that?"

"You have sad eyes. Would you like to talk about what's bothering you?"

"Not really. It won't change anything."

"Cole, for one day, let me be your friend," I said, resting my hand on his thigh. He looked at me, sighed, and stared back at the fire. The reflection of the flames seemed to dance off his eyes, making them sparkle despite their sadness.

"I have a hard time with the holidays. Watching you and your mother reminds me of how much I miss my mom. They say it gets easier with time when you lose someone, but I haven't found that to be true. I miss her so much, and I'm mad at myself for not being with her more when she got sick."

"Ashley told me you did the best you could, considering you had a contractual obligation. I understand you even took some time off."

"It wasn't enough. My mother deserved more. She deserved better than my father and me."

"Ashley said you were the light of your mother's life."

"That makes it even worse," Cole replied, taking a swig of his drink.

"Cole, your mom wouldn't want you to beat yourself up like this. At least you were by her side when she died. My grandmother, who was a second mother to me, died when I left to pick up a change of clothes after being glued to her side for a week. It took me a long time to get over the guilt."

"How did you manage that?"

"I told myself that she needed me to leave for her to let go. That at least her pain was over. She was finally reunited with my grandfather, who she missed. I also take comfort in that I feel her spirit is with me. I believe we are more than our bodies. Our souls live on when we die. I honor my grandmother daily by trying to live my best life."

"I gave up so much time with my mother to be a hockey player. Now, my career is over, and I can never get that time back. It seems like a waste."

"You would still be playing if it weren't for your injury. I think you need to be honest with yourself, Cole. Can you look me in the eye and tell me that you would do things differently if given a chance?"

"I don't know. I think that's impossible to answer until you're in that position."

"Maybe this is an easier question; Do you think your mother would have wanted you to give up hockey for her?"

"I know she wouldn't. She's not selfish like me."

"She's a mother, and a mother's greatest priority is her child's happiness. If you don't believe me, ask my mother, and doing something you love isn't being selfish."

"It is when that's all you do."

"You have a gift, Cole. It would've been a crime to waste it."

"Maybe. It still haunts me that I'm unable to play. I know I'm lucky to have the broadcasting gig, but it's agonizing watching the guys from the sidelines."

"I can only imagine how you must struggle with that, but I think playing a role is better than not being cast, even if it isn't the one you want."

"I don't mean to sound ungrateful."

"You don't. You're just being honest. Besides, this job allows you to stay connected to the team, and I can tell how much they care about you. In a way, they're your extended family."

"Yeah, tomorrow Brett Gillies is hosting a brunch. I'm going to play Santa Claus for the kids."

"I think your black heart just grew a few sizes."

"I get a kick out of it, but that's hard for me too."

"How so?"

"I feel like I'm missing out on something special when I watch the guys with their families."

"You are, but that is by choice. If you wanted a family, you could have one. However, it would mean giving up being the most eligible bachelor in Miami."

Cole gave me half a smile. "Thanks for listening, Newhouse," he said as he stared at the floor, avoiding eye contact. Cole clearly had a hard time dealing with emotion. I reached up and gently rubbed his back. I could feel his massive shoulder blade beneath the soft cotton shirt.

"Any-time, Cole. Why don't we get some dessert?"

"I'll be there in a minute."

I walked back to the table and saw Ashley and my mother laughing over a plate of sugar cookies Katelyn had decorated. "It's nice seeing you two get along. It's like a Christmas miracle," Ashley said with a smile.

"Don't get excited, little sister. When the clock strikes twelve, we'll be back to Prince Hans and Princess Anna."

"Just like in *Frozen*," Kate exclaimed.

"Yes, just like the evil prince in *Frozen*," replied Cole, as he lifted Katelyn onto his lap.

We finished dessert, which consisted of an array of cookies, pastries, and chocolates. "I think we must go before our food coma further consumes us. Thank you so much for having us. The thought of not being home for the holidays was so depressing. You guys made what would have been an ordinary day special, and you outdid yourselves with the meal."

"Thanks for coming. I know Ashley enjoyed having girl time. It was great meeting you, Theresa."

"Thank you for the delicious meal and the beautiful flowers, Cole. You and Ashley are incredible hosts. However, if you're not nicer to my daughter, you'll experience my wrath. Have I made myself clear?" my mother asked, slugging him in the arm.

Cole rubbed his bicep. "Wow, you have a hell of a hook. I guess I better stay on your good side. Goodnight, Theresa," he said, giving my mother a kiss on the cheek. "Merry Christmas, Newhouse. I'll see you in the office."

"Goodnight, Cole. Have fun tomorrow." He made no movement toward me. I thought of reaching over and giving him a kiss like he had given my mother but decided against it.

Ashley looped her arm in mine. "Come on, I'll walk you guys out." We said our goodbyes in the parking lot. My mother and I went home and kept our tradition of watching our favorite holiday movie, *A Christmas Story*. We went for breakfast the following day before I took her to the airport.

"I wish you could stay longer, Mom. I have so much to do right now, but I'll plan a trip home after hockey season."

"I'm just glad we could spend Christmas together. However, before I leave, I need you to make me a promise."

"Sure, Mom. What's that?"

"I need you to give Cole a chance."

"A chance for what?" I asked defensively.

"I see the way you look at him, honey. You can't deny you have feelings for the man. It's nothing to be ashamed of."

"I admit being attracted to him, but what woman wouldn't be? You seem to forget that we don't like each other. Cole does nothing but belittle me. Why would you want me to be with someone like that, and what makes you think he would want to be with me?"

"Beneath anger lies passion. If you didn't affect Cole, he wouldn't go to such lengths to keep you at a distance. I think he's afraid of his feelings for you. On the flip side, you're afraid of being rejected. Hence, you use sarcasm and degradation as a way of protecting yourself. I'm not the only one who feels this way. Ashley agrees with me."

"Even if you are right, even if Cole is interested in me, I'm not sure I want him. He's with a different woman every night. I need something more. Sure, we might have a great time for a few weeks, and then he would get bored and cast me aside for the next shiny plaything."

"He behaves that way because he hasn't met the right woman. You could change that."

"Why do I want to date a man I have to change? Did it occur to you that Cole likes his lifestyle? He's a player, and I'm past that stage in my life."

"That's a façade. I watched Cole. He is great with kids. He's loving and protective of his family. He's thoughtful and generous. Cole isn't the shallow man he pretends to be. If you let down your guard, you will see a different side of him."

"I didn't start this feud, Mom, and I've tried reaching out to Cole more than once."

"It's not like you to give up so easily, Layla."

"I don't want to get hurt, and you forget that I work with him. I can't afford to lose my job if things go south."

"There is no reward without risk, honey. Just think about what I'm saying. I only want your happiness."

"I know that, but Cole Pasternak isn't my happily ever after. Text me when you get home to let me know you arrived safely."

"Let me know what happens with your fundraiser. I want to see pictures, and Layla, I'm proud of you."

"Thanks, Mom. I needed to hear that. I'm glad to know someone has faith in me."

CHAPTER 16

"Layla, Gabriela, Darius, are we set for this weekend's fundraiser?" Leora asked.

"We're as ready as we can be," I replied, passing out instructions for the big event. "We've sold more tickets than I expected, thanks to the great job Gabriela has done with promotions. I'm hoping it will be a smashing success," I said, crossing my fingers. "I'm asking everyone to report to the arena by nine-thirty. The gates will open at eleven. We'll have an hour before the scrimmage for people to purchase refreshments and T-shirts. The scrimmage should wrap up by one. I would like Cole to introduce Shane and have him say a few words. After Shane speaks, I want to acknowledge our sponsors and encourage parents to head to the auction. Then, Cole and Addison will run pee-wee and junior skills hockey clinics. Families can take pictures with T-Bone throughout the day and write messages for the Predators on the mural."

"This list of sponsors is quite impressive," Leora said as she glanced over the program. "You did some job, Layla."

"Thank you. Everyone was quite generous with donations for the raffle. I think we should be able to raise a significant amount of money."

"I bet you'll be happy when this is all over," Leora replied.

"Relieved is more like it. I want to thank everyone who volunteered. I couldn't have done it without you. The generosity and helpfulness of this staff, and the Predators organization, never ceases to amaze me."

"Cole, thanks for the new advertising clients you brought in. I heard you agreed to make cameos in their ads."

"You're welcome, Leora. Anything for Shane and the station." I shot Cole a quick glance. I didn't realize he was using his influence to recruit new business.

After tossing and turning all night, I arrived at the stadium three hours early. Powered by nervous energy, I ran around like a chicken without a head, ensuring everything was going according to plan.

As the clock rounded eleven and the crowds began to arrive, I was ready to pass out. I was thrilled to see most spectators purchasing T-shirts, along with food and beverages, on their way into the rink. The crowd began filtering into their seats as Cole announced the lineup of the team members participating in the game. The scrimmage was entertaining to watch. It was evident that the players were having a blast on the ice. When it was over, Abby announced the opportunity to have pictures taken with T-Bone and our team captain while three Predators continued autographing shirts. After thirty minutes of picture taking, the ice would be prepped for Cole and Addison's clinic while photos continued in the lobby. I went to the foyer and assisted some kids with the mural. I was helping one little girl draw the Predators logo inside a heart when I felt a hand on my lower back.

"I didn't know you could draw," Cole said admiringly.

"I was in art club as a kid, but I'm no Picasso."

"Things are going great so far. I just wanted to check in and see if you wanted to introduce Shane."

"No, I think it's better if you do it."

"This is your gig, Newhouse. You should be in the spotlight, not me."

"I don't need to be the center of attention, and the introduction will mean more to Shane coming from you."

"Okay, if that's what you want." Cole picked up a marker and drew a picture of a helmet and skates.

"I see I'm not the only one with artistic talent."

"If you consider one step above stick figures' artistic talent," he replied modestly.

Cole walked away as I continued working on the mural. I had the feeling I was being watched and turned to see him standing by the auction booth. My eyes met his, and he gave me a smile so heartwarming I was afraid it would melt the ice.

I left the lobby when it was time for Cole to introduce Shane and his family. Cole's voice cracked from the emotion in his speech. You could tell how much he admired this man. This was the side of Cole I heard about from others. Maybe it was a blessing that I never experienced his soft side because the man standing before me would own my heart.

Shane's speech was equally touching. He thanked his family for their love and support. He expressed gratitude to the fans, team, network, and sponsors for making this day possible. Then Shane asked me to come down to the ice. I briefly took the opportunity to thank our fans and promote the upcoming auction and raffles. Forty-five minutes later, I returned to the rink to watch the skills clinic. What I saw floored me. Cole was amazing with the kids. He was funny, patient, and encouraging. In addition to the group instruction, Cole provided individual pointers to each participant. I could see where he would make an outstanding coach. Cole caught me watching and gave me a wave. His face was full of joy as he showed a little girl how to hold her stick. I never saw him so blissfully happy.

The crowd had dispersed by the late afternoon. I walked around the stadium with Gabriela, ensuring everything was left as it should be. We sold all the T-shirts and every piece of paraphernalia in the auction. The day was a huge success. I ended it by giving a big hug to Shane, who looked as drained as I felt. Cole escorted Shane and his family out of the arena. I assumed he was headed home from the parking lot until I saw him walk back into the stadium.

"Can I take you to dinner?" Cole asked. "You must be starving. I bet you didn't eat at all today."

"You're asking me to dinner?" I asked, looking over my shoulder to confirm he was speaking to me.

"Yes, I am. I'm sure you skipped lunch."

"You're right. I did."

"Then it's settled. We'll go in my car, and I'll bring you back here afterward."

"I should go home and change. I feel grimy."

"You look great."

"I'm not dressed to go anywhere nice."

"Don't worry. They'll make an exception for me if there's an issue with the dress code."

I walked with Cole to his car. He held the door open for me like a perfect gentleman.

"Is this a spot of dust I see on your dashboard?" I asked, running my finger along the leather. "It looks like you would benefit from my cleaning the interior."

"Maybe next bet," he replied, laughing. We arrived at Truluck Steak and Seafood House, where two men dressed in suits greeted us. "Hi Shanna, I know I don't have a reservation, but I was hoping I could get a table for two," Cole said to the hostess.

"Of course, Cole. I'd better sit you at Mia's station, or she'll kill me." We followed the hostess to an intimate corner table. Once again, Cole exhibited exemplary manners as he pulled out my chair.

"Hey Cole," an exuberant waitress called out as she made a beeline for our table. "I didn't know you were coming in tonight," the server said, hugging him.

"Neither did I. I was at a Predator fundraiser when I came across this famished young woman."

"It's Layla MacKenzie," the waitress said, eyeing me. "I love watching you two on TV."

"Thank you. Please pardon my appearance. We came straight from the stadium."

"How did the fundraiser go?" asked Mia. "I would have gone

if I didn't have to work. Chase would have loved to do your clinic."

"The fundraiser was a smashing success, thanks to Layla. Words can't describe the amazing job she did. I'm sorry you couldn't make it; Chase would have had fun. You know, I go to the rink with Shane's son Addison. I would be happy to have Chase join us one day."

"That would be awesome, Cole! You're the best. Now, what can I get you guys to drink?"

"We'll have a bottle of Dom Perignon to start. Layla, do you eat oysters?"

"No, and I don't think it's a good idea for me to drink."

"Nonsense, we're celebrating. Do you like shrimp?"

"I do."

"We'll have a jumbo shrimp cocktail, a dozen oysters, a Sonoma Greens Salad, some bread, and two five-pound lobsters for dinner."

"I'll get right on that."

"Thanks, Mia, you're a doll."

"Cole, I don't eat lobster."

"Why not?"

"For starters, the way they kill them is deplorable. I feel guilty when I look at my plate and see my food staring back at me. I hate eating anything that requires a struggle, and last but not least, it's too expensive."

"Have you ever eaten one?"

"Only stuffed in ravioli."

"This is ten times better. Nothing is tastier than a tender piece of lobster dipped in drawn butter. Trust me." Mia returned with the champagne on ice. "I'd like to make a toast," Cole said, raising his glass. "To an amazing day and an even more extraordinary woman." My face blushed. I wasn't comfortable with him being nice to me.

"To Shane and a speedy recovery," I countered, clinking my glass against Cole's.

"Your cheeks are turning red."

"I'm not used to you being so complimentary. I'm waiting for the other shoe to drop."

"There's no other shoe. I just want to show my appreciation for your hard work. I didn't realize until today the magnitude of this undertaking. Frankly, I don't know where you found the time to pull it off."

"I will admit, I'm glad it's over. I haven't had a minute to breathe between the skating competition, the job, and the fundraiser. It's like a huge weight has been lifted off my shoulders."

"You handled yourself well under all that stress. I promise to give you the rest of the week off before hitting you with another challenge."

"Please do," I said, sipping my champagne. Mia brought our bread and salad. It was a battle not to devour my food like a vulture eating its prey. I tried to eat with restraint but failed as I gobbled down three rolls before our appetizers arrived.

"Would you like to try an oyster? They're aphrodisiacs, you know."

"From what I've seen, that's the last thing you need," I replied. "Besides, they look gross. They're all slimy."

"Have you ever tasted one?"

"No, it's a texture thing."

"Don't knock it until you've tried it." Cole squeezed some lemon and placed some cocktail sauce on an oyster. "Watch and learn. You throw it back in your mouth and suck it down like you're drinking a shot." He slurped down the oyster and prepared one for me.

"I don't know about this. I don't knock-back shots, either. I tend to savor things slowly." Cole watched my lips as I took the oyster from his hand.

"I can imagine," Cole replied, as he continued staring at my mouth.

I sucked the oyster off the shell and swallowed it as quickly as possible without choking.

"Well?" Cole asked.

"I admit it was better than expected, but I still don't see the point of ordering something expensive only to force it down my throat."

"You must develop a taste for the finer things in life, Newhouse."

"I'm one of those people with champagne taste on a beer budget. Therefore, I refrain from indulging in things I can't afford, like this Dom Perignon. It must be a couple of hundred dollars a bottle."

"I'm beginning to think I should have taken you to McDonald's," Cole said, shaking his head.

"I'm just not used to being taken out for such expensive meals."

"I had you figured all wrong. Here I thought you were a spoiled brat."

"Far from it. Like you, I work for and appreciate everything I have. Since we're admitting to misconceptions, I confess that I've misjudged you as well."

"How so?"

"I was watching you with those kids today. You have a gift with children. You'll make a great father someday."

"I disagree."

"How can you say that? Did you see the way they respond to you?"

"I'm sure Ashley told you about our father. Let's say that family wasn't high on his list of priorities. I have no idea what fatherhood looks like. I never had a role model."

"That's where you're wrong. Your father showed you what not to do."

"Don't people follow in their parents' footsteps?"

"They can, but they also go in the opposite direction, which is what you'll do. That is if we can get you to have a relationship with an actual woman instead of a glorified cheerleader."

"Real women want real things," Cole said solemnly.

"Is that so wrong?"

"Not at all. I'm just not the guy to provide the loving, committed relationship most women want."

"I think you're selling yourself short. From our talk at Christmas, I know you long for the family you didn't have."

"Maybe. Did you forget that, according to you, I'm a conceited, self-centered, egotistical playboy? I wouldn't exactly consider that husband and father material."

"No, but that could change if you found the right woman. Ashley said you were very devoted to Haley."

"And look where that got me. Haley put a stake through my heart while my best friend put a nail in my coffin."

"And that's it for you? You love fiercely, Cole. I admire that, but you can't be through with relationships based on something that happened years ago. I didn't think you were that fragile."

"Have you ever had your heartbroken, Newhouse?"

"I admit to never having a breakup that left me completely devastated."

"Then you never loved somebody the way I loved Haley. I never cheated on her, despite having numerous opportunities. I planned to marry her and have a house full of kids with a dog in the yard and a white picket fence. Instead, the two people I trusted and loved more than anybody, aside from my mother and Ashley, betrayed me."

"Maybe it didn't have anything to do with you, Cole. You said you and Haley had been together since you were kids. Perhaps she just wanted to experience someone else before getting married and settling down."

"Then she should have told me instead of going behind my back."

"Would you have been receptive to that conversation?"

"Absolutely not!"

"That might explain why she didn't bring it up. I'm not suggesting what she did was right, and I admit her choice of men left a lot to be desired. I'm just saying she was young, and she made a mistake. It happens. Maybe you shouldn't take it so personally."

"How else would I take it? My girlfriend cheated on me. In my eyes, that meant I wasn't enough for her. When I think about it, the pain is as fresh now as when it happened. Why would I open myself up for that again?"

"Because there's no reward without risk, Cole. Is it worth living half a life because you're afraid of getting hurt? Can you honestly say you find your lifestyle fulfilling?"

"Guys would kill to live like me. I do what I want, when I want, with whomever I want."

"That's great for a while, but I imagine it grows old. Now that I know you better, I doubt you're that shallow."

"So, now you're an authority on me and relationships. This comes from a woman who's never truly been in love. Why aren't you in a relationship if you're such an expert?"

"I don't claim to be an expert on either topic. I haven't been in love because I haven't met the right person. I would like to be in a relationship, but I've been a little busy, if you haven't noticed."

"Well, things should ease up now that the fundraiser is over. Hopefully, you'll develop a social life, leaving you less preoccupied with mine."

"Message received. I'll leave you alone. It's instinctual for me to help others. I didn't mean to offend you. You just have so much to offer somebody. It would be a shame if you let that go to waste."

Cole's eyes grew thoughtful. "I've been thinking about becoming a volunteer coach, especially after my experience today."

"I think that's a great idea."

"I love broadcasting the games, but truth be told, if I can't play, I would prefer to coach. My job allows me to stay connected to the team, but that's a mixed blessing. It kills me to be on the sidelines. I think coaching would prove more rewarding."

"Why don't you start with a youth league? If you love it and you're good at it, which I'm sure you will be, pursue a professional coaching job. I imagine a team would love to have you."

"Coaching jobs are hard to come by. I'm not sure if I have

enough experience to coach for the NHL. I only played professionally for seven years, and then there's my vision issue."

"I think it's worth considering," I replied as Mia arrived with our lobsters.

"I might not have sold you on the oysters, but I'll be shocked if you don't love the lobster."

"Mia, do you think I could have another napkin?" I asked. I took the extra napkin and placed it over the lobster's head. Cole gave me a strange look.

"Is there a problem?"

"Several. I resolved the first issue. At least it's no longer looking at me. Now, if only I could figure out how to eat it."

"Here, let me help you." Cole slid his chair over to my side of the table. He picked up the nutcracker and broke open a claw. He reached in with another utensil that looked like a tool of torture from the dentist's office and pulled out a large chunk of meat. "Try this," he said, dipping the lobster in butter and then holding it to my mouth. I took a bite, inadvertently dripping butter down my chin. Cole took his index finger and gently wiped the butter off my face. Then he sucked it off his finger. Now it was me who couldn't keep my eyes off his lips. "Tell me that isn't an orgasm for your mouth."

"I don't know if I'd go that far, but I'll admit it's delicious." Cole started cracking open the body of the lobster. "Leave me the other claw. I want to crack it myself. It looks like a good way to work off some pent-up frustration."

"I can tell you many ways to do that, and cracking lobster doesn't make the list," Cole replied with a provocative stare.

"I think it's time for you to move back to the other side of the table," I said, feeling a hitch in my breath. Cole's thigh brushed against mine as he rose from the chair. I admired the way his jeans hugged his well-rounded buttocks. It was hard enough fighting my attraction to him when he was being a jerk. This version of Cole, the one that was complimentary and vulnerable, was irresistible. Mia came by to check on us. I could see he had the same effect on her by the way she looked at him.

"How is Chase doing with his video games?" Cole inquired.

"He spends too much time playing them. He said he needs to practice because he wants to be as good as you."

"Tell him that hockey players have abnormally good hand-eye coordination."

"You should come by and give him a rematch," Mia suggested. Cole grew quiet. I could tell he was trying to choose his words carefully.

"It would probably be better if you brought him to the rink. He would benefit from the exercise."

"The trouble is hockey is an expensive sport. I can't afford all that equipment, so I don't want Chase falling in love with it."

"There must be a junior league he can get involved with where sponsors subsidize the cost. Let me investigate for you. I'll also check with the team. I'm sure one of them will know where to get their hands on some old equipment."

"That would be awesome, Cole," Mia replied, but I could see the disappointment on her face.

"Is there a woman in Miami you haven't slept with?" I asked Cole after she walked away.

"Yes, you."

"I'm sorry to spoil your perfect record."

"I thought we were playing nice."

"We are."

"Let's change the subject. Tell me about figure skating. Was your goal to attend the Olympics?"

I nearly choked on my food. "Hardly. I wasn't that good."

"Would you have been if you were able to continue?"

"I doubt it. The most I could have hoped for was to compete nationally. I didn't have the innate talent for skating you have for hockey."

"You have to dream big to achieve big, Newhouse."

"I assume you always knew you wanted to play for the NHL."

"For as long as I can remember."

"How old were you when you started playing hockey?"

"I started skating when I was four years old. My uncle, Mike, got me started. When I was five, he enrolled me in an organized team."

"Did your uncle play?"

"He played at the college level. Mike knew my father was preoccupied with things outside the family. He felt bad for me and tried to be a pseudo-father figure."

"Was he related to your father or your mother?"

"My mother. My father is estranged from his family."

"I was surprised to hear Ashley is in contact with your father."

"That's her decision. Ashley's not always the best judge of character."

"She thinks he's changed. Don't you have any desire to see for yourself or meet your half-siblings?"

"He's a user, an alcoholic, and a conman. That doesn't change. Even if he's turned into father of the year, I don't need to see it. It would make me resent him even more. However, I do wish my uncle lived closer. Occasionally, I fly him down to see a game."

"Where is he?"

"He moved to Maine after my mother died. We're planning to meet in upstate New York to go skiing the next time I get a few days off. Do you ski?"

"Not well. I can stay on my feet, but ski trips were expensive, so I didn't go often enough to be good."

"You need a sugar daddy, Newhouse."

"Bite your tongue. If there's one thing I learned from the women in my family, it's the importance of being independent. I never want to rely on a man."

"Is your goal to become the next Katie Couric?"

"Noooooo! The TV business is so cutthroat at that level. I could never handle the competition. I don't want my career to consume my life. I want a family at some point."

"Would you be willing to give up your job to raise kids?"

"I shouldn't have to. I might be willing to take a couple of years off when they are small, but broadcasting is a tough business. If you're out of sight, you're out of mind. Besides, as a woman ages, it becomes harder for her to get a job in front of the camera.

Ageism is still alive and well in our industry, not that I would have a problem working behind the scenes, but I resent the double standard."

"I think things are changing for the better. There are certainly more women working in sports than ever before."

"That's true, but they're not treated equally to their male counterparts. You haven't spoken to as many women as I have. Sexism still exists, despite the MeToo movement."

"It's hard for anyone in the spotlight, regardless of gender. You must be hyper-vigilant about everything you say and do in this political climate. Social media has robbed us of our privacy, so I avoid it as much as possible. If you've noticed, I don't allow women to take pictures with me. My private life is private."

"That's true. Your nemesis, Tristan O' Shaughnessy, is all over social media."

Cole's eyes grew dark. "Why were you looking at Tristan's social media?"

"I was trying to find out why you two fought."

"You saw the fight?" Cole asked, looking alarmed.

"Several times. However, I can't figure out what started it. Certainly, nothing on the ice triggered that kind of violence. It seemed personal to me. Maybe I'll make you tell me when you lose our next bet."

"That topic is off-limits, even if you predict the Stanley Cup winner down to the number of shots on goal," Cole replied definitively.

I couldn't imagine why he was being so secretive. "If I cuffed you to the bed and plied you with alcohol, would you tell me?"

"As tempting as that sounds, the answer would still be no. Please don't bring it up again. It is an excruciating part of my past that will forever impact my future."

"You wouldn't know from looking at your face that you have a vision problem. You have the most beautiful eyes I've ever seen."

"Thank you. It is the nerve behind the eye that is permanently damaged." Cole's tone softened.

"Is it hard to do certain things without your peripheral vision?"

"I think I've compensated for it. I believe I could still play professional hockey if the owners let me. Even if I can't see what's going on to the side of me, my hockey sense lets me know where the puck and the opponent are headed."

"You need to get back on the ice, Cole. Why don't you play for a men's league?"

"That would be too anticlimactic for me at this stage. Maybe I'll change my mind when I'm older."

"I can tell by your talk with Mia that there is a need for a local junior league."

"That is something I plan to investigate more thoroughly. Speak of the devil."

"Can I interest you in dessert?" Mia asked.

Part of me toyed with ordering something because I didn't want our evening to end. "Not me. I'm stuffed. Dinner was delicious. However, I will have a cappuccino," I replied.

"I'll have a piece of Key Lime Pie and a Horse Soldier Barrel Bourbon straight up."

"I see you know your bourbons."

"I'm learning more. There are so many things I want to explore. I spoke to Emeril about giving me, and some of the guys from the team, a private cooking class during the off-season."

"That's impressive."

"Not as impressive as graduating from college with honors."

"I'm sorry I ever brought that up."

"Don't be," Cole replied adamantly. "You shouldn't let me or anyone else diminish your accomplishments."

"I can't help it if I'm sensitive."

"I understand. I'm not as insensitive as you may think."

"I'm starting to see that. I wish I could see more of this side of you."

"Sorry, Newhouse. Take it all in now. I have a reputation to uphold."

"Silly me," I said, shaking my head.

We talked more about the Predator's standings in the Presidential Trophy Race and their chance at winning the Stanley Cup. I would've been content talking about the weather if it meant I could keep staring into those baby-blue eyes.

"You look tired," Cole said thoughtfully. I should take you back to your car. Mia brought the check, and Cole handed her his credit card. As we rose to leave the table, he reached into his pocket and threw two one-hundred-dollar bills on the table.

"How expensive was this dinner?" I asked in horror.

"Don't worry about it. I like to leave her a little extra as a single mother." Cole's generosity touched me. The unpredictability of his actions never failed to keep me on my toes. When we returned to the parking lot, Cole came around to my side of the car and opened my door. "Thank you for accepting my invitation and all you did to make this day a success for Shane. You'll never know what this means to me."

"Thank you for a wonderful dinner."

We stood for a moment, looking into each other's eyes. I felt Cole's body lean toward me. Was he going to kiss me? Should I kiss him back if he did? Unfortunately, I never got the chance to answer those questions. Cole ran his finger down my cheek before reaching past me to open the car door. My heart sank with disappointment.

"Goodnight, Newhouse. I'll see you at the staff meeting tomorrow."

I told myself it was a blessing that his lips didn't touch mine. If his kiss was half as deadly as his eyes, he would wind up in my bed. I had to keep reminding myself why that would be a mistake. The man I spent the evening with wasn't the Cole I despised. Tomorrow we would be at odds once more. I crawled into bed and reached for my vibrator. Despite my exhaustion, I climaxed quickly. It was the first time I considered it a sorry substitute for the real thing.

CHAPTER 17

I woke up feeling as if Cole, and I had turned the corner. It took a lot of work, but I believed the fundraiser was the turning point that earned his respect. Maybe he finally realized I was not the enemy.

I walked into the staff meeting to receive applause from my co-workers and praise from Leora.

The proceeds from the day totaled ninety-six thousand and change. In addition to the donation for Shane, we had several new advertisers for the station, which was a feather in my cap from the perspective of upper management. When the meeting was over, Cole came to my office.

"Hey, I wanted you to add this to the check you're giving Shane." Cole tossed a check for five thousand dollars on my desk.

"Wow, this is very generous."

"I would give him more, but he won't take it from me. I figure this way, if we tack it on to the net proceeds, it will go unnoticed."

"I'm going to add munificence to your list of attributes. You better watch out, Cole; I may start to think you're a nice guy."

"Just don't tell anybody," he said with a wink.

"I think they already know. Thanks again for dinner last night."

"It was nothing compared to what you did for Shane. He was blown away. I saw the story made the local news and ESPN."

"Yeah, it truly was a great day. I think you should be the one to give Shane the check."

"I think that should come from you. You did all the work."

"I had lots of help, including you. Besides, you are closest to him."

"We'll see. At the very least, we should present it together. I'll catch you at the game later, Newhouse."

"Is there anything I should know about tonight's opponent?" I asked as Cole headed out the door.

"That's for me to know and you to figure out," Cole replied with a mischievous grin.

"Ugh, just when I had hope that you were a redeemable human being."

"Sorry to disappoint you. I'll see you later."

That night the Predators were playing the Demons. This was the second time the Predators faced this opponent. Based on statistics alone, they should beat them. However, when they met earlier in the season, the Demons emerged victorious. Unfortunately, tonight had the same result. Cole's prediction topped mine, but he let me off the hook. I guess he was still feeling some residual softness from the fundraiser. That ended the following day at the road game against the Scorpions. I didn't know what I did to set Cole off, but he sabotaged me with a unique form of attack. Usually, he would correct my mistakes publicly or render my viewpoint worthless to the audience. Tonight, Cole incorporated an arsenal of obscure hockey terminology into the narrative, making it difficult for me to follow up with an appropriate dialog.

At one point, our guys were scrambling in the corner of our 'D' zone, trying to get the puck. "Wow, Jordan blew a tire. Luckily, Andersen was able to cover with a butterfly," Cole exclaimed.

I knew Cole's statement had something to do with Andersen blocking the shot, but I didn't want to risk saying the wrong thing. "Maybe you want to clarify your comment for our viewing audience, Cole," I suggested.

"I'm sure the audience could deduce that Jordan lost his footing resulting in Tyler Headman taking a shot. If Bryce didn't drop to his knee, protecting the lower portion of the net in what is referred to as the Butterfly Technique, the Scorpions would have scored.

That was only the beginning of his commentary. Moments later, Austin McAvoy scored on a breakaway. "That cherry picker was lucky the saucer got past Jackson Kane, giving McAvoy the opportunity. There was nothing Bryce could do to block that one."

"Cherry picker?"

"You know, Layla, players who hang out on center ice, abandoning their defense but still hoping to get a pass. It usually doesn't work. Austin was fortunate that Clifton made an airborne pass high enough to skip over Jackson's stick."

"Like a flying saucer," I surmised.

"Exactly. Otherwise, it wouldn't be labeled a Saucer Pass."

The Scorpions were on the power play two minutes later. "Cole, I think Pierre Paquet is going to the box for interference."

"That was worse than interference, Layla. That's what we call a can opener."

"Excuse me?"

"A can opener is when a player puts his stick between another player's legs and twists it. It's an easy way to hurt somebody." The Scorpions wound up scoring on the power play. "I have to say that Kaprizoff is some dangler. It takes one hell of a clapper to produce a Datsyukian Deke."

I rolled my eyes as I felt my frustration continuing to build. "Cole, I know a deke is when a player stick handles the puck in a way that fools the defender causing him to go out of position. I've never heard of a Datsyukian Deke. Would you be kind enough to explain your comment? Because it sounds like a foreign language."

"If you call hockey talk a foreign language, I understand why you're confused. For the benefit of my co-commentator and anyone else new to hockey, a dangler is a player who is extremely skilled with stick handling. A clapper is another term for a slap shot. A Datsyukian Deke is a maneuver that sends the goalie to the opposite side of the net. Thus, leaving it empty on one side, enabling Kaprizoff to score. It was a beautifully executed play.

Layla, maybe I should have gotten you a book on hockey terminology for Christmas."

"I'm well versed in hockey terminology, Cole. Hockey slang is a different story."

"I assure you; I'm using legitimate hockey terminology. I can't help it if your vocabulary in this subject area is limited," Cole replied with a look of superiority written all over his condescending face.

"What are you trying to do?" I snapped when we went to a commercial break.

Cole tried to feign ignorance. "What do you mean?" he replied, shrugging his shoulders.

"What's with the ridiculous catchphrases? Are you trying to make me look clueless?"

"I'm just trying to broaden your knowledge like a good mentor."

"I have news for you, Cole. I've listened to countless hockey broadcasts, and never heard anyone mention these terms. I admit you're confusing me, but I bet you're baffling our viewing audience. If you don't knock it off with this obscure vocabulary, it will backfire on you, not me."

Cole couldn't help himself. During the following period, he insisted on pointing out that Matt Perrault missed a key passing opportunity. "I can't believe Perrault missed the beaver tap. He better regain his focus if the Predators hope to win this game."

I was trying to think if a beaver tap was some perverse sexual term when Cole asked me to define it for the audience.

"You must know what a beaver tap is, Layla. It's far from an obscure term."

"I can't say I do, Cole," I replied, opting for honesty over the embarrassment of an incorrect response.

"When a player slaps his stick on the ice to call for a pass like Koulak did, it's called a beaver tap. Perrault blew a key scoring opportunity by not passing him the puck." There were five minutes left in the third period when Killorn blew past our defense to tie the game at five to five. "It was disgusting how Killorn just deked through our entire defense to score that goal. Wouldn't you agree, Layla?"

My mouth dropped open. "I think disgusting is a harsh way of putting it, Cole."

"Are you saying you disagree that Killorn's ability puts him on a level superior to the average player?"

"No, I completely agree with that statement."

"The word disgusting, when applied to hockey, means a player is so good that it's bad news for the opposing team."

"I'm glad you clarified that, Cole. I'm sure our viewers were confused. I wouldn't want them to think you were disrespecting our opponent."

"No, quite the opposite," Cole replied with a smirk. As we headed into overtime, Cole declared the game 'one hell of a barn burner.'

"I didn't realize we were on a farm," I replied, thoroughly exasperated by Cole's bizarre catch phrases.

"What are you talking about, Layla? A barn burner refers to a close, high-scoring game."

"I assumed that was apparent by the five-five tie after three periods of high intensity, back-and-forth play," I replied in a caustic tone.

The Predators lost two minutes into overtime. I wouldn't look at Cole on the ride back to the hotel. "What's with the resting bitch face?" he asked, plopping down in the seat next to me.

"Are you being serious right now?" I hissed. "I don't know what you were trying to accomplish tonight, but that broadcast didn't reflect well on us. I had hoped we were past taking potshots at each other, especially on camera."

"I wouldn't call what I did taking potshots."

"I don't care what you call it. It was in poor taste." Cole seemed pleased that he had gotten under my skin yet again. I needed to take him down a peg. My urge to humble him made me resort to something I usually wouldn't do, stoop to his level. I stood up and walked to the back of the bus where the Predators were sitting.

"Hey, guys, I have something to show you that will lift your spirits."

"That would be great, Layla! We're all down about losing the game." I pulled out my phone and accessed the video of Cole coming at me wearing an apron and waving a feather duster. The players broke into uproarious laughter as the video made its way around the bus.

"What's going on back here?" Cole inquired over my shoulder. The guys hurled slews of wisecracks at Cole. It didn't take long for him to figure out what I had done.

"I watched you delete those pictures when you lost the last bet," Cole stated, with fury in his eyes.

"I did, but I archived the video just in case."

"In case of what?" Cole snapped.

"In case your ego needed deflating."

"C'mon, Cole, don't be upset. It's funny. We needed a good laugh," Travis Goodrow interjected.

"I'm glad I could elevate the mood," Cole said, his face softening. Travis handed the phone back to me. "Give me the phone Newhouse," Cole demanded.

"I proved my point. I'll erase the video now."

"Why should I believe you?"

"Here, you can watch me do it."

"Do you swear that is the last bit of evidence you have of my cameo as a French maid?"

"I do," I replied, making an 'X' over my heart. "Shall we declare a truce?"

"I'll agree to a tentative truce. However, if you pull a stunt like this again, I'll make you regret the day you crossed me."

The bus pulled into the hotel. I was surprised to see several puck bunnies gathered in the lobby. One of them walked up to Cole and asked if he would like a drink. He linked his arm around her waist and escorted her to the bar. I was seething with jealousy, an emotion that was becoming increasingly familiar. I shouldn't be surprised. My hard work on Shane's fundraiser earned me a temporary reprieve from Cole's degradation and a modicum of respect, but that was where it ended. I went to bed tossing and turning. By now, he was probably kissing her the way I longed for him to kiss me. Thoughts of Cole bombarded my brain throughout the night, making sleep elusive. I woke up the next day cranky and exhausted, with a dull throbbing between my legs. Nothing would change between us, so I needed to take Skye's advice and move on.

I stayed clear of Cole until our next home game two days later. His mood at the game was strangely sullen. His affect was flat. Cole didn't utter a single jab or one obscure hockey term. After the match, Morgan suggested we go out for a drink. The Predators roared back after their devastating loss against the Scorpions. The thrill of victory resulted in a celebratory mood. A few of the players, and the media crew headed to our favorite spot. Cole hung out with the players for a drink while I chatted with Abby and scanned the bar for a prospective date. My eye caught the attention of an attractive man. I smiled at him, and he came over and offered to buy me a drink. As he walked to the bar, I noticed Cole sitting on the corner stool with a bottle of bourbon in front of him. In the time it took my gentleman friend to return with our drinks, Cole had turned away two women. This wasn't like him. He was never anti-social when we went out.

I sipped my drink while encouraging my male friend to talk about himself, permitting my level of distraction to go unnoticed. I watched as Cole poured one shot after the next while staring at the TV screen. I knew something was wrong when an attractive female sat down beside him and he politely dismissed her. I knew I should mind my own business. Cole would resent my butting in, but I wouldn't be able to concentrate on anything else until I knew he was all right. My overwhelming concern was proof that no matter how hard I tried, denying my feelings for Cole was no longer possible. I vowed to keep this realization to myself. If Cole knew the truth, he would use it to further humiliate me.

My friend Bryan excused himself to go to the restroom, and against my better judgment, I made a beeline for Cole. "What's up? That poor girl looked incredibly dejected. It's not like you to turn away such a good-looking groupie."

"I don't feel like company," Cole replied, somberly. "That goes for you too, Newhouse."

"Is everything okay? You look sad." I thought he would ignore me as he diverted his gaze from mine, but I was wrong.

"Today is the anniversary of my mother's death."

"Oh, Cole, I'm so sorry," I said, gently rubbing his shoulder.

"Not as sorry as I am. By the time I arrived at the hospital, she was incoherent."

"At least she passed quickly. I don't know if you'll find any comfort in this, but my grandmother lingered longer than expected. The only thing I was allowed to give her was morphine. I sat by helpless as her body slowly deteriorated. I couldn't imagine what was keeping her alive. You wouldn't have wanted to watch your mom suffer. Maybe what happened was a mixed blessing for you both."

"I'll never forgive myself for not being able to say goodbye."

"She knows how much you loved her, Cole."

"I hope so," he said, pouring another drink. "I appreciate your concern Newhouse, but I'd prefer to be alone."

"Are you sure?" He nodded and threw back more bourbon.

"Cole, take it easy on the booze. Maybe you should eat something."

"Goodbye, Newhouse."

"Okay, I get the hint, but I'll be over there if you need me."

I went back to Bryan, who had ordered another round. "Is everything okay?" Bryan asked.

"I'm concerned about my friend. He's having a tough night."

"That's Cole Pasternak. I used to watch him play. He was unbelievable. It's too bad his career was cut short."

We continued our conversation until the bar began emptying out. I saw Cole attempt to get up from his chair. The bottle of bourbon was nearly empty, and he was far from steady on his feet. "You'll have to excuse me, Bryan. Cole needs some assistance."

"I'd like to see you again. Can I have your number?"

"My information is online. Why don't you email me? I'm sorry. I need to rush off. I enjoyed meeting you," I replied, racing to

Cole's side. He was clutching the bar to steady himself as he dug through his pockets in search of his keys. "Cole, you can't drive like this. You've had way too much to drink."

"I'm fine," he insisted.

"No, you're not. You're slurring your words, and you can't stand straight. I'm going to drive you home."

"I can take care of myself, Newhouse," he mumbled indignantly.

"I know you can, just not tonight. Do you want to risk getting a DWI or, worse yet, crashing that sparkling clean Porsche?" I asked, trying to lower his defenses.

"I drive myself home all the time after drinking. It's not a problem."

"Humor me. Who would I spar with if something happened to you? It's an Uber or me. You choose," I said, definitively.

"I'll be okay if I lie down for a little while."

"You can crash at my place until you feel better, and then I'll drive you back to get your car."

"If you insist," he replied indignantly.

"Lean on me," I said, wrapping my arm around him. I was relieved when the bartender helped me get Cole in the car. "Thanks for your help."

"I feel like this is my fault. I should have cut him off."

"Don't blame yourself. I know how difficult Cole can be. Have a good night." I didn't know where I found the strength, but I managed to get Cole into my apartment. I opened my front door, and he headed directly for my bedroom. He pulled off his shirt and collapsed on the bed. I brought him some aspirin and a glass of water. Cole swallowed the pills and passed out.

I wasn't sure what to do. I threw on a camisole and lounge pants and crawled into bed beside him. He rolled his head onto my chest and laid his arm across my waist. Cole was out cold. I gazed down at his muscular torso, watching his chest rise and fall. His thick hair and heavy breath felt warm against my skin. He was in such a deep sleep that he would never know if I touched him. He was the sexiest man I'd ever seen, even drunk and snoring. As I struggled with my urges, Cole muttered some words I failed to distinguish. I felt his breathing become more erratic as his mind wrestled with his inner demons. I whispered in his ear, "You're okay. You're having a bad dream." I stroked his hair and rubbed his back. Cole burrowed his face against my breasts. He appeared to be soothed by my whispers and caresses.

After a few hours of watching Cole, I gave in to sleep. I wasn't sure what time it was when I heard him get up to use the restroom. Cole crawled back into bed, so I didn't think anything of it until I felt his lips working their way up my midsection. I was half asleep when he pressed his stiff cock between my legs. I opened my eyes to find Cole naked on top of me. I couldn't believe this was happening. It was the last thing I expected. I panicked for a moment, not knowing what to do. My body was still in shock as I felt his fingers parting my labia. This wasn't the scenario I fantasized about. However, if I didn't give in, the opportunity might never present itself again. The logical part of my psyche would applaud if I resisted my urges, but in what universe did rationality trump lust?

"Cole, give me a minute. My body isn't quite on board," I whispered.

Cole was far from coherent, but I knew he heard me when he cupped my vagina with his hand. I couldn't comprehend his actions until I felt my body relax beneath the soothing warmth of his touch. Maybe he'd fall back asleep, putting an end to my indecisiveness. That thought was dashed as Cole's lips traipsed their way up my breasts. He gently nibbled and licked my nipples, alternating from one breast to the other. I felt my insides come alive as my tips hardened beneath his tongue. Digging my hands into his hair, I pressed his head against my chest. He took my breast in his mouth, sucking on it, swirling his tongue over my rigid bullets. I started to moan as searing heat burned through my body like wildfire.

"Kiss me," I whispered firmly. Cole's eyes were still closed when he released my breast to hover over my face. I raised my head and gently tugged at his lower lip. He placed his mouth over mine. His lips were firm, yet soft, if that was even possible. I parted my lips, but Cole was slow to respond to my invitation. Unable to wait, I placed my hands on both sides of his face. Coaxing his mouth open, I slid my tongue past his lips, slowly swirling it around his mouth. His tongue intermingled with mine, flirting, tasting, and quickly withdrawing. I wanted to object until his face moved to my neck, which he bathed in licks and kisses. My neck was so sensitive that I had forgotten about the hand warming my pelvis. Cole had taken his index and middle fingers and slipped them inside my slick channel. He began massaging my inner walls as he pressed his thumb against my clitoris. The pressure in my pussy intensified. My legs spread wider as my insides devoured his fingers. Cole applied more pressure causing my body to spasm with need.

I felt the tide of ecstasy rise as my release began to build. I didn't want to come without having him inside me. I put my arms around him and pressed Cole's magnificent torso against mine as my legs encircled his lower body. I felt his erection push against my opening. I arched my hips for a seamless entrance. The girth of his cock pervaded every inch of me until I thought I would explode. Pleasure assaulted my body as Cole battered me with his throbbing cock. Taking my legs and placing one at a time on his shoulders, Cole elevated my lower back slightly off the bed. The shift caused his cock to plunge even farther into my depths. I gasped as he buried himself to the hilt, stretching my insides. Cole's eyes were open now as he began thrusting deep inside me. He started slowly but quickly increased the power making my muscles strain against every inch of his width.

"My God, you're tight," Cole mumbled.

"Is that bad?" I asked in a sultry voice.

"Are you kidding? You feel fucking incredible. You're going to suck the cum right out of me." My senses were on overdrive as I teetered on the cliff of an orgasm. Now that I knew how good it felt to have Cole inside me, I wasn't ready for it to end.

"Slow down," I whispered. "My insides want to covet your cock." Cole switched his jolting thrusts to gradual, smooth strokes.

My insides clenched his erection, wanting to claim it. Cole was moaning now as his breathing became labored. I slid my legs off his shoulders, planting them alongside his hips. I was too over-wrought to be passive. I began thrusting against him. We rocked against each

other, moving faster than we wanted as the need within our bodies eradicated all control. I felt the waves of orgasm rushing the floodgates. There was no turning back this time. I arched my back and wrapped my legs so tightly around Cole that I was surprised he could move. I let out a guttural scream as my insides imploded. He took several long, hard strokes before his cock let loose. Cole collapsed on top of me. Our chests were heaving against each other as we embraced.

Neither of us said a word, as the sound of our breathing filled the air. I think we were trying to contemplate what had just transpired. I knew from Cole's reaction that he was as surprised as I was that we had sex. He rolled onto his back, and I leaned against his chest. I ran my nails over Cole's pecs as his heartbeat slowly returned to normal. Cole hesitantly kissed the top of my head while stroking my hair. I wanted to tell him how much I longed to touch him like this, but I was afraid to ruin the moment. I pressed into his side, trying to feel every inch of him. I kissed his wash-board abs, running my fingers down the trail of hair above his groin. My actions soothed us both to sleep. It was the first night in months that my body wasn't restless from thoughts of Cole incessantly bombarding my brain.

CHAPTER 18

I lay in bed with my eyes closed. Having sex with Cole last night seemed surreal. My mind raced as I tried to think of how we would respond to one another in the light of day. Cole's actions took us both off guard. I was sure he wasn't planning to have sex with me when he came to my apartment. If only I knew what he was thinking.

The sun seeped through my eyelids. It was time to face the day and the man whose actions continually keep me off balance. I turned to find an empty bed. How did Cole manage to leave without disturbing me? Relief and disappointment washed over me. I roamed the apartment in search of a note but failed to find one. As I got ready for work, I tried to predict Cole's reaction. Numerous scenarios passed through my mind, except the one I faced.

I went straight to Cole's office upon arriving at the station. I stood in his doorway, waiting for him to acknowledge me. Cole didn't lift his eyes from the computer screen, forcing me to knock.

"What is it, Newhouse?" His greeting was chillier than I anticipated.

"I thought we should talk."

"About what?"

"About last night."

"What about it?"

"For starters, how are you feeling?"

"I'm fine. Why do you ask?"

"You drank a lot, even by your standards. I figured you would have a nasty hangover."

"Not really."

I waited for Cole to go on, but he didn't. "Is there anything else, Newhouse?"

"We should talk about what transpired between us."

"What is there to talk about? I passed out. When I woke up, I Ubered back to my car, drove home, and got ready for work."

"Is that all you remember?"

"No. I remember you making a scene in the bar, insisting I was too drunk to drive. You embarrassed the hell out of me."

Is it possible he was so drunk that he blacked out last night? I asked myself.

"Am I missing anything?" Cole asked in an irritated tone.

"No, I guess not," I replied, unsure of what to say next. "I'm sorry I embarrassed you, but I didn't want you to risk getting a DWI or killing somebody. Forgive me for caring."

"It's not your job to care! I'm a grown man who's perfectly capable of handling himself," Cole yelled.

"Not from what I saw," I replied defensively. "I'm concerned you have a drinking problem that needs to be addressed." I knew my comment wouldn't be well received, but even I was shocked by Cole's reply.

"I don't recall asking your opinion. Why don't you mind your own business, you medaling cunt!"

I froze. My mouth dropped open in disgust. I didn't know how I expected Cole to react, but it wasn't like this. "I don't know who you think you're talking to, but nobody speaks to me like that. You've crossed the line. We're done!" I exclaimed, storming out.

"Newhouse, wait," Cole called out. I raced to my office and locked the door. Cole was right behind me. "Newhouse, please let me in. I didn't mean that. I'm sorry."

"You're only sorry because you fear the repercussions of your actions," I shouted.

"That's not true. Please open the door. Let's talk this through."

"Go away, Cole, or I'll call security. I mean it."

He continued knocking fervently. "Please hear me out. I never meant to speak to you like that."

"But you did, loud and clear. Now, get lost."

Cole waited for a few moments before retreating to his office. At least, that was my assumption. I would have stopped him if I had known he was headed to share our exchange with Leora.

"What did you do this time?" Ava asked Cole. "She seems really angry."

"Ava, could you tell Leora I need to see her immediately?"

"She's on the phone."

"Please tell her it's important." Cole stepped into Leora's office as she was wrapping up her call. "Hi Cole, what's so urgent?"

"I need to tell you something before you hear it elsewhere."

"Okay, I'm listening."

"It's about Layla."

"What have you done to that poor girl now?"

"We had a disagreement, and I called her a cunt."

Leora gave Cole a look that was a mixture of shock and horror. "That is irreprehensible, Cole."

"I know."

"How could you say something like that?" Leora bellowed.

"I didn't mean it. It just came out."

"Things like that don't just come out. I couldn't defend your actions even if I wanted to, which I don't."

"I wouldn't expect you to. I know what I did was inexcusable. I tried apologizing to Layla, but she won't speak to me."

"I don't blame her."

"I want you to know that I take full responsibility for my actions, and I'm willing to accept the consequences."

"You really crossed the line this time. I'm sure Layla will be taking this to HR. I can't guarantee what they'll do, but I'm suspending your pay for two weeks."

"I understand," Cole replied, nodding.

"I know the money doesn't mean much to you, but I must take some form of punitive action. You'll be lucky if you're not suspended. Layla could press charges for sexual harassment."

"I know. I can't tell you how much I regret what I did. You know me, Leora. You know I don't speak to women like that."

"You've had an issue with Layla from the moment she arrived. After all the ways she's proven herself, I would have thought things between you had improved. I never bargained for this. I'm your biggest fan, Cole, but I'm ashamed of you right now."

"Believe me, that makes two of us. Please let Layla know how sorry I am."

"May I suggest you pay a visit to HR, so we know what we're facing? Layla isn't ready to do the broadcasts on her own. If I need to shift personnel around, I'd prefer to know sooner than later."

"That's my next stop, Leora. I'm truly sorry for any problems I have caused you."

"It's not me; you owe an apology, Cole. I'll let you know if I hear anything."

"Hello, Chloe."

"Hi, Cole, what brings you to this department? I haven't seen you in ages."

"I want to let you know that Layla MacKenzie will pay you a visit if she hasn't already."

"I haven't seen Layla."

"I'm sure you will. She'll be filing a complaint against me."

Chloe stared at Cole in amazement. "I can't imagine why. I've seen you guys on television. You're so cute together, like an old married couple."

"I'm afraid we're getting divorced."

"I'm sorry to hear that, Cole. I think you're both great people."

"I want to go on record that anything Layla says is true. I'm not defending myself."

"If she files a complaint, we'll need you to sign an official statement confirming that."

"I understand. That won't be an issue."

"I hope you guys find a way to work it out, Cole."

"That's doubtful but thank you. Have a good day, Chloe."

"You too, Cole."

I was so upset that I couldn't work. At least we didn't have a game tonight, so I wouldn't have to face Cole until tomorrow. "Ava, I'm going to take the rest of the day off. If Leora needs anything, she can call me."

"I'll let her know, Layla. I hope everything is okay."

I went home, put on sweats, and parked myself in front of the TV with a bottle of wine. I didn't feel like talking to anyone, not even Skye. How could Cole treat me like that? I was only looking out for him. He should be thanking me. Then we finally consummated our relationship after months of internal torment, and he doesn't even remember it. I was simultaneously disheartened, disappointed, hurt, confused, and angry.

Sitting on my couch with a bag of chips, I sulked like a wounded child. I couldn't recall the last time I did this, if ever. I would give myself one day to have a pity party, and then I'd pull myself together. My immediate instinct was to find another job, but that wouldn't be easy. I hadn't made enough connections to make a move. Besides, why should I leave when he offended me? Cole should be the one to go, but I knew that would never happen.

I had just finished the end of my second depressing movie when I heard a knock at my door. I didn't want to see anybody. I just finished a crying binge, and my eyes were still puffy. It was probably an Amazon delivery.

The banging became more persistent. "Newhouse, please let me in. We need to talk." The balls on this guy! I couldn't believe he had the nerve to show up here.

"Get lost, Cole."

"Please let me in, Newhouse."

"I thought I made it clear. I don't want to see you."

"I know, but I'm not going away until we talk. If you want me gone, you'll have to call the cops."

Unbelievable! I didn't have the strength to argue with him.

Against my better judgment, I dragged myself off the couch and cracked open the door. "I have nothing to say to you."

"I know, but I have something you need to hear."

"Say your piece and leave."

"Can I come in?"

"I prefer you didn't."

"Please, Layla, what I must tell you isn't easy for me. I'd prefer not to do it in the hall."

He never called me Layla. Curiosity got the better of me, and I decided to hear him out. "Fine, come in," I said, opening the door in annoyance. Cole saw my puffy eyes. I was angry that he witnessed the impact his words had on me. He reached out to stroke my cheek with his finger.

"Don't touch me," I snapped.

"I'm sorry. I hate to see you so upset knowing I'm the cause." Cole took a seat across from me on the couch. "Do you have anything to drink in this place?"

"Really, you think you should be drinking after last night?"

"Can we please skip the lecture? It will help me get this off my chest."

"We have wine or vodka."

"I'll take a double vodka on the rocks." I poured Cole's drink, trying not to care if he got caught driving drunk. Maybe that would teach him a lesson.

"Here's your drink. Now say what you came to say." Cole sipped his vodka. He looked at the floor, then back at me, and then back at the floor. He was clearly struggling to find the right words.

"Layla, I know we slept together last night."

I looked at him with raised eyebrows. "Then why did you pretend you didn't remember?"

"Because I was ashamed of my behavior. I climbed on top of you like some sort of circus animal. That's not how I make love to a woman, and you deserve better. I like to cherish a woman's body and make her feel special. When it comes to sex, it's not all about me. I pride myself on pleasing my lovers. I feel like I ramrodded you and fell back asleep. It wasn't one of my finest moments."

I paused, not knowing what to say. "I've never been fucked that hard in my life."

A look of horror passed over Cole's face as his eyes met mine. "Did I hurt you?"

"No," I replied shaking my head. Cole let out a sigh of relief. "If we're being honest, it felt good. I never come like that with a man."

"I'm surprised you did since our level of foreplay was severely lacking."

"I still don't understand your reaction, Cole."

"I don't expect you to. I was mad at myself for getting so drunk that I needed you to take care of me. Then for crossing the line and sleeping with you. I know you were just trying to help, which I'm uncomfortable accepting. I turned my anger at my actions against you instead of inward, which was a horrible mistake. I'm not going to use alcohol as an excuse. I was in a bad headspace with it being the anniversary of my mother's death. I shouldn't have gone out at all, but I did. I regret everything that happened last night, especially our exchange this morning. I've never called a woman the C-word. If someone ever said that to Ashley, I'd break his jaw. I hope you believe me."

There was an unfamiliar sound of desperation in Cole's voice. His eyes, which were the windows to his soul, were full of remorse. I believed he was telling me the truth. "I want you to know that I'm prepared to face the consequences of my actions. I told Leora what happened, and I spoke with Human Relations. I told them I support whatever you say and will do whatever they deem appropriate."

"Why did you do that, Cole?" I asked, taken aback by his actions. "I have no intention of reporting you to either party."

"You should, Layla. I deserve to be officially reprimanded. Leora already suspended my salary for two weeks, a drop in the bucket compared to my infraction."

"I told you a while ago, I'm not a child. I have no intention of tattling on you. You must live with knowing you did a shitty thing to someone who didn't deserve it. I hope that thought eats away at your conscience."

"I assure you it does! Listen, Layla, I'm not here to ask for forgiveness. I don't deserve it, but I felt I owed you the truth."

"While we're being honest, there are a few things I need to know," I said, staring into Cole's eyes.

"Okay," he replied hesitantly.

"Did you know it was me you were sleeping with, or did you think I was some random woman you picked up?"

"I see you're going to make this even tougher on me," Cole said with a heavy sigh.

"I think I deserve to know if the man I slept with wanted me or somebody else."

"When I awoke and glanced over at the sea of thick, blond waves strewn across the pillow, I knew I was in bed beside you," Cole replied, diverting his eyes back to the floor.

"Last night, you said that I was beautiful. Did you mean that?"

"C'mon, Layla, you know you're gorgeous. Men's heads spin around like something out of *The Exorcist* when you walk by."

"I'm not talking about other men. I want to know what you think."

"I thought you were beautiful from the minute I saw you, even after you doused me with hot coffee. I've struggled with my attraction to you for quite a while."

"Is it because I bear a strong resemblance to Haley?"

"I admit you have similar features, except you're even more striking."

"Does that bother you?"

"It did at first, but I've gotten used to it."

"You seemed hesitant to make out with me. Why?"

Cole ran his fingers threw his hair as he took a swig from his glass. "I view kissing as a very intimate act. It sounds strange, but I try to keep full-blown make-out sessions to a minimum."

"Don't women find that odd?"

"I don't think they notice. My lips and tongue are too busy exploring the rest of their body for them to object."

I took a deep breath, fearing this response more than any other. "Did last night feel good to you at all?" I asked with trepidation.

Cole paused before replying in a soft tone of voice. "Of course it did. Listen, Layla, if you need to hear that I wanted to sleep with you, I obviously did, even if it was on a subconscious level. It was a terrible mistake, and it won't happen again." My heart sank. After all the nights I dreamed of making love to this man, I finally did, and he regretted it.

"It's not like you'll be heartbroken, considering you hate me."

"I don't hate you, Cole," I replied gently. "You just make it very hard for me to like you."

"I know I haven't treated you well, Layla, and that will change. I never gave you a fair chance. I didn't think you deserved Shane's job, and I wanted you to fail. I thought you were a spoiled rich girl who used her looks to manipulate people. I couldn't have been more wrong. You are one of the hardest-working, most genuine people I've ever met. I'm amazed by how much you've learned in such a short period. The guys on the team love you, as do the Southern Sports staff. Despite my attempts to undermine you, I have the utmost respect for what you've accomplished. Moving forward, if you have questions, I want you to come to me. I'm done stonewalling you."

"I appreciate that, Cole. Now I have something to say you won't want to hear."

"What's that?" Cole asked nervously.

"We didn't use protection last night."

His eyes flared in horror. "You're not on birth control?"

"Why should I be? I'm not in a relationship."

"I thought all young women are on birth control," he replied incredulously.

"I didn't see the need to screw with my hormones if I wasn't seeing somebody. Normally, I would have insisted you wear a condom, but everything happened quickly."

"That's my fault. I always wear a condom, even if the woman uses protection. Obviously, I wasn't thinking straight either."

"You don't have any diseases, do you?"

"Of course not!" Cole replied defensively.

"You can't blame me for asking, considering your level of

promiscuity."

"Are you telling me you could be pregnant?"

"I hope not, but it's not out of the question."

"Just when I thought things couldn't get worse," Cole replied, holding his head in his hands. "Layla, if God forbid something happens, let me know, and we'll work it out. I'm not one to shirk my responsibilities."

"That's good to know." An awkward silence fell over the room.

"Where does this leave us?" I asked.

"That's up to you. I'm hoping for friendly co-workers."

I felt like stabbing myself in the eye. I'm now stuck in the friend zone with the one man who consumes my mind, dominates my desires, and makes my body quiver when he enters the room. Logically, I knew it was better this way. A romantic relationship with Cole would leave me devastated. As it was, I felt a piece of my heart drifting away. "We can't be too nice to each other. Our viewing audience would go into shock," I replied, forcing a smile.

"I suppose they would. Are you okay with some sarcastic banter?"

"I'm an expert at sarcastic banter."

"I've noticed. Seriously, Newhouse, thank you for hearing me out. I know I'm the last person you wanted to see. I'm truly sorry for my reprehensible behavior."

"Thank you for being honest with me. I know that wasn't easy for you. I admit to hating what you did, but I can separate the action from the man."

Cole gave me a look of gratitude. "Can I give you a hug?"

"I don't think that's a great idea."

"I understand. Have a good night, Newhouse. I'll see you tomorrow."

My mind flooded with mixed emotions as I closed the door behind him. Needing to sort them out, I called Skye. "I don't understand, Skye. I should be relieved. Cole's going to be nicer to me. He agreed to serve as the mentor I was promised instead of my adversary. He wants to be friends. This is what I've been hoping for all along."

194

"Layla, I'm glad Cole's finally seen the error of his ways. Although any man who calls a woman the C-word is indefensible in my book. I hope you're able to work through it. If I were in your shoes, I'd find another job. I know that's the last thing you want to do, especially now that your hard work is starting to pay off."

"Cole admitted to respecting me. He said I'm doing a good job. Why am I still so unhappy?"

"Because you still refuse to admit that what you want more than respect is a relationship with this man. You need to accept that and come clean with him about your feelings. Tell him you don't regret sleeping with him. I think he's struggling just as much with his feelings for you. Otherwise, you wouldn't have evoked such a strong reaction from him."

"Cole said sleeping with me was a mistake that he regretted. I have my pride, Skylar. I won't chase a man who doesn't want me."

"That's what he said, Layla. It isn't necessarily what he feels. I think he's protecting his ego too."

"From what? It isn't like I rejected him."

"No, but it wasn't the experience either of you had hoped for, yet you both felt something. Cole has a reputation as a ladies' man. You are the one woman who hasn't fallen at his feet. He may not be as secure as you think. Plus, you work together, which you've admitted is a line he doesn't cross. The fact that he did tells me something, even if he was drunk."

"If I went out on a limb and Cole rejected me, it would be impossible to work with him. It's hard enough now."

"Then look for a new position. Ignoring your feelings for Cole isn't working."

"I can't give up my job. At least not yet."

"I understand. Then maybe you should try dating other men. I don't think it will change your situation, but it would be a distraction until you can make a move."

"I'll think about it. Being with Cole reminded me that I miss physical intimacy. Maybe it is time to start dating."

"I suggest you try to distance yourself from Cole and develop a social life outside work."

"That's a good idea, Skye. Thanks for the advice."

"Hang in there, Layla. You're too good for this guy."

"You're probably right, but that doesn't factor into my law of attraction."

The next day, I walked into my office and found Leora waiting for me. "Hi. Layla, I came to speak to you yesterday, but Ava said you went home."

"I hope that wasn't a problem."

"Of course not, especially in lieu of the circumstances. Cole filled me in on what transpired."

"I know. Cole told me when he came to my place last night to apologize."

"I'm glad he did that. I know he regrets his actions, but I'm not here to defend him. I want you to know that I will stand behind you if you decide to take this incident further."

"I'm not. I'm hoping something good will come out of this situation."

"Like what?" Leora asked, looking perplexed.

"I know you told Cole to be a resource for me, but he refused."

"That's not what you told me."

"I know. I figured I could handle the situation on my own."

"You shouldn't have to do that, Layla. I would have insisted that Cole adjust his attitude."

"I wanted that to come from him, not you. It was important for me to earn his respect, and I finally have it."

"I'm glad to hear that. You should have had it a long time ago. Cole's behavior toward you has been an anomaly. I'm sorry it took something like this to get him back on track. If you change your mind, I want you to know you have my support."

"Thank you, Leora. I appreciate that. I'm heading to the airport for the away game in a couple of hours. I'll see you when I get back."

"Have a good trip, Layla. I hope Cole finally recognizes what he has in you."

CHAPTER 19

Cole was noticeably standoffish toward me for the next week. We barely said two words to each other beyond a professional capacity. I kept telling myself the space was a good thing, even though I admit to looking for excuses to catch a glimpse of him. I even went on a date with Bryan. We had a lovely evening. He seemed like a good guy. Under normal circumstances, I would have pursued a relationship with him. However, it didn't seem fair when all I could think about was Cole.

I was reviewing the footage of tonight's opponent when I heard a knock on the office door. Cole was standing there with a beautiful bouquet of flowers. My heart skipped a hopeful beat.

"These just came for you," he said, placing them on my desk. Disappointment washed over me.

"Thanks," I said, opening the card." It read: "I had a wonderful time last night and look forward to doing it again soon, Bryan."

"Do you have a secret admirer?"

"No, they're from the guy I've been dating."

"I didn't realize you were seeing someone." Cole paused. "Is he a good man?"

"It seems that way."

"I'm glad. You deserve it," Cole said, matter-of-factly as he turned to leave my office.

"Cole, there's something you should know. I got my period this morning."

"Whew, that's a relief." He sighed, allowing his raised shoulders to relax. "The possibility of you being pregnant has been weighing on me. Thanks for telling me, Newhouse. I'll see you at the game unless you have questions beforehand."

Cole had been true to his word about being a resource. His commentary at the games changed from trying to find fault with my analysis to complimenting my insights. Oddly enough, I missed our sparring. It was as if the sexual tension went out the window now that we were no longer adversaries. I feared the mystery had died for Cole since consummating our relationship. Apparently, I wasn't as enticing as his harem of nubile chicklets. I could accept that. What I couldn't bear was the awkwardness between us. I decided to ask Cole to get a drink following the game to clear the air. That thought vanished when I saw one of the girls from the Predator's crew meet Cole at the sound booth. She had blonde hair down to her waist and annoyingly perky breasts. She couldn't have been more than twenty-two.

"See you tomorrow, Newhouse. If you have questions about the Tampa Bay Thunder, let me know," he called out.

"I will. You guys have a good night."

I felt sick as I watched them walk away. I had to find a way to reel in my jealousy. I called Bryan and met him for a drink to soothe my wounded ego. He wanted to go back to my place, but I didn't have the energy to fake it. I wanted to get home and look at more footage on the Thunder. As the other local Florida team, they were the Predators' biggest adversary. This would be the first time I saw Cole and Tristan O'Shaughnessy in the same building. I was interested to see Cole's reaction. Could he remain impartial in his commentary? From what I read in the statistics, Tristan was having a good season. I was sure it ate away at Cole that he was sidelined while Tristan was in the top two for goals scored by a defenseman.

The game lived up to the hype. The players on these two teams were familiar with each other's styles. I could see frustration building as both teams' scoring attempts were thwarted. The temperature was rising, as were the tempers. The game went from being physical and wrought with infractions to fighting. Tristan saw more of his share of the action, delivering and drawing penalties. He was involved in two fights. One that he instigated and the other where he came to the aid of a teammate. Cole kept his commentary to play description, keeping his opinions to a minimum.

By the time the game ended, I was convinced there would be a brawl on the ice. In the last two minutes, the Predators went ahead to earn a two-to-one victory. Pushing and shoving broke out in front of the Thunder goalie following the game-winning goal. The crowd went wild when Tristan and Matt Perault dropped their gloves. A punching match ensued until Tristan knocked off Matt's helmet, causing the referees to intercede. After looming on the ice following the final buzzer, both teams reluctantly headed to their locker rooms.

Cole was in a great mood following the Predator win over our archnemesis. The crew decided to head out for a celebratory drink. We were finishing our first round when Tristan entered the bar, accompanied by a handful of teammates. My eyes immediately darted to Cole. His body language changed instantaneously from relaxed to rigid. I heard Morgan ask Cole if he wanted to leave. "Absolutely not," Cole replied defiantly. "I'm not giving that jerk the satisfaction of running me off." Cole turned his back to Tristan, attempting to ignore him. I decided to sit at the bar within proximity to the Thunder players. It didn't take long for Tristan to approach me.

"Why if it isn't Layla MacKenzie. May I say you are even more beautiful in person?"

"Thank you, Tristan," I replied, tossing my hair over my shoulder.

"I'm flattered you recognize me," he replied.

"I research all the teams we play, and you're one of the Thunder's star players. Additionally, you're one of the top-scoring defensemen in the NHL. You use your physicality as a weapon. You're infamous in these parts because of your brutal fight with my co-commentator. I know you were drafted the same year as Cole. You came out of Michigan and have a younger brother who was drafted by the New Jersey Demons last year."

"Wow, you really did your homework."

"The one thing I didn't encounter in my research," I said casually, "was what caused the brawl between you and Cole."

"I think we can find way more interesting things to talk about," Tristan said, staring at my breasts.

The man standing before me held the missing piece to the puzzle, and I was determined to use my powers of persuasion to get it. I appealed to Tristan's overblown ego with flattery while plying him with alcohol. I hoped the combination would prove lethal enough for him to spill the truth. "Let me buy you a drink. Tonight's loss must have been tough to swallow, especially when you played such a great game."

"I'm surprised someone from the enemy camp is willing to acknowledge that."

"How could I not? The way you maneuver on the ice is captivating," I replied, batting my eyelashes.

"I think I should buy you a drink for your kind words. Maybe this evening isn't a complete loss after all."

After three drinks, Tristan was becoming quite flirtatious. His hand started on my knee, slowly moving up my thigh. His body was inching closer to mine as he whispered in my ear. His other hand ran up and down my arm, stopping to intermingle his fingers with mine. The strange thing was I enjoyed it. Tristan O' Shaughnessy made me laugh. He was a great storyteller, exceedingly charming, and all alpha male. However, what attracted me the most about Tristan was his impact on Cole.

Cole hadn't taken his eyes off us since we started talking. I couldn't generate a reaction from him no matter how hard I tried, until now. My insides rejoiced as I watched the agitation emanate from Cole's body. Tristan caught me looking at his nemesis. "You guys aren't together off-camera, are you?"

"Who, me and Cole? Nothing could be further from the truth. I'm not a fan, which seems to be something we have in common."

"Yeah, I noticed Cole hasn't given you the respect you deserve. I think you're doing a great job. Your play analysis is accurate, and I like your interviewing style."

"Thank you. I see you're a man of good taste," I replied, leaning into Tristan.

"Cole is a fool for not appreciating you. What do you say we finish this discussion in a more private setting? This way, I can show you just how special you are."

His offer was tempting. My sex life had been non-existent, aside from the random night with Cole. The moisture building between my thighs told me my body was willing. My mind jumped on board when I realized this would be the ultimate way to burn Cole. Tonight, he could watch me go home with someone, as I'd seen him do countless times. If this man had any feelings for me whatsoever, my leaving with Tristan would be the action to trigger them.

"You lead the way," I whispered in Tristan's ear. "My car is here, so I'll give you a lift to the hotel." Tristan extended his hand to me as I hopped off the barstool. His arm encircled my waist, and we headed for the exit.

"Layla, can I speak with you?" Cole asked, grabbing my arm.

"I'm on my way out, Cole. Whatever you have to say can wait until tomorrow."

"No, it can't!"

"Get lost, Pasternak. Layla wants to experience a real man."

Fury flashed in Cole's eyes as his hands clenched into fists. The last thing I needed was for a fight to break out. I wanted Cole to be emotionally tormented, not physically hurt.

"Please, Layla," Cole implored in an urgent tone.

"Tristan, give me a moment," I said placing my hand on his chest.

Cole's face was flushed. His cheeks were as red as Dorothy's slippers in *The Wizard of Oz*. My interaction with Tristan was clearly making his blood boil. "Come with me," Cole said, pulling me aside.

"What is it, Cole?" I asked in feigned annoyance and inner exuberance.

"You aren't seriously thinking of leaving with him?"

"I'm doing just that. Apparently, you're not the only one who has a way with the opposite sex."

"Layla, you're making a huge mistake. I know him. You don't."

"I don't know what transpired between you two, but I find him charming and extremely sexy."

"He's dangerous."

"I'm sure he is, in all the right ways," I replied, with a mischievous grin.

"Layla, I'm not joking," Cole's grip on my arm intensified.

"Let go of me, Cole. You're hurting me."

"Is there a problem?" I heard Tristan call out.

"No problem," I responded, turning to walk toward him, only to have Cole pull me back.

"I'm begging you, Newhouse. Please don't go home with him."

"What's the problem, Cole? You don't like it when the shoe is on the other foot?"

"You can sleep with whomever you want, except for him. I'm saying this out of genuine concern for you."

"That's news to me. Goodnight, Cole," I said, yanking my arm from his grasp. I took Tristan's hand and walked out. He continued his seduction in the car. I felt Tristan's hand slide between my legs as I stopped for a red light. My insides grew moist beneath his touch. "Tristan, I would stop that unless you want me to crash the car."

"It's a good thing we're close to the hotel. I can't wait to get you out of these clothes," he replied, nuzzling my neck.

When we reached the hotel, Tristan ordered a bottle of wine from room service. A combination of sexual tension and nerves caused my belly to tighten as he opened the door to his room. It wasn't like me to have a one-night stand.

It was too late for second-guessing as Tristan came up behind me and spun me around. He held me against his colossal frame. At six-foot-four and two hundred and twenty-five pounds, he was even bigger than Cole. Tristan grabbed my neck as he pressed his mouth on mine. He slid his tongue toward my throat, devouring my lips with his. Why couldn't Cole kiss me with such deliberation? I shut my eyes and imagined Cole's face. Tristan kissed me with intensity, making it hard for me to catch my breath.

I was almost relieved when we were interrupted by room service knocking on the door. Tristan poured us a glass of wine. I took a sip before he removed the glass from my hand. "Where were we?" he asked as he pushed me back against the desk. Tristan stood between my legs, prying them apart. He reached beneath my skirt, his fingers probing for my wet slit. I tensed as he pressed his long fingers inside me, swirling and twisting them as he dug deeper. I tried to shift back on the desk, allowing my body to adjust to his invasion. Tristan pinned my shoulder against the wall. My gasp was smothered by his mouth over mine. It was a combination of excitement and discomfort. Tristan had a wild gleam in his eye as he pulled his shirt over his head. He removed his fingers from my vagina and shoved my skirt around my waist. Tristan's fingers tore the silk panties off my body with ease. His strength was overpowering.

"Tristan, we should take this down a notch."

"Take it down? I was just about to turn up the heat," he replied, with a low growl.

"You have such a great body. I want to take time to explore it."

"You want to feel something? Try this." Tristan stripped his jeans off, revealing a monstrous erection. He walked toward me, lifted me off the desk, and tossed me onto the mattress. In a matter of seconds, he was crawling on top of me.

"I've been wondering what these look like all night," he said, ripping the buttons off my silk blouse. I felt his rock-hard cock against my thigh as he reached behind me and unhooked my bra. He pinned the bra around my neck while taking my breast in his mouth. What started as nibbles on my nipples quickly turned into bites. He was hurting me. Worse than that, he was scaring me.

"This isn't working for me, Tristan. We need to stop," I said firmly, pushing against his chest with my hand.

"I'm just getting started," he said, pressing the bra more firmly against my neck. I coughed in reaction to the restriction. "That's it. We're done!" I snapped, attempting to push him off me.

"I'll tell you when we're done," he said, putting his hand around my throat and pushing my head back down on the mattress.

Fear shot through me as I realized he was out of control. My mind was swimming as I pictured my violated body lying on the bed like garbage strewn by the side of the road. Time was running out. I had to act fast. With lightning speed, I slid my knee into his ball sack. It stunned Tristan momentarily, enabling me to escape. I leaped off the bed and dashed toward the door.

"You're not going anywhere," he yelled. I yelped in pain a Tristan used a fistful of hair to pull me to my knees.

"I'll scream if you don't let me go."

"Not if you know what's good for you," Tristan replied sternly. He raised his hand and delivered a sharp slap across my face, knocking me to the floor.

"Help! Somebody help me," I screamed. Turning feral, I began biting my assailant's arms and pounding my fists against his torso. Tristan cupped his hand over my mouth while pinning me to the floor with his massive frame. Bile worked its way up my esophagus into my mouth, making it difficult to cry out.

"Are you going to be quiet? Tristan asked, wrapping his other hand around my throat. I tried to kick him again but couldn't move my legs. I dug my nails against his chest, breaking the skin, yet he seemed unscathed. I tried to let out another scream causing Tristan to increase the pressure on my throat. He was going to crush my windpipe. I felt myself getting dizzy from a lack of oxygen when I heard a pounding on the door. I let out a muffled scream. The door gave way as Cole came rushing into the room. He pulled Tristan off me and punched him in the face. "Get out of here, Layla!" Cole yelled, delivering another strike that knocked Tristan to the ground. Cole straddled him, dispatching a steady stream of blows. Tristan tried to block his face with his hands as Cole pummeled him. I watched in horror as blood spurted over

Cole's fists and face. Apparently, Tristan wasn't the only one who snapped.

"Cole, stop it! You're going to kill him!" I tried to grab Cole's arm, but he pushed me away, allowing Tristan to deliver a blow. I watched as blood ran from Cole's nose.

"Layla, leave now before you get hurt."

I ran into the hall and began yelling for help. Fortunately, some of the other Thunder players were staying on the same floor. "Please come quickly. Cole and Tristan are fighting. Someone's going to get seriously hurt."

I heard yelling and watched several members of the team pile into the hall and head for Tristan's room. It took three guys to pull Cole off Tristan. I peered into the room, but all I could see was blood spattered on the carpet and Tristan lying motionless on the floor. "Let's get out of here," Cole said, grabbing my hand. "Here, take this," he said, removing his shirt and pulling it over my head. I forgot I was naked from the waist up with all the commotion. We ran to the parking lot and hopped in Cole's Porsche. We passed the ambulance approaching the hotel as we sped away.

"Are you okay?" Cole asked, his breath erratic.

"I'm fine. It's you I'm worried about. Your nose is bleeding."

"I'll be all right," Cole said, wiping away the blood. "It could have been much worse. If I didn't get the jump on him, the outcome would have been different." Cole grabbed his gym bag, and we headed into my apartment.

"Here, put your head back," I said, wrapping some ice in a washcloth. "Do you think your nose is broken?"

"I don't think so," he replied, while I poured us both a double vodka. As I went to hand Cole his drink, I noticed my hands were shaking. "Are you okay, Newhouse? You must have been terrified."

"How did you know where we were? Did you follow us?"

"No. I asked the other guys from the team where they were staying."

"Thank God you arrived when you did."

"Are you sure you aren't hurt? Your face is bruised," Cole said, grazing my cheek with his fingertip.

"I'll be alright, thanks to you. How did you know I was in trouble?"

"I didn't, but I know Tristan can be volatile. I was listening outside the door. I knew I had to break it down when you cried for help. I tried to warn you."

"I was more afraid for you than him. I thought you were going to kill him."

"I should have," Cole said, smacking his fist into my table.

"Cole," I said, gently taking his hand in mine. "You need to tell me what transpired between you and Tristan. You were so brutal it scared me. I need to know what caused that kind of rage."

"I couldn't let him hurt you, Newhouse."

"The wheels were set in motion long before tonight. I think you owe me the truth."

Cole took a swallow of his drink before meeting my gaze. "Who is the one woman I would die defending?" Cole asked softly.

I thought for a moment. "Of course," I replied, as the realization hit me. "Ashley."

Cole gave me an affirmative nod. "Tristan and I were friends at one point. He went to Michigan while I played for Minnesota. We traveled in the same circles for years, meeting at various competitions and training camps. One night after a game, players from the Predators and the Thunder decided to grab a drink."

"Even though you were enemies?"

"We were only adversaries on the ice. We'd take out our aggression there and leave it behind. Ashley was at the game. She decided to come out with us. She and Tristan hit it off. They started dating."

"That must have upset you."

"Not really. At the time, I didn't think Tristan was a bad guy. However, I did warn Ashley that he had a reputation as a womanizer." Cole ran his fingers through his hair as he continued to gather his thoughts. "Things between them were good for a while, but it was hard for them to see each other. She was in college. He was on the road. Tampa isn't around the corner from Miami, and Tristan wound up straying. Pictures of him with other women appeared on social media. Ashley gave Tristan an ultimatum, and he broke up with her. A few weeks later, Ashley found out she was pregnant. She confronted Tristan, and he denied it. He accused her of sleeping around. They got into a huge fight, and he hit her."

"Oh my God, Cole." I gasped. "That's awful! Did he abuse her while they were dating?"

"No, but they had a very volatile relationship. Tristan has always had an issue controlling his temper. I figured he worked it out on the ice like I did. Anyway, I accompanied Ashley to the clinic, but she changed her mind about having an abortion. Tristan denied being the father when Ashley told him she was keeping the baby. I hired an attorney. We had a court-ordered paternity test that proved Tristan is Katelyn's father. Tristan didn't want to be tied down with a baby. He agreed to a generous child support settlement if Ashley promised to keep his identity a secret. Apparently, upper management wasn't happy with Tristan's media image, and he didn't want the situation going public."

"Ashley was okay with this?"

"Not at first, but I convinced her she was better off with Tristan out of her life. The next time our teams faced each other, Tristan and I had words on the ice. He knew what I thought of him and that I was instrumental in Ashley's legal victory. At one point, we were fighting to get control of the puck against the boards. Tristan trashed talked Ashley. He called her a worthless slut, and that's when I lost it. I was overcome with rage. It was a brutal fight that resulted in some significant injuries. We were both at fault, so no charges were pressed. I received a settlement from a civil suit because my injuries were career-ending. Now, you know what started the feud and how I knew he was dangerous. I couldn't let him hurt another woman I care about."

Cole's comment took me by surprise. "I thought tonight's violent display was residual anger over losing your NHL career."

"That anger will always be there, but my actions were motivated by the need to protect you. I admit my plan was to stop Tristan, not beat him half to death, but I couldn't help myself."

"I'm eternally grateful, Cole. I'm also wrought with guilt."

"Guilt, what for?" Cole asked, looking perplexed.

"Tristan isn't the man I wanted," I said, staring directly into Cole's eyes.

"What are you saying, Layla?"

"I admit to finding Tristan attractive, but I agreed to go home with him to make you jealous." Cole stared back at me with incredulous eyes. "Why didn't you just talk to me?"

"Would you if you were in my shoes? First, you pretend that you don't remember sleeping with me. Then when you owned up to it, you described our night together as a mistake you regretted. Let's not forget our acrimonious relationship up to that point."

"I said I regretted sleeping with you because of our working relationship, and I thought that was how you felt. Given our history and the way that night went down, I was protecting my ego. I made love to you with all the finesse of a jackhammer when I should have explored every sensual curve, crevice, and nuance of your beautiful body. Ever since we slept together, all I can think about is your wavy blonde hair, toned legs, the slope of your breasts, and sun-kissed skin. The vanilla aroma that emanates from your sweet center makes me want to taste every inch of you. Let's not forget your eyes. They're like sunflowers with irises as dark as night nestled in flecks of gold. If I were to be honest, just being near you arouses every impulse in my body, sending my senses into overdrive. I want to suck those pillowy lips and nibble on that flippant tongue. My defenses melt away beneath the tenderness of your touch. I've been with countless attractive women and have always been able to stay detached. I was determined to bury my attraction to you. To douse my desire to be inside those tight, wet walls that drip like honey. Just the thought of massaging those oh-so-responsive brown nipples makes my cock hard. That's why I vowed to stay away from you. It isn't that I didn't want you, Layla. I didn't want to want you."

I was stunned and incredibly turned on by his confession. This

209

was the man I caught glimpses of beneath the arrogant façade, and I found him intoxicatingly alluring. I took Cole's face in my hands, forcing his eyes to meet mine. "You once told me that you like to savor a woman when you make love to her." Cole nodded in agreement. I took my fingertips and ran them down his face, brushing them over his lips. "Show me."

Cole responded to my request with a look of uncertainty. "Are you sure that's what you want? You've had a rough night. I would think you're still pretty shaken up."

I leaned over and pressed my lips against his. His reaction was very different this time. He began fervently kissing me as he pulled me into his arms. Cole's tongue outstretched into my mouth, claiming it, exploring every crevice with deep deliberation. When he finally withdrew to take a breath, I leaned in and took his lower lip between my teeth. My lips caressed his, sucking and nibbling on his mouth before sliding inside to taste him. This was the intimacy I longed for as passion poured through my veins. "Lift your arms up," Cole said, as he reached and slid his shirt over my head. His eyes drank in the image of my naked torso. Placing his hand beneath my breast, Cole softly encircled my nipple with his thumb pad. "You have the most incredibly sensual nipples. They're so large and responsive."

"I've never been happy with my breasts. I always wanted them to be bigger."

"You're so hard on yourself. Your breasts are the perfect size for your body. They fit like they were molded for my hands, and that's all that matters," Cole said, replacing his thumb with his tongue. I gasped as my bud became erect, swelling with sensitivity between his lips. With his eyes locked on mine, Cole released his hold on me and removed his shirt. I went to reach for him, and he pulled back, evading my touch.

"Lie back," he instructed. I couldn't imagine a woman ever saying no to those bedroom eyes. I did as I was told.

"Lift your hips slightly," Cole said, sliding my skirt off. He rose off the bed, removing his pants in an excruciatingly slow fashion, allowing me to admire every curve and cut on his sculpted physique. My abdomen grew taut, and my center slick as I imagined him inside me. "I want you to decompress and let me take complete control."

"I don't think I can do that. You have no idea how badly I want to touch you."

"After the evening you've had, you need to relax and let me do all the work."

I went to raise an objection, which Cole silenced with his lips. I watched his massive frame straddle my body. Cole reached above me, placing an extra pillow behind my head. His chest was inches from my lips. I went to kiss him, inhaling his musky scent. Cole wrapped my hair around his hand, gently forcing my head back onto the pillow. He hovered over my face, stroking and kissing my eyelids. I felt my throat hum with pleasure. "Remember what I said, Layla; just lie back and enjoy."

"Where are you going?" I asked as he slid off my torso and positioned himself at the end of the bed.

"I'm going to start at the bottom and work my way up."

"I don't think I can wait that long."

"You can, and you will. I don't want to hear another word," he chided.

Cole took my foot in his hands. With his fingers on top, he kneaded the bottom, applying deep pressure with the pads of his thumbs. I wasn't a fan of feet. I ignored mine apart from the mandatory pedicure, but this felt incredible. Holding my heel in one hand, Cole pinched the back of my Achilles tendon, releasing the tension. Placing my foot against his chest, Cole made circular motions on the top of my foot, gently tugging at my toes. He bent over and licked the skin covering my ankles, sending shivers up my spine. "My God, that feels incredible!" I murmured.

"The skin is thin there, making it especially sensitive. I want you to keep your foot pressed against my chest while I rub your calves."

Cole ran his hands up and down the length of my calves, alternating the pressure with each stroke. He ended by holding my ankle as he penetrated my calve muscles with circular motions from his knuckle. Cole placed my feet back on the bed, separating them enough for him to kneel between my legs. He rubbed my thighs with prolonged strokes of deep pressure. The feeling straddled the line of simultaneous pain and pleasure. My breathing got heavier as his skilled hands manipulated my tight muscles. My legs spread farther apart as he bent his head to lick and nip my inner thighs. I braced to feel his face between my legs when he shifted his body to my waist. He grazed his fingertips back and forth across my abdomen, causing me to buck as he skimmed my ticklish navel. "I see I found one sweet spot. I suspect this is the other."

Cole pressed his thumb into my clit, massaging it in elliptical motions. He rubbed my belly with his other hand, stretching the skin on my abdomen upward, exposing my clit and making it even more sensitive. Splintering contractions consumed my insides as he continued to assault my senses. Cole removed his hand from my stomach, placing it on the side of the bed for leverage. He leaned in and blew his warm breath into my core as he massaged my clit between his thumb and index finger. I felt him encircle the area around my belly button with his tongue. I was panting as the tip of his tongue dipped down to explore the folds of flesh in my center. My back arched as I pressed my core into his mouth and my throbbing nub against his fingers.

"Cole, please," I pleaded.

"Just relax," he whispered.

"I can't. My nerve endings are firing on all cylinders."

"Take some deep breaths. I have a ways to go."

I tried following his advice, hoping to slow my speeding heart. That hope vanished as I felt him rubbing my nipples between his thumbs and index fingers. At least he released my clitoris, which was far more sensitive than my breasts, or so I thought, until I felt Cole pressing against them as he ran his tongue along my cleavage. He pinched my nipples, sending electric shocks through my chest. Alternating between twists, pinches, licks, and kisses, Cole forced me to feel every ounce of scintillating pleasure and pain. My senses were on overload as I clenched his hair and pulled his face away from my overstimulated torso. Cole responded by coating my neck in kisses. He scooped my hair and placed it on the pillow over my head, enabling him to home in on my highly sensitive nape. I felt my body trying to writhe free, but his frame resting on my abdomen prevented me from moving. I felt myself sinking into the mattress beneath his weight as Cole scaled my torso, nibbling my earlobes like a savory snack. He traced the outline of my ear with his tongue, stopping only to blow his warm breath inside. Every fiber of my being pulsed with desire as Cole drove me slowly out of my mind.

"Cole," I said, trying to relay my growing sense of urgency.

He silenced my pleas with another seductive kiss. There was no use trying to object. Cole had an agenda that he planned to follow regardless of my body's incessant demands. Teasing me with his tongue fell high on the list as he lightly ran it against my inner wrists. His mouth meandered up to my elbow, sucking on its crease before returning to my hands, where he massaged my palms and sucked on my fingers. I felt the cream seep past my opening onto my thighs. "Cole, you're making me crazy. Fuck me before I explode."

My outcry fell on deaf ears as Cole ran his finger down my cheek and over my breastbone. I would be remiss if I didn't visit one more spot," he said with a devilish gleam in his eye. He inched his way back down my torso bathing me with kisses along the way, stopping at my drenched vagina. I felt him parting my legs as he repositioned himself between them. Placing his hand beneath my buttocks, he lifted me slightly, tilting my pussy toward his mouth.

"Cole, this will send me over the edge. Don't do this. I want you inside me."

"Don't worry, baby, there's no way that won't happen."

Cole bowed his head and ran his tongue up and down the length of my outer lips. I spread my legs farther in the form of an invitation. He slipped his fingers inside me, stretching them against my clenched muscles until settling behind my clitoris. He circled my walls with his fingers until they rested against my G-spot. I wasn't convinced the G-spot existed until the pressure emanating from Cole's hand proved otherwise. Lowering his head, Cole ran his tongue up and down my slit before focusing on my clit. He placed his mouth over my tender nub barraging it with the tip of his tongue. My swollen sex throbbed, dangling on the edge of release. I was moaning uncontrollably as my body writhed against the onslaught of sensation.

Sensing I was close, Cole withdrew from me, peeling off his remaining piece of clothing. His rock-hard erection sprang up, relieved to be free from its confines. I slid my arms around his back as my legs locked around his waist. Cole guided his penis up and down my crease, stopping to rub its head against my clitoris. I shifted my lower body, trying to push him inside. My juices dripped onto Cole's cock. I felt him dip his finger in my secretion and run it down the length of my butt crack. He was pushing me to the brink. I dug into his shoulders as I tried to stave off my impending orgasm.

I was about to lose my last shred of control when Cole slid his cock inside me. I could feel his member throbbing. I expected him to bury himself to the hilt, knowing his need was as great as mine. I was wrong. Instead, he slowly inched his way into my depths, taking long lingering strokes. We were settling into a rhythm when I felt Cole's cock pulling back. The change in angle enabled the top of his head to rub against the bottom of my clitoris as Cole eased his way back in. I pumped my hips against him, urging him to thrust faster. Cole caved into the pressure. We groaned with every stroke, as he sheathed his cock deep within my tight pussy. Knowing I was about to peak, Cole placed his hands beside my shoulders for leverage. His cock mimicked a jackhammer as he pounded me with swift, staccato strokes. My orgasm ripped through my body like a tsunami. Unrestrained screams emanated from my throat. My inner walls bore down on his penis, quivering around him. Cole took several long thrusts before burying his release inside me. We were both moaning uncontrollably as our hearts raced through our heaving chests.

Cole collapsed on my torso, allowing me to feel the weight and warmth of his body. I held him in a full-body hug, keeping him pinned inside me. "I should move. I must be crushing you," Cole murmured.

"Not a chance. I love holding you like this. You barely let me touch you," I lamented.

"I owed you from last time."

"I'm hoping you don't view this as a business transaction or, even worse, settling a score?"

"How could you think that?" Cole asked, with an incredulous stare. This was as personal as it gets for me, Layla," Cole replied, lifting his head to meet my eyes. "I felt you in my core."

"I think it was another way for you to torture me," I replied with a smile.

"Hopefully, the sweetest form."

"I liked it a lot better than your usual style."

"Me too," he said, kissing my forehead. "I think I need to clean up. Can I get you anything?" Cole asked.

"No, you gave me everything I need. I feel better than I have in a long time." I lay in bed, enveloped by the residual warmth from our encounter. Cole took a quick shower. He was still speckled with blood from the fight. Now that my body was satiated, the evening's events crawled back into focus, leaving my mind unsettled. "I hope you're not planning to leave," I said.

"Not if you want me to stay."

"I would like that. I'm still feeling a little shaky."

"Let me hold you," Cole said, wrapping me in his arms.

"Tonight feels so different from the last time we were together. You know you broke two of your cardinal rules. You slept with a co-worker and had a marathon make-out session."

"I know, but that's because the days of us being co-workers are about to end."

I sat up in shock. "Why would you say that?"

"Because I'm out of a job. At the very least, Tristan will demand my resignation."

"He can't do that. You were defending me!"

"That doesn't matter. I burst into Tristan's room and attacked him. He'll claim it was unprovoked."

"I'll dispute that."

"You're not going to say one word! I mean it, Layla," Cole said gripping my shoulders. The sternness of his reply took me by surprise. He tipped my chin to meet his gaze. "You need to stay out of this. If you go public, you'll be dragged through a media circus. The press will probe into your background and make you look like a slut."

"Let them try. They won't find anything."

"That doesn't matter. The media twists things to suit their needs. You know women don't fare well in these kinds of cases. The fact that Tristan didn't rape you will make it your word against his. Witnesses saw you leave the bar hand in hand. You willingly went to his hotel room. Regardless of the outcome, your career won't survive the scandal."

"I don't care. I won't let you lose your job because of me."

"I made a choice. I knew the consequences when I broke the door down, and I'm prepared to accept them."

"Well, I'm not!" I said defiantly.

"I don't want you to worry," Cole said, pulling me against his chest. "I'm a grown man, Layla. I can handle myself."

I knew there was no point in arguing with him. I would tell Leora, the police, the media, and whoever else needed to know that Cole wasn't at fault.

"Regarding our make-out session," Cole said, changing the topic, "I've wanted to kiss you for a long time. I finally decided to surrender to my feelings. Fighting them was exhausting."

"I'm so glad you did," I said, pressing my lips against him.

"It's been a long night. I think we should get some sleep," Cole said, stroking my hair.

We crawled under the covers. I fell asleep lying on Cole's chest until I awoke two hours later with an irresistible urge to touch him. I ran my fingers through Cole's chest hair while listening to him breathe. I felt my insides stir at the feel of his skin beneath my fingertips. I slid down to his waist and cradled one of his testicles

216

in my hand while wrapping my lips around the other. My tongue slowly swirled around his circumference. I moved from one to the other before stroking the length of his shaft. I heard Cole groan as I wrapped my hand around the base of his cock, taking the head into my mouth. I bathed it with kisses, pressing my tongue where the head and shaft collided. I felt Cole's penis grow hard as I took him in my mouth, sweetly sucking his girth. It felt so good to finally taste him. The increase in his groggy moans told me he was enjoying it too. When his cock was fully engorged, I straddled his waist and enveloped him with my pussy. Cole batted his thick lashes at me as he struggled to open his eyes.

"Now, it's your turn to enjoy the ride," I whispered softly. I began slowly gyrating on his cock, feeling every inch of him seeping into my depths.

"You look so beautiful with the moonlight streaming through the window, like an X-rated angel," Cole murmured.

"I didn't know there was such a thing."

"Neither did I until now. Toss your hair behind your shoulders so I can see your breasts."

Cole was more alert now. He fixated on my erect tips as I began massaging my nipples. My eyes found his, undeterred by the dark. "You look so fucking hot." Cole's hips shifted, enabling him to drive his cock farther inside me. I pressed my palms against his torso, increasing the speed of my thrusts and grinding my pelvis against him in circular motions. A burning sensation emanated through my core as I devoured his cock with each stroke of my swollen folds. His torso became taut as his breathing grew increasingly erratic. "I'm getting close," he uttered breathlessly.

My hips went full throttle as I elevated my ass cheeks off his abdomen for the final throes. Cole gripped my waist as his release filled my channel. I gave several more commanding thrusts, cutting the night's silence with a scream of ecstasy. I lay on his chest as Cole cradled my head in his arms. "Where did that come from?" he asked. "I would've thought you were exhausted."

"I had this residual need to touch and taste you. Are you complaining?" I asked lightly.

"God, no. I wish I could wake up like that every day."

"That could be arranged," I whispered in a seductive tone. Cole wrapped his hands around mine. I pulled them toward me and kissed his bruised knuckles.

"Your hands are so swollen. They must hurt."

"Pain is the last thing I'm feeling right now."

"Can I get you some ice?"

"No. I just want to blanket your body with mine. I don't want to feel any boundaries between us." We fell asleep spooning. I knew tomorrow would be a rough day, but at this moment, everything seemed right with the world.

CHAPTER 20

Cole was sitting beside me on the bed when I awoke the following morning. "What time is it?" I asked.

"It's early. Go back to sleep," he whispered.

"Come back to bed and snuggle."

"I'd love to, but I need to go home and get some clothes before heading to the office. I should talk to Leora before the shit hits the fan."

"If you give me a few minutes, I'll come with you."

"This is something I need to do on my own. Besides, you must be exhausted. Get some rest."

"How are your hands?"

"They're swollen. I'll throw some ice on my knuckles when I get home."

"I'm sorry for this mess, Cole."

"It's not your fault, Newhouse."

"Everything will work out. I'll fix it. I promise."

"You just take care of yourself." Cole pulled the blanket over my shoulders. He leaned over and kissed me on the cheek.

"Goodbye, Newhouse," he said, dusting his fingertips along my face. There was a strange tone to his voice. I didn't recognize it until later that morning when I got to the station. It was the sound of him leaving me for good.

Cole was busy boxing up his office when Leora knocked on the door. "Come in, Leora. You were next on my list."

"I see you're packing," she replied.

"I wish I didn't have to."

"That makes two of us. I got the call from Tristan's attorney this morning. Tristan is still in the hospital. He has a broken nose, jaw, eye socket, cheekbones, and several missing teeth. Tristan will require major reconstructive surgery. He'll probably miss the remainder of the season. What did he do this time? Did he hurt Ashley again?"

"I'd prefer not to talk about it, but I promise you he deserved a beating."

"I wish there were something I could do for you, Cole, but my hands are tied."

"I understand. I'm sorry for causing you such grief. You've always stood by me, Leora. You gave me a chance when other stations wouldn't touch me."

"Do you have any idea what you're going to do?"

"The only thing I've figured out is I'm leaving Miami. It's time for a fresh start."

"Where will you go?"

"I'm not sure yet, but I'll let you know when I'm settled."

"I'd be happy to give you a reference if you need one."

"I appreciate that."

"Did you tell Layla you're leaving?"

"No, and I want you to swear that you won't share my where-abouts. It's better for Layla if she has nothing to do with me."

"You really care about her, don't you?"

Cole sighed. "I'm not sure how that happened, but I do."

"Take care of yourself, Cole," Leora said, hugging him. "I'll talk to you soon."

I listened to the news on my way to work. There was nothing about the fight. I took that as a sign that Tristan didn't want to risk going to the cops. I went to Cole's office to see if he had heard anything. My stomach plummeted when I saw that his desk had been cleared out. I raced down the hall to see Leora.

"She's at a meeting with corporate. She won't be back for at least another hour," Ava said.

"Tell her I need to see her as soon as she gets in. It's urgent! Ava, did you see Cole today?"

"I did, and I got the impression he's not coming back."

"Did they fire him?"

"I don't know. Nobody's said anything."

I raced into my office and called Cole. He didn't pick up. I texted him and asked him to contact me. He ignored my text. Fifteen minutes later, I texted him again, pleading with him to call me back. He refused, so I tried calling him but got no response. I didn't wait for Leora to take a seat before barging into her office. "You can't fire Cole. It wasn't his fault. He was protecting me."

"Slow down, Layla. Take a deep breath and start at the beginning."

"Did you fire Cole?"

"Not officially, but our attorney is drawing up the paperwork."

"You can't do that. This is all my fault."

"What are you talking about?"

"Last night after the game, a bunch of us went out for drinks. Tristan showed up at the bar. We started talking. He invited me back to his hotel room, and I went. Cole warned me not to go. He said Tristan was dangerous, but I didn't believe him. Tristan's attitude changed when we got back to his place. He became more aggressive, and I was turned off. I told him I was leaving, but he refused to let me go. He slapped me and pinned me to the floor. I started to scream. That's when Cole broke the door down. He was waiting outside in the hallway, listening. He pulled Tristan off me and began beating him with his fists. I called for help, and a couple of Tristan's teammates intervened. Cole grabbed me, and we fled to my place. If Cole hadn't shown up, Tristan would have raped me."

"My God, Layla! Are you okay?"

"I'm fine, thanks to Cole."

"At least that explains his actions. I couldn't imagine what provoked such brutality."

"So, you see, you can't fire him. I'll be happy to talk to the police and corporate. Cole didn't want me to say anything. He fears the situation will backfire on me, but I don't care. His reputation shouldn't be tarnished for coming to my rescue."

"I'm afraid there's nothing we can do, Layla. I received a call from Tristan's attorney this morning. Tristan will need several reconstructive surgeries."

"Will he be able to play again?"

"The doctor thinks so, but at the minimum, he will miss the rest of the season."

"At least he didn't lose his career, like Cole. Now he's trying to take another position away from him. I can't let him do that. I'll charge him with attempted rape."

"Layla, if we say anything to damage Tristan's reputation, he will have Cole arrested for assault and attempted murder. Between the public fight they had last time and the extent of Tristan's injuries, Cole would go to jail. I don't see any way around it."

"So, Tristan gets to walk away unscathed again," I replied incredulously.

"I'm afraid so. Even if you want to press charges, Layla, you have no proof that he tried to rape you. He's a famous athlete. Women hit on him all the time. It would be a tough case."

"Cole heard him hit me. He saw my torn clothing and bruised face."

"Cole isn't going to be seen as a credible witness. On the flip side, several guys from the Thunder will testify that Cole was enraged, and you left the bar willingly with Tristan. I hate to say it, Layla, but Cole is right. You're not going to come out on top of this one. Why do you think Ashley didn't go after Tristan?"

"You know about Ashley?"

"I wouldn't hire Cole unless he told me what happened. Nobody wanted to employ him after that violent public display. Tristan would have lost his job if he wasn't one of the Thunders star players."

"It's just so unfair," I lamented as tears spilled down my cheeks.

"I know it is, but Cole will be okay. Tristan agreed not to press charges if Cole loses his job, pays an undisclosed settlement, and doesn't publicly discuss the fight."

I felt sick. It was like someone repeatedly kicked me in the gut. "I need to see, Cole."

"You can leave after you do that insider interview with Andre Perrault."

"That's not important."

"I disagree. You're finally starting to get the respect you deserve, Layla. Don't undermine your hard work."

"Fine. I'll do the interview, but then I'm going to see Cole. He hasn't returned my messages."

I wrapped things up at the studio and sped to Cole's penthouse, where his doorman greeted me. "Hi, Milo, I'm here to see Cole."

"I'm sorry, Ms. MacKenzie, Mr. Pasternak is gone."

"What time will he be back?"

"I'm afraid he's not coming back."

"How can that be? I just saw Cole a few hours ago."

"He packed a bag and said his sister would send the rest of his things. One of the rookies from the Predators will be leasing the penthouse starting next month."

"Did he say where he was going?"

"Even if he did, I wouldn't be at liberty to share that information."

"I understand. How long ago did he leave?"

"A few hours ago. Mr. Pasternak seemed to be in quite a hurry."

"Thanks, Milo. If he contacts you, please let him know I came by."

I sat in my car and tried calling Cole again, to no avail. I texted him not to leave but got no response. This couldn't be happening, not after the way we bonded last night. I called Ashley. She wasn't accepting my call either. I drove to her condo and camped outside her door. There was no way I was leaving until I saw her. Luckily, she arrived within the hour.

"I can't help you, Layla," Ashley blurted out defensively before I could say anything.

"I'm assuming Cole told you about the fight," I replied.

Ashley nodded. "I'm so sorry for both of you. None of this would've happened if I hadn't fallen for that monster."

"It isn't your fault, Ashley. I can see how you were taken in by him."

"Unfortunately, my brother continues to pay the price for Tristan's bad behavior. I should have gone after him when I had the chance."

"I know you're going to be sending Cole his things. Please tell me where he's going."

"I can't. Cole made me swear not to."

"I need to see him, Ashley. Things can't end like this, especially after what he did for me."

"He doesn't want you following him, Layla. In his own way, he's protecting you."

"That's not fair. Cole should at least speak to me. I can't even get him to return my calls."

"He has a lot on his mind right now. I agree he should have told you he was leaving, but he thought you would try to stop him if you knew. Cole wants you to move on."

"Let him tell me that," I pleaded.

"I'll encourage him to call you, but I wouldn't get my hopes up. If it's any consolation, I know how you feel. I miss him already."

"At least you weren't the reason he left." I walked away from Ashley feeling despondent. The best thing in my life was slipping through my fingers, and I couldn't seem to stop it.

The next few days were a blur. I felt like I was sleepwalking through my life. Leora arranged a meeting for me with the station's attorney. He, too, discouraged me from pressing charges against Tristan. I couldn't fathom how the victim would still be on trial in this day and age. It was maddening.

Morgan was filling in for Cole while Leora searched for his replacement. I called and texted Cole every day, but he never responded. I registered with several background check websites to see if he recorded a change of address, but nothing came up. Thoughts of Cole consumed my every waking moment. Where was he living? Was he okay? Did he think of me? I needed answers. The way he cut me off was driving me insane. I had to find a way to make him reach out.

Word of the fight escaped the local news but not the sports world. Tristan O'Shaughnessy was out for the remainder of the season, which was big news in the NHL. Rumors were flying that the injuries resulted from an ongoing feud between Tristan and Cole, but neither party would confirm. Cole resigning his position at Southern Sports lent credence to the gossip. I texted Cole and told him I couldn't stay silent any longer, and I was going to call a press conference. I wasn't lying. The ugly truth had burned a hole in my gut since he left. My conscience couldn't negotiate Cole ruining his career for me. My text generated an immediate response.

You can't do that, Layla. I signed a gag order forbidding me to discuss the circumstances of that night.

You signed it. It has no bearing on me, I texted back.

Inadvertently, it does. You need to let this go, Layla, for both our sakes. I wouldn't fare well in jail, and that's where I would be headed. I reached a resolution with Tristan. Now you need to move on.

I can't move on until I know you're okay. Where are you? What are you doing?

He didn't respond.

Cole, I can't have closure without answers.

I'm fine, Layla. Don't waste time worrying about me.

How could you leave without saying goodbye?

It felt like an eternity before Cole typed his reply. "I did. You just didn't realize it." My mind flashed back to his voice the morning Cole left. He knew he was going then.

Could we at least talk?

Goodbye, Newhouse. Take care of yourself, was his last and final text. Three weeks later, I headed for an away game with the team when Brady Caulfield said, "Hey Layla, isn't it great news about Cole getting the job with the Buffalo Blaze?"

"Cole is working for the Blaze?" I said, trying to sound nonchalant.

"I figured you knew."

"No, we haven't spoken since he left. What is Cole doing?"

"He's the assistant coach. It's rumored the head coach is getting ready to retire at the end of the season, and he's considering Cole for his replacement."

"I'm assuming the Blaze are a college team."

Brady nodded. "They are the hockey team for Buffalo University."

"I'm happy for Cole. I know he wanted to get into coaching."

"Yeah, the poor guy has had a couple of rough breaks. I hope this works out for him."

"I'm sure it will. Cole has great coaching skills."

The minute I had time alone in my hotel room, I Googled the Buffalo Blaze. I found the article announcing Cole's recent addition as an assistant coach. The report said that Cole made the transition because he was passionate about coaching and couldn't think of a better place to embark on a career than the area where he grew up. The reporter speculated that the head coach was retiring at the season's end, and Cole was being groomed for his position. It ended by saying the Buffalo organization hoped Cole's leadership would turn the tide in the team's struggle to secure a wild card in the playoffs.

I tossed and turned into the wee hours thinking of Cole. I hadn't slept well since the night I spent with his body softly cradled around mine. I had hoped by now the aching need to touch him would have subsided, but it grew more agonizing by the day. No matter how hard I tried or how busy I stayed, I couldn't temper my desire for Cole. Thoughts of him bombarded my every moment. Memories of his scent, the way he tasted, his seductive kiss, and those blistering eyes consumed my every breath. The ache to feel him filling me, stretching me, making me beg for more, swallowed me. My body longed to be anchored beneath his, riding each other until we reached a bone-shattering release. The kind of explosion that came from my core and didn't stop until it rocked every ounce of my being, leaving me spent and blissfully content.

I had never been with someone that had this kind of effect on me. I was clearly obsessed. I couldn't imagine ever being attracted to another man like I was to Cole. What if I never met someone who made me feel the way he did? I lay in bed clutching the pillow each night, hoping it would make it feel less empty. Without Cole, a piece of me was missing. My feelings transcended lust. I wanted to share everything with him. I longed to care for him, hold him. I had never been in love. Cole and I weren't even dating. Until recently, we were barely civil to each other. Could I be in love after such a short time? My mind said no, but my shattered heart indicated otherwise. I thought back to the devastation Cole described when things ended with Haley. Now I understood what he was going through. If only love could break your heart, I was hopelessly in love. Unfortunately, Cole didn't return my feelings. He couldn't love me and cut me off the way he did. Unless I could find a way to make him care and want me as much as I wanted him, I was facing a future laden with despair.

It took me several days of inner turmoil, followed by more sleepless nights, before I went to see Leora. She had hired Cole's replacement. He was a former goalie for the Jersey Demons.

"Hi, Layla; how are things going with Kevin?"

"They're going well. Kevin is easy to work with, unlike his predecessor. We're learning a lot from each other."

"I appreciate you bringing him up to speed."

"Leora, I hope you know I'm eternally grateful to you for the opportunity you've given me here at Southern Sports."

"Why do I hear a 'but' coming?" Leora replied hesitantly.

"I'm thinking of going back home. Miami isn't where I belong."

"I can't say I'm surprised. You're going after Cole."

"Am I being stupid? You can tell me woman to woman."

"You're taking a big risk. I recommend going for a quick visit before you do anything drastic. Talk to Cole. Find out what he's feeling. Get answers to your questions. Then decide if it's worth uprooting your life."

"If Cole thinks staying in Miami is an option, he'll send me away. Moving to Buffalo is my only shot at convincing him to give us a chance. You know him, Leora. Am I crazy to think he cares for me?"

"His actions point to that but getting him to admit it is another story. As your friend, I think you should follow your heart, Layla. As your boss, I would like to tell you that your job will be waiting if things don't work out, but I can't make that promise."

"I understand."

"Will you at least stay long enough for me to hire your replacement? I still have the list of candidates for Cole's position, so it shouldn't take long."

"Of course I will. Do you have any connections in Buffalo?"

"I think your former supervisor will be a better resource in that regard, but I'll be happy to make some inquiries. It goes without saying that I'll give you a wonderful recommendation."

Two weeks later, I received a call from the local Buffalo news station. They had an opening in their research department. The position was a step-down, but I was confident that the interview was a formality. The likelihood of secure employment swayed my decision. I gave my notice and prepared to leave. If things didn't work out with Cole, I could always move back to Syracuse and be by my mother and Skylar. I never felt comfortable in Miami. I needed the change of seasons and oversized sweaters, not string bikinis and cosmetic surgery. Even if this job didn't work out, I was sure I'd land on my feet. My experience at Southern Sports was a valuable addition to my resume. It was early enough in my career to recover if I was making a mistake. What I couldn't live with was the regret I'd feel if I didn't try to make things work with Cole. I knew it could be too much to hope for, especially since he refused to speak to me. However, I couldn't shake the feeling there was something between us. He could deny it, but I couldn't rest until I knew for sure.

I had a farewell drink with Ashley before I left town. "Ashley, please give me Cole's address," I implored. "I don't want to humiliate myself by showing up at the university until I run into him."

Ashley shifted uncomfortably in her seat. "I can't break my promise to Cole, Layla. I'm sorry."

"Do you think he'll agree to see me?"

"All I can say is he asks about you every time we talk."

"That's encouraging."

"I wouldn't get my hopes up. My brother is a hard nut to crack. He'll be mad that you resigned. That's the last thing he wanted."

"He's not the only one entitled to make decisions. It's my life," I snapped. "You know we could be good together Ashley," I said, regaining my composure.

"I agree, but I'm not the one you need to convince. You're taking a huge risk, my friend. I hope you're not disappointed."

I hugged Ashley and made my final round of goodbyes to the team and Southern Sports staff. I was disappointed that Ashley wouldn't divulge Cole's whereabouts. I knew she wanted us to be together. What would I have done if I were in her shoes? At the very least, I would tell my brother to put on his big boy pants and do the right thing. I should have known that's exactly what Ashley did.

"Cole, pick up. I need to talk to you."

"What's up? Ash."

"I just saw Layla. She resigned from her position at Southern Sports. She's interviewing with the local news station in Buffalo."

"Why the hell did she do that? How could she be so stupid? This is what I was trying to prevent. Can't you talk her out of it?"

"I wouldn't try. It's what she wants. Layla's been miserable since you left. She'll be arriving in Buffalo tonight on the ten-thirty flight. I know you have feelings for her. Stop being a coward and face her. You owe Layla that."

"I'm anything but a coward," Cole snapped, defensively. "I gave up my job so she could keep hers. I left town to save her reputation. She would have gone to the press if I had stayed. They would have destroyed her."

"Those sound like the actions of a man who cares."

"I never said I didn't."

"She needs to hear that, Cole. In your twisted logic, I know you think you're protecting her, but you're wrong. Stop being an idiot and meet her. You need to talk, even if you guys can't work it out.

The way you left things is tormenting her. If you don't do it for her, do it for me. Better yet, do it for yourself. Don't let your chance at love walk away. I love you, Cole. I just want my brother and my friend to be happy."

"I love you too, Ash. Thanks for the call."

CHAPTER 21

As the plane touched down on the runway, panic washed over me. I must be crazy to give up everything for a man, especially one who left me. My stomach mimicked the first time I gave a speech in junior high. I was so terrified that I forgot what I was supposed to say. The kids laughed as I stuttered and stammered my way to the end. I was mortified for days. Was I opening myself up for that kind of humiliation again? Maybe I should have thought this through before abandoning my life in Miami. It was too late for regrets. I had to trust my female intuition and hope for the best.

I was immediately struck by Cole's piercing blue eyes and athletic frame when I stepped into the baggage area. "What are you doing here?" I asked as my heart ricocheted from head to toe.

"My sister told me you were coming. She didn't want you fending for yourself at this time of night. There can be some unsavory characters hanging around. Let me take your bag." Cole grabbed my carry-on without giving me a hug. I was trying to read his body language, but all I could get were mixed signals.

"Are you hungry?" Cole asked. "There's an all-night diner not far from the airport. We can grab a bite after collecting the rest of your luggage."

"That would be great. I'd love a cup of coffee."

We barely spoke on the ride to the restaurant. Once we were seated, I congratulated Cole on his new position. He told me how happy he was to be coaching. Cole asked for my feedback on his replacement. I was pleased to hear that he still watched the broadcasts. Cole gave me an update on Shane. The new treatment appeared to be shrinking his cancer. We talked about Cole's plans for the Blaze and the Predators' chances for the Stanley Cup. It was as if we were afraid to broach any topic of substance.

"It's getting late. Where are you staying?" Cole asked.

"I booked a room at a Marriott extended stay. I'll start looking for an apartment tomorrow."

"When is your interview?"

"In two days."

"Why don't you come back to my place? I'm leasing another penthouse. I'm happy to say money goes further in Buffalo, considering I just took another salary cut."

"Are you sure you wouldn't mind?" I asked, surprised by his invitation.

"I have plenty of room, and I'm uncomfortable leaving you alone in a hotel this late at night."

"Okay, I'd prefer to sort things out tomorrow when I'm rested." I took Cole's offer as a positive sign, especially when he placed my luggage in his room.

"I didn't realize your guest bedroom isn't set up yet."

"I'm afraid I haven't had time to go furniture shopping. I'll sleep on the couch."

"I don't want to put you out," I said, disappointed by his reply.

"I offered. Can I get you a cup of coffee or a drink?"

"I'll have another cup of coffee." He poured himself a bourbon, handed me my coffee, and we sat on the couch sipping our drinks. Finally, Cole broke the silence.

"Why are you here, Layla?" he asked pointedly. My stomach muscles tightened into a knot. I still couldn't gauge if he was happy to see me. Was this the right time to go out on a limb?

"You know I was never a fan of Miami. It didn't feel like home," I replied.

"So, you're in Buffalo because you're homesick?" Cole asked, in disbelief.

"I missed the snow."

"They get plenty of snow in Syracuse, where your mother and best friend reside." As usual, Cole wasn't making this easy on me. I decided it was better to know sooner rather than later where I stood. I took a deep breath. There was no point postponing the inevitable.

"The truth is, I think I'm falling in love with you," I replied, unable to face him. Silence fell over the room as Cole's eyes diverted between mine and the floor. It felt like an eternity before he replied.

"I'm sorry to hear that," he said, taking a deep breath.

His words shattered my heart into a million pieces, like shards of glass that could never be pieced together. How could I have put myself in this position? Now I had no job, no place to live, and no feelings of self-worth. Tears welled up in my eyes. I tried to fight them back as Cole lifted my chin to meet his gaze.

"I'm sorry to hear that because I know I'm in love with you." It took a few seconds for the words to sink in, flooding my veins with anger and adrenaline.

"You're incorrigible. I loathe you," I said, pummeling him relentlessly with my fists.

"So, you've told me multiple times." He laughed.

"How could you torture me like that? Do you know how hard it was for me to say those words?"

"I do, but that doesn't mean messing with you is not still one of my greatest pleasures."

"That was an awful thing to do," I said, continuing to hit him.

"You're right. My bad. Forgive me. Now you better knock it off before I report you for domestic abuse," Cole said with a smile. He grabbed my hands and pinned me to the couch. "I think we just had our first fight as a couple. We had better kiss and make-up," Cole said, lowering his face to mine. I parted my lips. Our tongues tangled as Cole claimed my mouth, probing deeper with each kiss. Longing coursed through every inch of my being as I unbuckled his belt. "Are you sure you're not too tired?"

"I hope you're joking," I quipped.

My need was overwhelming as Cole scooped me up and carried me into the bedroom. We stripped off our clothes in record time. My legs spread wide as I admired his engorged cock. I clawed at his back and used my calves to drive his body into mine. Cole let out a sigh of relief. "I dreamed of doing this from the moment I left. I missed you, Newhouse."

"I missed you too, Cole. Now fuck me like I'm yours," I said, pulling his mouth against mine. We took turns thrusting against each other as we rolled around the king-sized bed. I fought off the urge to come within seconds of feeling his cock consume my insides. He must have been struggling with the same issue because he suddenly withdrew.

"What are you doing?"

"Making it last," he replied, licking and nibbling my neck while his hands played with my nipples. Pleasure engulfed my body as I buried my hands in his hair, kissing and stroking his head. Cole sat back on my waist, and my hands reached for his cock.

"He looks angry," I said, referring to his throbbing member.

"Not angry, just demanding," Cole said, flipping me onto my belly. He put his hands on my hips, pulling me onto my knees. I was on all fours as Cole entered me from behind. "Go down on your elbows," he commanded. "The shift will enable me to go deeper."

Broken groans and pants emanated from my mouth as Cole propelled his cock up the length of my pussy. If his cock burrowed any deeper, I would feel it in my throat. He released one of my hips as I thrust back against him. Cole placed his fingers against my clit, firmly rubbing back and forth. My insides were so saturated that my juices spilled onto his hand. Using my secretions, Cole ran his moist finger between my buttocks and around my anus. I lurched in reaction to the new yet highly erotic sensation.

"Cole, I can't hold on any longer."

"That makes two of us." He gasped, grinding his pelvis against my buttocks. I felt his cock shudder as his release coated my insides. I emitted a cry from my gut as my body bucked beneath Cole's staggering thrusts. My limbs shook like a five on the Richter scale as my orgasm engulfed me.

We collapsed onto the bed where our exhausted bodies remained intertwined. I buried my head in the nook of Cole's neck as I tried to catch my breath. "I have a confession to make," I mumbled, unevenly. "I've never come that hard in my life. My skin has goosebumps."

"That's what I was aiming for," Cole replied, stroking my back. "I tried to get deep enough to stroke your A-spot."

"Where and what is my A-spot?" I asked, in a perplexed tone.

"It's another erogenous zone on the front of your vaginal wall about two to three inches past your G-Spot. It's the female equivalent of the prostate."

"I never heard of it."

"Sometimes it's referred to as the deep spot because of its location. It's reached during deep vaginal penetration with a cock or sex toy. A-spot orgasms are usually more intense and longer lasting than typical orgasms, but they're not always easy to achieve."

"I'm fairly sure, that's what I just experienced. How do you know about this, and I don't?"

"I do my research," he said, pulling me against him.

"Well, you graduated at the top of your class," I said admiringly.

"Thank you. I plan to become an expert when it comes to pleasing you. There are so many experiences I want us to share."

"I'm already happier than you could ever know."

"I have a pretty good idea," Cole replied, dusting my neck with his lips.

We moved into a spooning position as sleep claimed our satiated bodies. In the morning, I awoke to Cole's tongue tantalizing my ear. He shifted his hand under my buttocks, lifting my upper thigh to rest on my lower leg. Cole's hand found my center, petting the outside of my pussy before sliding his fingers inside me. I pressed against his rotations as moisture flooded my channel.

"I'm normally not horny in the morning," I grumbled.

"Your body disagrees."

"You've persuaded it to see another point of view." I felt Cole's penis ease into me, sliding softly back and forth against my opening. "I've never had sex lying on my side," I murmured.

"The nice thing about this position is it prevents me from going too deep or too fast, prolonging our release."

"That's normally not my preference, but I can feel the merits of this approach."

Cole withdrew his cock from my pussy. Wrapping his hand around his erection, he rubbed his swollen head against my clitoris. I panted uncontrollably as he swirled his crown against me before returning to my core. I grabbed his hand and pressed it between my legs.

"Are you ready for me to go a little deeper?"

"Always," I uttered, my voice cracking in anticipation.

"That's my girl," Cole responded as he elongated his thrust.

I placed my hand over his, grinding it into my pussy. The floodgates burst. Cole withdrew his cock, sliding it snugly between my glutes. He slid his cock back and forth, penetrating my anus with his slippery thumb. I lurched forward as I felt Cole's orgasm sputter onto my lower back.

"Good morning," Cole whispered as he encircled me in a full-body hug.

"That was some wake-up call," I replied with a grin.

"Can I make you breakfast?"

"If you cook the way you make love, I'm never touching the stove again."

Cole laughed. "It's hard to screw up bacon and eggs."

"After breakfast, I'd like to shower, and then I should probably check into my hotel."

"Why would you do that?" Cole asked, getting dressed. I gave him a quizzical look. "Layla, I want you to stay."

"You mean for the day?"

"No, I mean permanently."

I took a moment to weigh the gravity of his words. "Are you asking me to move in with you?" I asked, not sure if I was dreaming.

"Did you enjoy last night and this morning as much as I did?"

"You know the answer to that."

"Then stay. I have plenty of room. We wouldn't have to run back and forth trying to see each other. I want to come home to you at night and wake up with you in the morning." My mind was racing. I never bargained for this conversation. "Tell me what you're thinking," Cole implored.

"This is all happening so fast, Cole. I'm not sure it's a good idea."

"What are your concerns?"

"Do you want the truth?"

"Always."

"I was thinking about how much more experience you've had sexually compared to me. You've been with numerous women where I've only had a handful of lovers."

"That doesn't matter," he replied, dismissing my reply.

"It does when you're used to having a different lover every night. If we embark on a relationship, I need it to be exclusive. I'm not willing to share you."

"I wouldn't expect you to. I'm thirty years old. I've spent years avoiding commitment. Now I want one with you, only you."

"You're going to get bored with me."

"You're being silly."

"Not in my mind. I don't think man whores turn into monks overnight."

"They can with the right motivation."

We had a bit of a Mexican standoff as we plotted our next move. Cole was the first to break the silence.

"Come here," he whispered. Cole pulled me onto his lap, affixing his beautiful blue eyes to mine. "You have nothing to worry about. If you're willing to commit to me, my days of being a player are over."

"I want that more than anything."

"Then live with me. Let's find out if we've got what it takes for the long haul." Cole saw the doubt in my eyes. "I swear I can be monogamous, Newhouse. It would be hard not to be with you living here."

"Where there's a will, there's a way, especially with you being on the road."

"Let me prove it to you."

"How many women have you slept with since you've been in Buffalo, Cole?"

"That's not fair," he protested. "I never dreamed we would be together again. If it's any consolation, casual sex left me feeling empty after being with you. Listen Layla, I can't change what I did in the past. I can only pledge to be the man you need moving forward. Why waste time and money getting an apartment when I want you to be with me?"

"I wasn't sure you would agree to see me, let alone ask me to live with you. It's a bit overwhelming."

"You're not the only one who's scared, Newhouse. Caring puts me in a vulnerable position where I swore I'd never be again. However, a wise woman once told me, 'There's no reward without risk.' Were those just words, or did you mean what you said? This took me by surprise too. I didn't foresee asking you to move in with me, but now that we're together, it feels so right."

"Living with me won't be easy, Cole, especially from the stand-point of a carefree bachelor."

"I consider myself forewarned."

I paused for a moment, trying to collect my thoughts. My head was saying slow down while my heart was doing somersaults. This was the reason I came to Buffalo. I'd be foolish to reject Cole's offer. "If you're sure this is what you really want, Cole, I'd be willing to give it a try."

Cole picked me up and spun me around. "It is," he replied, beaming. "Now that our living situation is settled, I think we should seal the deal in bed." I rose from Cole's lap and held out my hand. He cocked his head to gaze at me and placed his hand in mine. "Layla Mackenzie, you are one insatiable woman." We laughed and walked into the bedroom. "Hold your arms over your head," Cole instructed, slipping off my night shirt. "I want you to lie on your stomach," he murmured, rubbing my shoulders.

"I hope you don't plan to be this domineering in other aspects of our relationship. I'll give you some leeway regarding sex, but don't forget who the boss is ."

"I'm assuming that's you," Cole replied in amusement.

"That's correct," I replied, sprawling across the mattress.

"This will be a partnership between equals," Cole countered.

"That's a perfect response. I wouldn't want to date a pushover."

"I know," he said in an annoyingly confident tone. "However, even the boss needs to learn how to submit." Cole opened the top drawer of his nightstand and pulled out a pair of handcuffs. "If I remember, these intrigued you the last time you were in my bedroom."

I swallowed hard. "I'm not sure we're at that stage in our relationship."

"Do you want to please me, Layla?"

"You know I do."

"Do you trust me?"

"Not completely."

"Fair enough. Consider this the first step in building trust. Put your hands behind your back." Cole snapped the handcuffs around my wrists. A pang of exhilaration shot through me. Then he reached into his bottom drawer and pulled out a black rope. "This is bondage rope. It's softer and more pliable than regular rope. It's designed to be easy to manipulate without being hard on your skin."

Cole went to the bottom of the bed and tied my ankles together. My muscles grew taut with nervous anticipation. I felt my lower legs being elevated off the mattress as Cole tugged on the rope. My knees began to bend, bringing my feet closer to where my hands were secured on my lower back. It didn't take long to decipher that Cole was fastening my ankles to my hands. My chest and legs were raised from the tension of my constraints. Cole kneeled beside the bed, making his face level with mine.

"How are you feeling?"

"Exposed, powerless, and strangely turned on. It's freaky not having control over my body."

"Surrendering control can be liberating."

"Not to a control freak."

"Maybe not initially. Give it time."

Cole returned to the nightstand and retrieved an implement that resembled a riding crop. He climbed back onto the mattress and began massaging my neck and shoulders. I groaned with pleasure beneath his masterful hands. As I felt my body melting into the bed, Cole picked up the flogger and ran it over my back, occasionally stopping to deliver a slap on my buttocks. I yelped at the sting, which turned into tingling when Cole soothed the sore spots with his kiss. He used his hands, lips, and the flogger to send a variety of sensations surging through my skin. The unpredictability of his actions kept me on pins and needles as I tried to anticipate his next move.

"The flapper has a small head, which delivers a concentrated blow. That's why I'm only using it on your buttocks. My hand covers a larger surface area, spreading the impact. When you spank someone, it is a good rule of thumb to start slow and increase the intensity as the body adjusts." Cole's hand struck my cheeks as he finished his sentence. He followed the contact with tender kisses and a fingertip massage. Cole raised his hand higher for the next blow, generating an outcry from the recesses of my throat.

"Are you okay?" he asked. I gave him an affirmative nod. "Let's switch it up," he said, delivering several small staccato blows to my cheeks. Each strike incorporated a slightly higher level of intensity. I felt my buttocks turning red, but that wasn't the only place the blood flowed. Cole finished with several firmly executed smacks.

"I wasn't even a bad girl," I objected.

"That's why I didn't punish you. If I had incorporated more

force or used the flapper on more delicate parts of your body, you would have had a different sensation."

I was not sure whether it was the novelty of the experience tantalizing my body or the combination of pleasure and pain, but I wanted more. "Show me," I replied as my breath became uneven.

Cole slid back on the bed to meet my eyes. "Are you sure? I thought we would take this nice and slow."

"I'll let you know if it's too much."

Cole rose from the bed, hovering over my bound body. He took the flapper and delivered several slaps to the bottoms of my feet before dragging it up and down my legs. The flapper landed more strikes on my inner thighs, which Cole coated with kisses. He turned me onto my back. I braced myself as I felt the tip of the leather head graze the length of my labia, settling against my swollen clitoris. To my surprise, Cole set the flapper down and sank his face between my legs. He ran his tongue up and down my slippery slit as his fingers orbited my clit. My restraints began to frustrate me as my limbs writhed against them. "Cole, untie me. I want to touch you."

"As the submissive, I'm afraid your wants are immaterial. Fortunately for you, my desire is to make you come." Cole moved his fingers inside me as he began sucking my clitoris. He used the tip of his tongue to apply pressure to my trigger point, causing me to crest in record time. My muscles strained against the rope as convulsions tore through my body.

"Cole, release me now so I can please you."

"No worries, you're about to."

Cole grasped the bondage rope and yanked me onto my knees. He picked up the flapper and positioned himself, so we faced each other. Kneeling between my spread legs, Cole pushed his cock inside me. I sighed as he raised the flapper, delivering a blow to each nipple. He massaged my aching buds with one hand, pulling my face close to his. Cole simultaneously invaded me with his cock and his tongue. It only took a few strokes to trigger his climax. Upon withdrawing, Cole untethered me from my restraints. We lay on the bed, holding each other.

"This is what I missed being bound," I said, caressing his face.

"What's that?"

"The freedom to touch you."

"Aside from that minor sacrifice, I think you're a fan."

"Let's say I'd be willing to try it again," I replied with a devious grin.

"I love a woman with a sense of adventure," Cole said, kissing my nose.

We were playfully rolling around the bed when his phone rang. "Do you have to get that?" I whined.

"It's for you," Cole replied, handing me the phone.

"Me?" I replied, thoroughly confused. "Hello, who's this?"

"Layla?"

"Ashley?"

"Are you with my brother?"

"I am. He talked me into staying last night."

Ashley's delighted squeal filled the room. "I'm so happy for you both!"

Cole took the phone from my hand. "Since Layla said she only thinks she might be in love with me, I told her to live here until she figures it out. Are you happy now, sis?"

"I'm over the moon," exclaimed Ashley.

"Good. Now get off my back," Cole replied affectionately.

"Tell Layla I'll call her later. I'm very proud of you, big brother."

"Thanks, Ash. We're thrilled. I love you. Bye." Cole hung up the phone and turned to me. "As much as I would love to stay in bed and devour you all day, I think the time has come for us to shower and venture out. When is your car arriving?"

"Tomorrow."

"Arrange to have it delivered here. In the meantime, I'll show you around, and you can drop me at practice and meet the team."

That night, I made dinner, and we spent the night making love. My heart was bursting with joy as I whispered in Cole's ear, "You know I love you, don't you?"

"There's no doubt in my mind," he replied, half asleep. I picked up a pillow and smacked him over the head.

242

"What was that for?" Cole asked, disoriented.

"There's the arrogant egomaniac that makes my blood boil," I said, hovering over him.

Cole pulled me into his arms and kissed my forehead. "I know you didn't move to Buffalo because you missed the snow and wanted to move down the corporate ladder. Only love or hate would motivate such a poor decision."

I smacked him with a second pillow. "Now you're insulting my intelligence."

"No, I'm saying that women are ruled by their hearts, not their heads."

"So, you would have never reached out to me if I didn't make the first move?"

Cole gave me an affirmative nod. "I wouldn't out of love for you. I didn't want you to make a mistake and resent me for it."

"Then don't give me a reason to."

"If I promise not to, will you let me get some sleep?"

"I'll consider it if you answer a question for me." Cole sighed and propped his head on his elbow in resignation.

"When did you know you were in love with me?"

Cole's face grew pensive. "That's a tricky question. I developed respect for you after our competition on the ice. Your physical and mental toughness impressed me. I always admired how you stood your ground and didn't take my crap, no matter how I tried to bait you. However, it was after the fundraiser that my feelings started to shift. Watching you with the kids and experiencing all you did for Shane touched my heart. I think I was falling in love with you then, but the realization didn't hit me until you were threatened. I told myself I reacted on adrenaline, but I was driven by the need to keep you safe. Any ambiguity regarding my feelings became clear when we made love later that night. The way we connected told me everything I needed to know."

I gave him a tender kiss, gently teasing his tongue with mine. It was the first of many wonderful nights to come.

CHAPTER 22

Things seemed to be falling into place. I was hired at the local network in Buffalo. Cole transitioned from assistant to head coach when his boss retired at the end of the season. The Blaze made it to the playoffs but lost during the first round. The Predators finished the year losing in the Stanley Cup finals. Cole flew to Miami to watch the final round with Shane who was in remission. After hockey season ended we went to Paris for a week, where we took turns tying each other to the bed. Coaching proved to be the next best thing to playing for Cole. Over the summer, we worked together to start a hockey league for disadvantaged youth.

By the end of October, I was promoted from research to correspondence. My new position required me to cover local interest stories, putting me back in front of the camera. In my spare time, I organized a raffle to help fund our junior league. I found a sponsor to pay for uniforms and an equipment upgrade. Tonight, I was meeting him at the Blaze game to do an interview for my news story on the volunteer organization. Cole arranged for me to take a few moments to publicly thank our sponsor and promote the raffle between periods. After Kevin Kessler from Prudential exited the ice, Cole appeared by my side. He took the microphone from my hand. "Isn't she terrific?" Cole asked, addressing the crowd. "Thanks to Layla's tenacity, our youth league has doubled in size, making a difference in the lives of future Buffalo Blaze recruits. Layla gives me all the credit, but the truth is I couldn't have done it without her. She is the best partner a man can have, and that's why"- Cole got down on one knee and pulled a black velvet box from his jacket pocket. - "I'm hoping she will make me the happiest man alive by agreeing to be my wife."

I was stunned as Cole took the ring and slipped it on my finger. He stared at me with those beautiful eyes. The ones that made me relinquish all reason, resistance, and rationality from the moment I saw them. "Are you going to leave me on my knee, or do I hear a yes?" Cole asked, snapping me out of my fog.

"Yes, a thousand times over, yes!" I exclaimed. Cole rose, and I jumped into his arms. The audience gave us a standing ovation, and the team emerged from the locker room, applauding. I fisted Cole's hair pulling his lips on mine for a long, lingering kiss. I was flying so high that I didn't feel my feet didn't touch the ground after he set me down. The Blaze won the game, making the best evening of my life even more perfect.

I was the happiest woman alive heading into the holiday season. My only quandary was what to get the man who had everything for Christmas. It was December twenty-third when the perfect gift arrived. Cole accompanied me to the airport, thinking we were picking up my mother. As we waited for the passengers to disembark, I said, "I really struggled to find you the perfect Christmas present."

"I don't want anything, baby. You already gave me everything I could ever need when you agreed to marry me."

"I think you'll want this," I replied mysteriously.

Cole looked at me with a raised eyebrow. "Uncle Cole!" Katelyn yelled as she rushed towards him. Cole's face beamed as he tossed Kate in the air. I threw my arms around Ashley, who was struggling with one too many bags.

"Ash, you told me you couldn't get away from work this holiday."

"I couldn't, but I couldn't spend Christmas without my big brother either, so I quit."

"I'm thrilled you're here, but was that wise?"

"It is if I plan to stay in Buffalo."

Cole appeared dumbfounded as I wrapped my arms around his waist. "This is your present. I found Ashley a condo five minutes from the penthouse. She's moving back home." Cole's face lit up. He hugged me so hard I thought I would break.

My mother arrived later that night, followed by Cole's uncle Michael. I had never seen Cole so happy, that is, until our surprise guest showed up for Christmas dinner. Ashley ran to answer the door, and in walked Cole's father, Patrick, with his wife and two kids. Cole's body stiffened. Anger flashed in his eyes as they darted past me and rested on his sister. We made introductions, and I took their coats. I was against springing this on Cole, but Ashley insisted. Knowing that he secretly dreamed of a big family gathering for the holidays, I played along. I was beginning to question my judgment when Cole went to the bar and poured himself a drink without saying a word to anyone.

I was putting out appetizers when I saw Patrick approach Cole from the corner of my eye. "From the look of things, you weren't expecting me. If you don't want us here, we can leave."

"No, stay. My sister seems happy you're here," Cole conceded.

"Congratulations on the head coach position. I see you've already had a positive impact on the team."

"I'm surprised you follow my career, considering I'm no longer an NHL star. You must be disappointed."

"I'm sorry you think that. The truth is I couldn't be more proud of you. I know you lost both jobs defending the women in your life. What you did took guts. You're more of a man than I'll ever be."

"I certainly didn't learn chivalry from you," Cole replied, with distaste.

246

"I know. Your mother did a wonderful job raising you. You have a great life, and Layla seems like a terrific woman."

"Layla's the best."

"Look, son, I'm not asking you to forgive me. I know I was an awful father and an even worse husband. I can't change the past, but I'm hoping we can move forward."

"My memory isn't as short as Ashley's, but you're welcome to stay for dinner," Cole replied.

"Would you object if I came to see a couple of Blaze games?"

"That's up to you. I can't control who buys tickets," Cole said, shrugging his shoulders.

"Cole, I'd like you to meet your half-brother, Clayton."

"It's great to finally meet you," Clayton said, shaking Cole's hand. "I remember watching your games as a little kid with Dad. I'm a big fan."

"Thanks. Do you play hockey?"

"I mess around. Football is my sport. I play for Buffalo State. I'm a freshman."

My gaze darted back and forth between the men. I was relieved to see Cole being cordial to his half-brother, who seemed genuinely excited to meet him. I decided to abbreviate the cocktail hour and serve the main course in case Cole's patience wore thin. Dinner turned out better than I expected. Cole warmed up to his half-siblings. He even engaged them in conversation. Patrick's second wife appeared to be a good match despite being younger. Ashley was beaming, just having everyone together. Uncle Mike and my mother turned out to be the biggest surprise. They seemed to hit it off immediately. As the evening came to a close, Cole offered to get Clayton tickets for the upcoming Blaze game.

"Would you mind if I brought my dad?" Clayton asked.

"You can bring whomever you choose," Cole replied. The evening was as close to a Christmas miracle as I could ask for.

That summer, Cole and I got married. Many of the Predators, along with Shane, and Cole's family were in attendance. Cole and his father would never be close, but at least they were civil. Clayton and Cole forged a bond over time. Clayton became a volunteer coach for our youth league. Before I knew it, Halloween was here again. It had been two years since I arrived in Miami. I could've never dreamed that I would be married to Cole and living in Buffalo. Life had come full circle. I was remarkably content yet incredibly exhausted. I hadn't been feeling like myself for weeks. My mother decided to relocate, and I'd been busy finding her an apartment. I was simultaneously organizing a fundraiser with Ashley for the youth hockey team. Maybe I was anemic. I hadn't been exercising or eating the way I should. Whatever the reason, I could barely keep my eyes open.

One night, Cole came home late from a road game to find me asleep on the couch. "Hey baby, I didn't mean to wake you."

"That's okay. How was the game?"

"Great, we won. Did you eat?"

"No, but there are some leftovers in the fridge if you want to warm them up."

Cole opened the refrigerator. "What's this?" he asked, grabbing a piece of paper I taped to the casserole dish. His eyes gazed at the image and then back at me. "Is this what I think it is?"

"It's a picture of your son," I replied, trying to wake up.

"You're pregnant!" Cole exclaimed.

"That's why I've been so tired. I should have realized it was possible since I haven't had my period, but you know my cycle is irregular."

"I thought we were using birth control."

"We were, but I got my shot late, which voided my protection for the month. I've been so busy with everything that I haven't been keeping up on things the way I should." A look of shock and panic passed over Cole's eyes as he waited for the realization to sink in. I walked over to him and cupped his hands in my face. "Are you happy?" I asked.

Cole lifted me up and spun me around. "Ecstatic. It just took a minute to register." We stood holding each other as we wrapped our heads around the news.

"How do you know it's a boy?"

"I won't be positive for another month, but I'm craving salt, my feet feel like icicles, and I'm getting headaches instead of morning sickness."

"That sounds like an old wives' tale. Not that it matters. I'm thrilled either way," Cole replied.

"It's a good thing I'm moving my mom here. We'll need a babysitter."

We fell asleep that night with Cole's hand resting on my belly. He was as attentive as he could be when his schedule allowed. When Cole was on the road, my mother and Ashley took turns pampering me. Six months later, Graydon Michael Pasternak was born. He came home from the hospital wearing a Predator onesie. I reflected back to how far Cole and I had come from the day we met. I never dreamed that spilling coffee on a man's crotch would be the catalyst behind my happily ever after.

To My Readers,

I hope you enjoyed my debut novel, *Fire on Ice*. If you enjoyed Layla and Cole's journey from enemies-to-lovers, I would greatly appreciate you leaving a review on the site where you purchased it. Reviews provide useful feedback and enable me to work even harder to craft an engaging story. As an unknown author, reviews are critical to my success moving forward. I thank you for your support.

If you enjoy a steamy read, look for my next book, *Seductive Games*.

If you could spend one week with a gorgeous stranger, would you?

Kaylee, a beautiful Boston psychologist, hasn't been on a date in two years. Realizing her life had become all work and no play, Kaylee embarks on a mental health weekend to the Berkshires. When her car spirals out of control, Kaylee is rescued by Will, a charismatic software executive, who tenderly nurses her back to health.

Will isn't relationship material. Amid a contentious divorce, he offers Kaylee the one thing he knows he can deliver, a week of seductive games and the best sex of her life. Intrigued by his proposal, Kaylee agrees to play. Wagers are won and lost as Will ignites Kaylee's deepest desires, renewing her faith in love.

Blinded by passion, Kaylee ignores Will's character flaws in the hope of having a real relationship. That dream is shattered when an enemy from Will's past threatens their future. Shocking secrets are exposed, revealing Will's dark side, and leaving Kaylee caught in a web of deception. Kaylee knows she should run but the thought of losing the potential love of her life tempts her to stay. Torn between fear and desire, Kaylee can't decide if she should save the man who holds her heart or save her heart from the man who has the power to destroy it.

ABOUT THE AUTHOR

Kim Kane's life was going according to plan until a momentary lapse of reason caused her to retire prematurely and leave behind everything she knew and loved. Flawed, funny, and trying to learn from her mistakes, Kim looked for ways to recreate herself. A decline in stress and an increase in spare time enabled Kim to return to her creative roots and love for writing. Feeling stronger and more enlightened from her journey of self-exploration, Kim uses her blog, humor, and erotically charged novels to connect with women.

A lover of music, blue eyes, and French martinis, Kim is a caffeine-addicted, OCD-driven football/hockey nut who is deeply devoted to those she calls friends. Kim is a native New Yorker who recently relocated to North Carolina with her husband and hopelessly spoiled French bulldog. As an only child who muddled through a dysfunctional childhood, she draws on her counseling experience to craft deeply flawed characters on a journey for redemption. When she isn't writing, she exceeds the speed limit, works out, takes classes, and meets new people.

Connect with Kim at:
Kimberlykane8@gmail.com
Twitter@figuringfifty